INSATIABLE MONSTERS

H. L. MACFARLANE

To Kirsty, again. I think the greys got darker.

THE BEGINNING OF THE END

NICK

"Do you have the building for the auction finalised yet?"

"With some bribery we've managed to secure it for early May."

Nick rubbed his twitching temple; it wasn't the answer he wanted to hear. "It can't be earlier?"

Carlos shook his head. He and Sam were responsible for organising the auction directly beneath Nick. "Not unless you want to raise suspicion. What with the police all across Europe on high alert after what happened in Scotland…"

"Damn *Kapros*," Nick spat. A migraine was blooming in his skull, so he pushed his fingertips against the pressure in his head in the hopes it would alleviate the pain. When it did nothing he sighed. "Fine, May it is. You have no excuse not to find the highest-quality specimens with six months at your disposal. If a fucking goat can do it then we can do it, too."

Sam and Carlos murmured in agreement before vacating Nick's office. His father's office, in truth, but Franco Richardson was away in New York on business. It had been left to Nichola, his only child and heir to the Richardson empire, to fulfil the food shortage left in the wake of Dorian Kapros' treachery.

Nick still couldn't believe the satyr had managed such a thing.

With a grunt Nick opened his laptop and searched for an update on the debacle that had been the Highlands Adrenaline Sports Facility. Nobody from the Outdoor Sports Society was supposed to have survived, keeping entirely in line with every other auction the Kapros family had been responsible for organising over the last one hundred years.

Thanks to Poppy King most of the thirty members of the club had escaped their deadly fate – though not all of them unscathed. It was a mess that had everyone on high alert: Dorian Kapros' face was now widely known across Europe, and the guise of sports facilities for human trafficking was on the radar of every police precinct from Scotland to Italy to Turkey.

"Where are you, Poppy King...?" Nick muttered, using every news network available to him to try and identify where she and Dorian might be next. He was assuming she was travelling around with him, though in reality Poppy could just as likely be hiding on her own.

Except Poppy wasn't the kind of person who hid, and Nick knew it.

He rubbed the side of his neck when it tingled at the thought of her. Despite his scales protecting him from the worst of the inferno that engulfed the Highlands facility Nick had still suffered from minor burns to his neck and stomach. He wanted to be furious with his adversaries for injuring him. For evading capture. Instead all Nick felt was respect and a rising excitement to meet their challenge.

And chase them down.

After all, if Dorian was full of Poppy's blood then he was

going to live as close to forever as a monster could imagine. He was a god walking amongst mere mortals. Nick planned to *join* him, not destroy him.

And steal Poppy from him in the process.

"Poppy King, Poppy King," Nick sang as he scanned the news, leaning back against his chair with the kind of relaxed satisfaction only one who was certain of victory could achieve, "run all you want. I'll find you."

There were dozens of monsters and humans at Nick's disposal to track them down; no matter how well Dorian protected Poppy he could only go so long before he made a mistake and left her unguarded.

For Dorian was hungry, and Nick knew it. He had seen it in the satyr's eyes, even with Poppy's blood inside him healing his every wound and preventing him from dying.

Eventually Dorian would have to leave Poppy's side in order to give into his insatiable urge to feed on human flesh, for Nick doubted he'd risk Poppy witness such a thing. Even if it were for thirty or fifteen or even five minutes Poppy would be alone.

That was all the opportunity Nick required to steal the goddess away from the god she had created.

The Richardson empire – and the very future of every monster on the planet – depended on it.

AN UNEXPECTED GUEST

FRED

A WEEK HAD PASSED SINCE FRED last saw Poppy and Dorian. A week. Seven days. One hundred and sixty-eight hours.

It felt like a lifetime.

The month following the Outdoor Sports Society's escape from Dorian's facility had, conversely, passed in a blur. There had been so much to deal with: police reports, interviews, hospital check-ups, teary family reunions and, above all else, the shock of their entire terrifying summer for the Society to wrap their heads around.

But now the worst of that was over, and most of Fred's questions had been answered thanks to Dorian, Poppy, Patrick and Casey. Which left...nothing.

Fred had no idea what to do next with his life. It felt like a distant, ridiculously banal dream that he'd ever tortured himself with what followed university regarding his career. For all Fred cared he could happily *never* have a career. A steady income and a secure place to live were insignificant goals in the grand scheme of things.

For how could he worry about a job where there were

monsters lurking in the dark, waiting to tear him limb from limb whilst he screamed for his life? Fred shuddered simply thinking about it.

And yet that fear was nothing compared to the terror Fred's memories of ripping Poppy apart instilled.

He had done that. Not a monster.

Not for the first time Fred wondered if that qualified him as one.

Yet there was no physical sign Poppy had ever been hurt by Fred, thanks to her blood. Dorian had called it immortal. The idea still baffled Fred even though he had witnessed its effects first-hand, for how had Poppy King of all people ended up with such a wonderful, tragic, dangerous ability?

He was desperate to fully understand how it worked. Perhaps that desperation was a result of Fred's well-honed instinct to research all things unusual – an instinct shared with Poppy, given their six years of forcibly studying for identical biology degrees together.

He wondered how much Poppy actually knew about it herself. How did it feel, to have such a substance coursing through her veins? Did it feel different than regular blood? Could Poppy even discern between the two?

But it was too late to find out now. Poppy and Dorian – as well as Casey and Patrick – made no mention of when Fred, Andrew, Rachelle and Nate would see them again. Or, at least, if his friends knew anything about when they would next see Poppy, they hadn't let Fred know. They hadn't spoken to him once since they'd all met up the week before. He knew he couldn't blame them, but still it stung.

For all Fred knew he'd forever be left in the dark about the subject of immortal blood, and he'd lost all his friends in the process.

"Frederick Sampson."

He shivered at the cold breeze that blew through his bedroom window and the words which accompanied it alike. Because Fred recognised the low, sultry, feminine voice that spoke, but it was out of place. A voice from another, nightmarish time. Reluctantly he turned to face the woman who had spoken.

Aisling smiled broadly, her perfect teeth gleaming.

"You here to eat me or something?" Fred asked, flat and dispassionate despite the throbbing of his heart and the adrenaline coursing through his body.

"Maybe later. I have a job for you first, though."

Interest piqued despite himself, Fred muttered, "What kind of job?"

Aisling's dangerous smile grew wider. "A manhunt, if you will. Help me find Dorian Kapros and Poppy King."

Fred laughed. He couldn't help it; the garbled, humourless sound escaped his lips even as the smile was wiped from Aisling's face.

"I wasn't aware that what I said was so funny, Sampson."

"You ask me to do this as if it's somehow possible." Fred shrugged his shoulders in what he knew was a frustratingly arrogant fashion. "In case the entire summer spent working for Kapros wasn't long enough for you to work it out, Poppy hates me. Why on earth would you think I know how to find her?"

Aisling's eyes flashed. "Perhaps you don't know directly but the rest of your group of friends certainly will. So unless you want me to bother pure, sweet Andrew with such a task..."

All at once Fred stop laughing, and his blood ran cold. The last thing he wanted was for Aisling to go near Andrew or Rachelle or Nate or anyone else from the Outdoor Sports Society. Fred had to keep her as far away from them as possible.

Going by the fact Aisling was demanding *he* locate her, Fred could only conclude that she did not know about the fact he'd tried to kill Poppy King. *She can* never *find out, otherwise she'll go to someone else for help.* "What's in it for me?" Fred demanded, crossing his arms over his chest and trying his best to sound unperturbed in the face of a monster who could easily rip him to shreds. *What was it Poppy said Aisling was?* Fred wondered, thinking hard. *A harpy? Was that it?*

He couldn't even visualise it.

Aisling circled him like he was prey. Fred supposed he was. "Find them for me – bring King *directly* to me – and I may consider sparing your life," she said silkily. "Try and run and...it won't just be you who feels the sting of my talons."

There was a photo collage behind Fred hanging on his wall; Rachelle had made it for him back when there were still dating. Aisling's sharp gaze locked on those photos now, leaving Fred with no uncertainty as to what she was insinuating.

He forced a grin to his face. "So it's Poppy and Dorian's lives for mine, then? I guess I can think of worse bargains."

"I knew there was a reason I liked you."

"Is there a time limit on this? I don't imagine it will be all that easy for me to find them. Considering you came to me rather than doing it yourself I can only assume there's a reason you're not looking for them directly."

Aisling flicked her long, luxurious hair over her shoulder as she made her way back to the open window through which she had entered Fred's bedroom. An unhappy scowl curled her lips. "Quite frankly I'm not stupid enough to face an immortal monster without picking the setting myself, and Dorian has an advantage over me if I don't have the space to...spread my wings. Much better for you to locate them and bring them to a place where *I* have the advantage."

Fred supposed that made sense. If Aisling was a harpy and she came across Dorian in a place where she couldn't take advantage of flight then Fred imagined Dorian's wickedly strong legs would make quick work of caving in her skull.

"And the time limit?" he pressed, pushing the thought of

Dorian's deadly hooves from his mind.

"Just so long as you get your precious Outdoor Sports Society president to me before Nick finds her I don't care how long it takes. Though I'd rather like if it were sooner. To keep my good looks and all." Aisling let out a sultry laugh. "And who knows, Sampson: if you do well maybe I'll be inclined to keep you as a pet, just like Dorian has done with Poppy. You'd like that, I think."

"Then you think wrong."

"We'll see. I'll be in touch."

And with that the monster masquerading as a woman was gone as if she'd never been there in the first place, leaving Fred with a new purpose for his life he really rather wished he didn't have.

But one thing was for sure: he needed to find Poppy King whether she liked it or not.

Both Fred's life and hers depended on it.

The Friends She Left Behind

ANDREW

"You know, I didn't believe I'd ever take my ordinary life for granted but by god is it boring."

"What, in comparison to being in a murder camp?"

"Well when you put it like that—"

A knock on the door followed swiftly by Andrew's mother walking in paused Nate and Rachelle in their tracks. The look of disapproval on her face told them everything they needed to know about the fact she had overheard their comments. But Andrew had long since learned that Nate used humour as a means of dealing with stressful situations. It wasn't how *Andrew* dealt with such things, but it wasn't up to him to judge his friend's way of coping.

And besides, Nate wasn't wrong.

"What are the three of you up to?" Andrew's mum asked. She glanced at Rachelle, who was perched on top of Andrew's bed with a laptop on her knees. Nate was sprawled over the floor, whilst Andrew's was sitting stock straight on his spinning desk chair. It was expensive black leather; Andrew had been desperately trying to save up his money to buy it for two years now. As soon as he returned from the nightmare that was the Highlands Adrenaline Sports Facility his parents immediately bought it for him.

To unsuspecting eyes Andrew, Nate and Rachelle looked for all the world like they were studying or discussing a film or organising a game. Banal things. Easy things. The kind of things friends in their twenties did together. Not that Andrew had ever been able to have more than one friend at a time in his bedroom, before. But things had fundamentally changed for Andrew after summer, and not just because of monsters.

"We're closing down Poppy's social media accounts, Mrs Forbes," Rachelle said, smiling sadly for the woman.

At this his mum investigated Andrew's face for a sign that he was about to have a meltdown. It was an understandable, expected reaction, but Andrew kept himself together. "That's very kind of you all to do," his mum said, addressing the room at large. "Honestly, I think it would be a whole lot easier on everyone if her parents would hold a funeral."

"We have to let them deal with things their own way," Nate chimed in, rolling up into a sitting position to accept a packet of crisps from Mrs Forbes' tray. "If I were them I wouldn't want to believe that...well."

Andrew had never been good at finishing the implied meaning of unfinished sentences but he knew what Nate meant loud and clear. For why should Poppy's parents believe that she was dead? She wasn't. It seemed impossible for her to be dead, even if she *wasn't* in possession of immortal blood. Poppy was the most invincible person Andrew had ever met. That any of them had ever met.

But Andrew knew Poppy would never show up in front of her parents again. She couldn't risk it. Perhaps his mother was right; perhaps the best thing for them was to hold a funeral.

Andrew knew he couldn't face such a thing.

"Thanks for the snacks, mum," Andrew said, wiping at the stinging in his eyes before the woman could realise he was close to tears. "You can go now."

"But Andrew—"

"You can go."

Realising she wasn't going to win this argument with her son she exited the bedroom on quick, quiet feet, though she kept the door open an inch or two. The moment she was gone Andrew rushed over and pushed the door closed properly. He leaned against it, sliding a hand over his face.

"What is that, the seventh time she's come in?" Nate asked, counting on his fingers. When he popped open his bag of crisps Andrew flinched.

"The eighth," Rachelle said.

"She can't leave me alone for even five minutes anymore," Andrew said, sinking back onto his seat. It was somewhat of an exaggeration, but it certainly didn't feel like it at that precise moment in time. "After we came back from Dunoon to see – well, you know" - Andrew cast a furtive glance at the door, suspicious that his mum might still be listening - "she hasn't let me out of her sight. Dad's the same when he's at home. But I'm an adult. I can handle itself. Surely this summer proves that—"

"*We* know that, Andrew," Rachelle soothed, reaching out from her position on the bed to gently stroke Andrew's arm, "but your mum and dad...they thought they lost you. They didn't know what was going on. And now they know you're different, and you don't need them anymore. That must be hard for them to take."

"It isn't that I don't need them anymore," Andrew grumbled. "It's just that—"

"That you want to do things your own way," Nate finished for him, nodding in understanding. "I get you. After all, it isn't as if mine or Rachelle's parents can stop us going outside any more than yours can. Not that Mum didn't try her damnedest to convince me to move back home." He chuckled, but even Andrew could tell it was forced. He wondered if Nate's sense of humour would forever be tainted by experiences that were entirely unfunny, or if he'd be able to get over it.

If *any* of them could get over it.

After he crunched his way through half his bag of crisps Nate asked, "Anyway, Rachelle, how's the social media take-down going?"

"Almost done. Twitter is done and I'm just waiting for the Facebook and Instagram requests to be accepted. I shut her Snapchat down yesterday."

"She doesn't have a MySpace account we don't know about, does she?"

Rachelle laughed but Andrew didn't, since he didn't understand the joke. "If she has one then Poppy can delete it herself. Well, if she ever gets somewhere that's safe for her to log into her accounts without revealing her IP address."

"Have Patrick and Casey heard from her lately?" Andrew asked, hurting at the fact that someone other than him might have been in contact with Poppy since their trip to Dunoon over a week ago.

Rachelle clicked her tongue, which meant the answer was *no*. "Casey told me that Patrick calls and messages Dorian all the time, but he rarely replies. He hasn't said anything about Poppy."

"She'll contact us when she's ready," Nate said, though he didn't sound convinced.

"She'll contact us when Dorian *lets* her."

"He doesn't control her like that," Andrew said, disliking the tone of Rachelle's voice. "Even if he asked Poppy not to contact us, she wouldn't listen."

"And how do you suppose that?"

"Because she never listens to anyone if she doesn't love them, and she doesn't love Dorian. She told me so herself."

Nate's eyes widened before he burst into guffaws of laughter. "Of course you asked her about that, Andrew. Hell if I wasn't curious about it. Still, Poppy might listen to Dorian if it's the only thing keeping them alive. And away from Nick."

"Maybe. But I still think she would contact us if she really needed to."

For a few moments Rachelle mulled this over, clearly very unhappy with the entire Poppy and Dorian situation. Andrew knew fine well she wasn't the only one. Then she sighed. "Speaking of people contacting us..."

"Ah, yes, Fred," Nate said, guessing where the conversation was going. "Did he call you today, too?"

Rachelle nodded. "He's off searching for Poppy. Won't tell me why."

"Wait, you asked him?"

"God no. I haven't replied to anything he says. I just figured he'd tell me why he was looking for her if he wanted to hear a word from me."

"He messaged me yesterday saying he was staying in Berlin for a few days. Obviously wanted me to ask why, but I haven't been replying either."

They had all agreed not to contact Fred, though Andrew had drafted several messages to him over the last several weeks. But he hadn't sent them; he wasn't about to break his promises to his friends like that. Still, despite what Fred had done he was the one who perhaps knew the most about what happened during summer other than Poppy herself. To that end Andrew was desperate to talk to him.

And punch him in the face. Andrew wanted to do both.

"He went there because someone matching Dorian's

description was seen in Berlin, didn't he?" Rachelle asked, scrolling on her laptop screen. They'd been tracking Dorian and Poppy as best they could based on news and internet gossip, though lately the three of them had taken to researching a far more macabre topic.

Namely, past human auctions.

It was getting easier and easier to spot them now they knew what to look for. After being told that Dorian had been organising them every four to six years across Europe, Rachelle was getting rather adept at figuring out what had likely been a front for an auction and what had been something else entirely. From this information Nate then tracked the victims to discover where and how they had first disappeared, and Andrew worked on identifying patterns to how the victims were taken.

Isolated sports retreats had clearly been Dorian's favourite front. There had been a mountaineering expedition in the Alps, a caving trip in the Yorkshire Dales, a diving group off the coast of Greece. Each and every time the humans had befallen tragic, unfortunate accidents. They'd gotten lost in a blizzard on the face of the Matterhorn. Part of the cave system had collapsed. The oxygen tanks had been faulty.

The state of the half-eaten Outdoor Sports Society members as they were helped out of Dorian's facility lingered in the back of Andrew's head. The memory of it never quite left his brain.

"Do you think Dorian will organise a new auction, to save face?" Nate asked, thinking out loud. Andrew was grateful for it simply to escape his own thoughts.

"I don't think he's safe from his own kind," Andrew said slowly. "It seems like they'll kill him for betraying Nick, Aisling and Steven. Didn't Poppy say that Nick was the monster equivalent of a prince?"

"Then he *definitely* has the means to find Dorian and kill him."

"*If* he can kill him..." Rachelle muttered. She and Nate were still trying to get to grips with the fact Poppy – and, by extension, Dorian – were full to the brim with immortal blood. It was a mere theoretical concept to them, since they hadn't knowingly seen it in action. But Andrew had, so he knew how difficult the act of killing Dorian would be. It wouldn't be impossible; had Andrew and Dorian not saved Poppy from Fred's horrific mental breakdown she would likely have been long since dead and gone.

Andrew gulped and begged the intrusive thought away.

"So do you think someone else will organise an auction instead?" Rachelle asked, too busy looking at her laptop to notice that Andrew was close to a meltdown. "If the monsters in this part of the world still need to eat then they'll surely have to organise *something.*"

"That's what I was thinking," Nate said, "so I thought we should start keeping track of random disappearances on the street. Pretty hard to do though, given how often people go missing."

"What was it that Poppy said? Monsters prefer to eat fit, able-bodied people?"

It was much easier to focus on the idea of monsters eating hypothetical people than it was to think of Fred trying to murder Poppy, so Andrew said, "That would narrow the search, if we focus on athletes. But what do you want to do if we find out what's going on?"

"Who knows." Rachelle closed her laptop shut with a snap. "I just want to feel useful. I can hardly go back to finishing my masters or work a part-time job when all of this is going on." She waved around emphatically. Nate and Andrew both nodded in agreement. Life seemed pointless now, all things considered. For what was the point of studying or working or travelling when at any moment a monster could snatch them from the street and consume their body and soul?

Now more than ever, Andrew wished he could run off to

New Zealand with Poppy.

"Ah, crap," Nate muttered, glancing at his phone when it buzzed in his pocket. "I didn't realise how late it was. Do you want a lift home, Rachelle?"

"I'd appreciate that. Andrew, are you free this weekend?"

"Yes. Could we go climbing at the centre?" he asked, hoping Rachelle would agree simply to give Andrew something physical to do.

She smiled as enthusiastically as she could muster. Which wasn't much these days, but Andrew appreciated the effort. "That sounds great. I'll see you then."

After Nate and Rachelle left Andrew's mother was quick to come into his bedroom and fuss over him. "It's all right if you want to spend some time at home alone," she said, stroking his hair. "You don't need to push yourself by seeing your friends so much. I know you found it hard to be around people for so long in the past."

But Andrew pushed her affection way. "They're my friends. I want to be with them. I'm okay, I swear."

It was clear his mum wanted to say that, in fact, no, Andrew was very much not okay, but she resisted. There was a set to her son's face that told her he would argue all night if she did so. So she left his bedroom, once again not quite closing the door. Andrew stalked over and slammed it shut.

He collapsed onto his bed and wondered what to do now. Though it was midnight he wasn't anywhere close to tired, and his bed smelled of Rachelle's vanilla perfume, which didn't smell like his shampoo at all. The only perfume Andrew had ever liked was Poppy's, and that was because it smelled of lemons and was, more importantly, *Poppy's.*

Andrew pulled out his phone and stared at the blank screen. He wanted Poppy to call him. Willed for her to contact him.

But nothing happened. As it had for weeks his phone stayed

resolutely silent.

INTERLUDE I

Carla didn't like being out so late at night. If her sister hadn't sent her a photo of her boyfriend with his tongue halfway down another woman's throat Carla wouldn't have been out at all. But, alas, her sister had sent such a photo, so now Carla was currently storming down side street after side street to reach the swanky west end bar she'd recognised from the photo.

"Stupid taxis," Carla muttered, turning up the volume on her headphones in order to drown out the sound of a group of drunk and rowdy men on the next street over. She'd tried and failed to book a taxi to pick her up but, because it was prime nightclub time, it had been impossible. At least Carla would be able to queue for one on the main street once she'd invariably thrown a drink in her boyfriend's face.

Possibly a punch, too.

Something punched her, instead.

"What the fu—" Carla bit out, but then a hand on her mouth smothered her cry. Two scaly - scaly - arms wrapped around her chest, whilst another equally inhuman hand wrenched Carla's phone from her shaking grip and tossed it onto the pavement.

Then she was thrown into the back of a van and plunged into silent, heavy darkness.

FOOD SHOPPING FOR HUMANS

POPPY

IT FELT STRANGE, TO BE IN a supermarket. Never mind the fact the signs in the supermarket were in Dutch. Never mind that it was three in the morning. Never mind even that this wasn't the first supermarket Poppy had been to with Dorian since their near-fatal escape from the Highlands Adrenaline Sports Facility – or as close to fatal as such thing could be for either of them.

Being in a supermarket with a satyr disguised as a man was, at the end of the day, very, very strange.

"Why do you fill your body with this crap?" Dorian muttered when Poppy threw two large bags of paprika crisps into her shopping basket. It was a flavour that wasn't easy to obtain in the UK, but in Amsterdam they were everywhere.

"I can eat what I want," Poppy replied, tossing in another bag just to spite him.

"You never ate this poorly back when—"

"Careful, you might just publicly admit to running a murder

camp."

"You know what I mean." Poppy didn't need to look at Dorian to know he was glowering at her. He'd been doing that a lot lately: glowering. Poppy took it as some kind of sick, twisted victory against him, though she knew in her heart that it was unfair.

Dorian had just been doing his job. His kind needed to eat humans, and he'd been providing them with top-of-the-line specimens so they didn't have to eat as frequently.

Except he'd played a cruel and disturbing game with Poppy throughout it all simply because he could, and now here she was tied to him forever.

Poppy chucked several bars of chocolate, a multi-pack of Haribo and eight Kinder Buenos into the basket.

"Fine, ignore me," Dorian said, clearly used to it. For the next fifteen minutes they perused the shop in silence, Dorian pretending he was interested in consuming anything but the alcohol lining the shelves whilst Poppy – reluctantly – padded out her unhealthy purchases with substantial, nutritious food.

When it came to buying the food Poppy took centre-stage. Dorian was a wanted man, after all, and she was presumed dead. Even with his hair an unwashed mess and the collar of his woollen jacket popped up to obscure the bottom half of his face Dorian was still a noticeably tall, handsome man. He was the type of person someone remembered – especially the young female cashier.

But nobody ever recognised a pale woman with no make-up on and a hood hiked over her hair. Poppy was, for all intents and purposes, a ghost.

After she paid for their shopping Poppy and Dorian made their way back to their apartment, which was a fifteen minute walk away. Wordlessly Dorian took all of the shopping bags from Poppy. She elbowed him in protest.

"I can handle them!"

"Just let me do something, please."

"You paid for it."

"I hardly think that counts, all things considered."

One of the things that infuriated Poppy most ever since she and Dorian had gone on the run was how gentlemanly he was acting. How polite. How caring. Aside from their meeting with Patrick, Casey, Nate, Rachelle, Andrew and – lord help her, Fred – Dorian had taken it upon himself to cater to Poppy's every whim.

Even though it was paired with his substantial glowering she couldn't stand it.

"I used to eat all this shite with Rachelle and Casey," Poppy eventually admitted, when they returned to their apartment and Dorian immediately began unpacking the shopping. "Feels kind of hollow to eat it alone, though. You never stocked this stuff back at your facility so...yeah. I never ate it."

Dorian stilled, his hands around a box of chocolate cereal Poppy couldn't buy back in Scotland. He was shaking, just slightly, but it was enough for Poppy to feel bad for him. His entire life had been destroyed because of her. His kind wanted him dead because of her.

But Poppy King was human, so she had limited sympathy right now for the monster masquerading as a man in front of her.

After taking off her coat and shoes Poppy made her way through to the bathroom, dragging the band that kept her tangled hair tied up in order to brush through it. At Dorian's insistence Poppy had dyed the silver-faded-to-blonde streak from the front of her hair. He'd even cut several inches of split ends for her, far neater than Poppy herself could have ever cut it. Her hair hadn't been shoulder-length and so uniformly ash brown since her undergraduate degree.

Poppy didn't actually look that terrible, considering what she was currently going through. She reasoned this was because Dorian was looking after her to ensure she ate and slept.

Watching her reflection Poppy turned this way and that, ignoring the unforgiving fluorescent light of the bathroom to inspect her general appearance. Yes, she'd definitely put on a little weight. By the time they fled the Scottish Highlands Poppy had been a few pounds away from skeletal, so the weight gain was welcome. Another few weeks of eating properly and Poppy would look as if she'd never been subject to the horrors of Dorian's facility and the truth of her blood. She'd look almost normal.

When Poppy returned to the apartment proper she saw that Dorian had frozen in place in the kitchenette, forgoing putting away their shopping in favour of staring at nothing. He did that a lot lately.

Poppy sat upon the bed and patiently waited for him to stop disassociating.

When Dorian finally sighed it was as if the weight of the world was upon him. Poppy thought that he looked older than he did back at the facility, even though he would never age another day with her blood inside him. *And neither will I,* Poppy reminded herself unhelpfully. She was yet to fully process this, just as she was yet to process Fred's attack and what the true extent of Andrew's feelings for her were.

Andrew.

Poppy hadn't messaged any of her friends since their last meeting, not even him. Upon her request Rachelle and Nate had taken over Poppy's social media – her parents had been glad for this, Poppy had been told, since they never knew her passwords – in order to deal with the messages that had flooded in. To delete her online presence from existence, so that Poppy would never have to see what the rest of the Outdoor Sports Society's members had said to her privately after their rescue. It was too much for Poppy to bear.

The thanks for saving their lives.

The curses from people who had lost their friends.

The incoherent ramblings from those who had been irrevocably damaged.

It was almost worse than the fact Poppy could never see her mother and father again. That they thought she was dead. Almost, but not quite. She'd always been an independent soul. Running around outside whilst her parents worked their high-flying, travel-heavy jobs. They'd never been a particularly physical, affectionate family, but they were a family nonetheless.

And Poppy would never see them again.

"Poppy?"

"Huh?"

Dorian had stopped unpacking to cross the room and sit beside Poppy upon the double bed that took up much of the apartment. His eyes were full of damnably genuine concern. He wiped a tear from her face. "You're crying."

"No I'm not."

"Yes you are."

Poppy stared at him until her guilty tears stopped. Close up she could see how gaunt Dorian was. How thinly his skin was scraped across his bones. She knew it meant something dangerous.

He told me, in the beginning, that monsters who ate high-quality humans didn't have to eat for four or five years. So when did he last eat? Poppy's blood would sustain him, she knew, but Dorian had once compared it to eating stale toast.

She dragged her hair away from her neck.

"Poppy, what are you...?" Dorian wondered, though out of the corner of her eye Poppy saw the immediate shift in Dorian's mood.

"You haven't drank since we escaped the facility," she said, which was true. The two of them had maintained a distance that had been uncomfortably easy to maintain, even when sharing the same bed. They were strangers, separate, apart, unconnected, even as they depended on each other to survive.

Even though they knew what the other intimately felt like, and Poppy knew Dorian craved her as much as she did him with every hungry, stolen glance in his direction.

Dorian pulled away. "I can't."

"But you need to!" she protested, touching Dorian's jaw in order to turn him back around to face her. He grew very still and careful beneath her touch. A predator poised to spring at the barest warning, trying its level best not to move.

"I have enough blood in my system to last me several lifetimes," Dorian said, and then, with a wry smile, "providing nobody bleeds me dry tomorrow."

"But—"

"I don't need it, Poppy."

That stung, especially because Poppy knew Dorian was saying it for her benefit. He didn't want to be a monster to her. He didn't want to be feeding off her, like a parasite.

No, Dorian wanted Poppy to view him as something else entirely. Something that they both knew she could never truly accept.

"*I* need it," Poppy murmured, to herself. Then, stronger, "I need it, Dorian. I'm too...full. I'm so used to you draining me that I can't...I can't function properly. So please."

It was true. Poppy had felt this way for much of her captivity in the Highlands facility, though she'd never admitted as much to Dorian. To tell him now – to assuage his guilt, no less – was a sensation Poppy wasn't sure how to deal with.

Dorian's eyes widened in delicious excitement, though they weren't his real eyes and therefore weren't the eyes Poppy badly wished to lock her down. For they were human blue. Ordinary blue. Not glacial nor luminescent. His pupils weren't barred.

But they were heavy-lashed, earnest, and focused entirely on Poppy.

He leaned towards her – closer than he'd gotten in weeks. "Can I really?" he asked, his voice a low growl that was music to her ears. Water over gravel. Wind through trees.

A waterfall crashing within a tiny forest, hidden upon a cliffside.

"Would I have offered if not?" She tilted her neck further, feeling her artery throb as her heart rate accelerated.

"...no."

"Then do it."

For a moment Poppy thought Dorian would refuse. But then he lowered his head to Poppy's exposed neck, and his very physical presence flickered. Poppy blinked several times against the odd visuals presented before her, as if that would somehow allow her eyes to focus.

Then she gasped.

Dorian's teeth sunk into her neck and drank greedily from her.

Poppy's hand threaded through Dorian's hair, pulling him closer but with a grip that could just as easily yank him away – for all the good she could do against Dorian's real strength. But Dorian wasn't in the mood for anything but compliance, and as he drank from Poppy all she was aware of was the feel of his lips against her skin, and of how his arms instinctively wrapped around her to pull her into his protection, and how her fingers clung to his jumper and she gasped in anything *but* pain when Dorian drank particularly deeply for the briefest of moments.

She wanted him to drain her of everything. She wanted so badly to feel it all go away, but she also wanted to live. The two sensations lived separate but concurrent in her head, irreconcilable in their differences.

Dorian yanked himself away long before Poppy was ready for his absence, his entire body heaving with every breath he took. She watched as he licked his lower lip of her blood.

"You should have told me I was taking too much," he complained, his hugely dilated pupils scanning Poppy for a sign that something had gone wrong.

"You...didn't." Speech was coming much too slowly.

"I did. Much too much. Lie down. I'll...I'll put the rest of the shopping away."

Poppy didn't need telling twice.

She was already asleep.

HUNTED

DORIAN

Each day that he and Poppy managed to fly under the radar Dorian breathed a sigh of relief. But his relief was short-lived. For as soon as one day ended another began, and the cycle of evading authorities, private investigators and creatures that walked on more than two legs began anew.

Dorian's nerves were frayed. He was exhausted. He was drained.

He was starving.

Poppy was asleep in bed, though it had taken a while for her to reach such a state. Dorian knew her sleep would neither be deep nor dreamless. Most all of her waking and sleeping moments alike were plagued by nightmares.

It was Dorian's fault.

Knowing he himself would find no solace in sleep Dorian got out of bed, slipped on his boots and wrapped himself in the wool jacket he knew he'd need to combat the cold outside. It wasn't quite November but Amsterdam had taken a remarkably quick turn towards winter over the last week.

Silently Dorian edged open the door of their apartment and stalked into the darkness outside. It was beginning to rain, so Dorian hiked up the collar of his jacket to help protect his neck from the fat, freezing drops of water that threatened to chill him to the bone. He wouldn't be surprised if the rain turned to sleet and snow within the next hour.

This wasn't the first time Dorian had left Poppy's side in the middle of the night to go walking. He needed time without her observing him, listening to him, judging him. For even though it was dangerous to leave Poppy's side, Dorian couldn't help it.

He was hungry, and if he couldn't eat the least he could do was *watch* his food.

There was a jogger going past the apartment who looked promising. She kept a steady thumping beat against the pavement, her lithe figure effortlessly fighting against the rain that was now falling in earnest. She laughed when her companion – a tall man twice her size, red cheeks huffing shallow breaths as he lagged behind her – tripped over the storm drain and just barely avoided falling flat on his face.

The woman reminded Dorian of Poppy. *Except she would run at two in the morning* without *anyone backing her up,* he thought, watching as the pair of joggers ran out of sight. Dorian's stomach grumbled painfully when he could no longer see them, clawing at his resolve. For whilst Poppy's blood kept Dorian alive it did nothing to sate his hunger.

He hadn't eaten in years; it was growing unbearable to watch people walk past him, blissfully ignorant of how easily Dorian could rip them to shreds and consume their flesh. His hands began to twitch – a sign he was close to dropping his human form entirely. Poppy would never need to know. She was asleep in bed, and Dorian was alone.

He took a step towards the direction the joggers had taken, and—

A vibrating in Dorian's pocket dragged him back to the

present. Immediately guilt overwhelmed him. He couldn't betray Poppy by eating her kind behind her back. Whether she found out or not wasn't the point; Dorian knew in his soul that she would never forgive him. If the price demanded of him in exchange for her immortal blood was to feel forever hungry then Dorian had no choice but to accept.

So long as he could resist his base nature.

Dorian pulled out his phone, which was the source of the vibrating, more as a distraction from his hunger than out of any intention to respond to whoever was contacting him. He knew it would be a message from Patrick, after all – one of many over the last few days.

He cringed at the sight of all his friend's messages lined up one after the other. As Dorian began once more walking through the rain he scrolled through them, though the raindrops on his phone screen blurred the words and made it difficult for Dorian to read. He hadn't replied to any of the messages, though he knew he should. But what was he to say to Patrick, when Dorian had been insistent that Poppy stay away from her friends and maintain radio silence? If he responded to Patrick then that made Dorian a hypocrite.

But Dorian lingered on the newest message from his best friend regardless, a heavy sigh escaping his lips whilst he waited at a pedestrian crossing for the light to turn green. There weren't any cars passing by, but Dorian had always been a stickler for obeying the laws of the road. Patrick had said all the usual things. That he missed Dorian. That Casey missed Poppy. That they both wanted to help them. Nick and Aisling knew who they were, after all, never mind that they also knew who the rest of Poppy's friends were. If they really wanted to – especially Nick – they could get their claws into everyone Poppy cared about in their attempts to grab her.

Dorian was painfully aware of this. Of course he was; he wasn't stupid. But if everyone was left in the dark then nobody would be able to tell Nick or Aisling where Poppy was. The main problem with this, of course, was that the monsters after them would have no qualms about doing whatever they needed to get information out of Poppy's friends, even if those friends didn't actually know anything. Perhaps the best thing to do was to meet with everyone and try to come up with a more coherent plan to keep them safe from harm.

Unknowingly Dorian bit his thumbnail deep enough for it to bleed, which meant he was biting with a monstrous amount of pressure. But all he had to do was pull away from the wound and it healed before his very eyes: physical, visible proof that Dorian's body was near impenetrable.

He licked at the stray drops of blood left on the pad of his thumb before looking back in the direction of his apartment. Dorian knew he should return to Poppy's side. Her sleep was fitful and shallow, and if he wasn't careful Poppy would wake up and discover him gone. Dorian couldn't do that to her, not least because he was the reason she was alone in the first place.

But *he* was alone, too.

Dorian sincerely wished to see Patrick because of this. He missed him. Right now Dorian was all frayed edges; talking to his best friend might be exactly what he needed to get back on even ground. For he and Poppy weren't talking particularly honestly to each other right now. Even though Dorian had thought there was nothing left for them to hide from each other after she'd betrayed him to free her friends, and they'd run off together in order to save their lives. But now everything they said was laden with deeper meanings, none of which the other person could understand. But Dorian *wanted* to talk. About their situation, about how Poppy was handling things.

About his hunger.

When his phone began vibrating in earnest once more Dorian jumped in fright. Thinking it was Patrick, and desperate to simply hear him speak, Dorian accepted the call.

It wasn't Patrick.

"I never thought my network would actually get this number," Nick drawled. Dorian heart stuttered to a stop. He swung his head wildly left and right, looking for who must be tailing him. Nick had found him so easily. He had—

"Don't hang up, Kapros," Nick urged, sensing Dorian's panic. "I just want to talk. What's the point of tracing this call when I know you'll be hundreds of miles away come morning?"

Dorian considered this. It was highly likely Nick was attempting to goad him into handing over information he could use against him. But Dorian could likewise do the same.

He didn't hang up.

"What is it, then?" Dorian asked carefully, keeping constant watch over his shoulder as he hastily made his way back to the apartment.

Nick laughed. "You know what I want. Hand Poppy over to me."

"Bye, Nick—"

"Let me finish, let me finish. Hand Poppy over and I can assure your safety and forgiveness from the rest of our kind. You know I'm just about the only one who *can* assure that for you."

Dorian said nothing.

"Given how special Poppy is," his former friend continued, voice low and steady as if Nick was already certain of his victory against Dorian, "I can understand why you did what you did. I commend you for it, truly I do. I probably would have done the same thing. That's why I'm giving you the chance to fix things, Dorian."

"And how can I trust that? How could I ever take you at your word?"

"I could just as easily ask you the same thing. You went back on your word to me, didn't you? So I guess you'll have to trust me and leave it at that. Besides...why would I lie to someone I want to work with?"

"Work with you? The hell is that all about?"

"Given the recent absence of food for European monsters, I find myself organising a live auction in your stead. Would be a hell of a lot easier with you on board, though."

Here Nick was, offering Dorian a better deal than he could ever hope to have. A blank slate with his kind, the ability to continue his job - something he loved - and the sparing of his life.

All he had to do was give up Poppy King.

"Thanks, Nick, but I think I'll pass."

"*Kapros—*"

Dorian hung up.

Giving Poppy up was off the table. Nothing would make Dorian hand her over, not even a full pardon. For how could he give up someone he so desperately, painfully loved just to save his own skin? He had no doubt Poppy would try to find a way, somehow, to end her life, if she were to be handed over to Nick. But Dorian knew Nick would never allow that. Poppy's life would be an endless torment. She'd be a prisoner forever, more so that she had ever been back in Dorian's facility.

He could never do that to her. He couldn't live with himself if he did.

Hunger gnawed at Dorian's stomach once more as he stood in the middle of the lonely street. The urge to eat was growing unbearable. *Ignore it, ignore it,* Dorian told himself, miserably shaking his head of rain as he headed back to the apartment. He had no idea what to do next except follow exactly what Nick expected him to do: wake Poppy and flee hundreds of miles from Amsterdam.

Anything after that was blank.

OBSERVATION

FRED

Fred had been to Berlin twice in his life. The first time was with his family when he was seven: his mother's side of the family were German, but they moved to Scotland after the First World War. He didn't remember much of the trip, truth be told, other than the fact the weather had been awful and he'd spent much of the time meeting distant relatives Fred knew he'd never meet again.

The second time had been during the first year of his master's degree. Fred, Rachelle, Nate, Poppy and Casey had travelled to Berlin for a long weekend getaway in June after everyone's exam results had been released.

Of course Fred hadn't wanted to go on holiday with Poppy. But, as was always the case with having the same group of friends, it had been an inevitability. Fred wanted to visit Museum Island and get a multi-day pass to visit every exhibit it had to offer.

Poppy had staunchly refused.

"Why waste our time inside stuffy museums when it's so hot out, Sampson?" she'd said, dismissing his plan in one fell swoop. "Come back in winter to visit them all."

Fred had hated how quickly Poppy singularly derailed the entire trip to suit her own agenda at the expense of his. Looking back on it now, however, Poppy had been right. Their friend holiday was much better spent under the sun, drinking German beer, exploring parks and rooftop bars and taking the train out to visit a range of castles, rivers and, one night, a secret rave.

Still, Fred had hated Poppy, so he hated that she tossed aside his far more cultural plan for Berlin.

Now it was late October, and Fred was in Berlin for the third time. Perfect museum weather – if he went by Poppy's view of things. The irony of returning to the city in the vain hope of finding her was not lost on him.

Going by the news someone fitting Dorian's description had been spotted in Berlin recently. Fred wondered if he could truly be lucky enough to find both him and Poppy on his first attempt at seeking them out.

"I highly doubt it," Fred spoke aloud, simply to hear his own voice. He hadn't spoken to anyone since Aisling blackmailed him into helping her four days ago, not even his parents. Rachelle, Andrew, Nate and Casey still refused to pick up his calls – though he'd left all four of them a voicemail explaining what he was setting off to do – so Fred shoved some clothes into a rucksack, emptied his savings account and slid his passport into his pocket without telling a soul where he'd gone.

Realising how terrible that was for his parents after the horror of the Outdoor Sports Society retreat, Fred quickly unlocked his phone to send his mother a message explaining that he'd be gone for a few days. She'd called him a dozen times whilst he was up in the air en route to Berlin; Fred pushed his guilt to the side for now. He didn't know how to talk to his parents about what he'd been through, and he definitely couldn't fabricate a reasonable excuse off the top of his head for seemingly spontaneously travelling to Germany.

Dealing with his parents would have to wait for another day.

When Fred reached Museum Island he stared at the façade of the Pergamonmuseum, shivering when a breeze laden with the sinister chill of winter found its way into his jacket. It was the primary museum he'd wanted to visit last time.

He turned from it and headed north-west along the River Spree, instead. *Ruining my trip even when she's not around,* Fred mused, though given that he wasn't actually in Berlin to have fun he couldn't find it in himself to be angry or upset with Poppy. *And besides, it's no fun on my own.*

But alone was what Frederick Sampson was, and it was nobody's fault but his own.

The sky was a solid blanket of grey cloud above him, reflected back on the perfectly still surface of the Spree. The pavement was grey. The lampposts were grey. The buildings were grey. Fred wondered if it looked so monotonous because of his current state of mind or whether it truly was as grim as he observed it.

Eventually, after an hour or two of aimless walking – during which time Fred searched for possible hotels and hostels to check out in case Poppy and Dorian were staying at them – he came across an old building that looked like it was part of a university or a hospital. Curious despite himself at the welcome break from flat grey stone, Fred deviated from the river to check out what the sign outside the building said.

"Museum of Medical History," Fred murmured, understanding what the German words said without needing to look at the English translation written in smaller type below the main sign. And though it served no purpose to his search, Fred found himself walking up the broad stone steps, paying for entry to the museum and hanging up his jacket in the cloakroom.

The museum was about as macabre as Fred had expected it would be. Medical museums always ended up being the same: deformed bones; unborn foetuses in jars; cancerous tumours of increasing size pinned to white boards; photos of diseased indigenous folk from long-ago highly unethical studies. It should have distressed Fred to realise how desensitised he was to such obviously upsetting material, but he was numb to it all.

If it wasn't the blood of Poppy King painted across his skin, Fred could no longer be disturbed.

Because it was mid-morning on a Wednesday the museum was largely empty of other guests. Fred was therefore surprised when he spotted a man with a flash of shockingly pale blonde hair upon entering a more modern room of the museum, detailing the current state of medical research undertaken by the university in recent years. Going by what the man was wearing Fred assumed he worked for the museum. Then the man turned to face him, and all thoughts of whether the man was a visitor or employee were chased straight out of his head.

Fred was looking at himself.

"So the Fred Sampson at the Highlands facility really *was* you," the man said. The room they were in was small and claustrophobic; it swallowed his voice until it was barely a whisper, though the man had spoken at a normal volume.

Fred could only stare. *Just what is happening? Who is this man? Why does it feel like I'm looking in a mirror?*

The man coughed self-consciously into his hand. "It's rude to stare, Frederick, even at your own relatives."

Caring about being rude was the last thing on Fred's mind. Something impossible was happening right before his very eyes, after all. But nothing would come of him remaining stunned and silent so, blinking furiously, Fred forced his brain to reboot so he could take a proper look at the man who stood in front of him.

The man's hair was several shades lighter than Fred's sandy colouring, and his skin was pale and clear where Fred had a spray of freckles across his cheeks and the last vestiges of a summer tan. His nose was straighter, too, and his eyes were a glassy blue instead of Fred's bottle green.

They were of a similar height, but the man's lanky and

slightly stooped posture suggested he shied away from the kind of physical sports Fred adored. In fact, the spidery frame of the man very much suggested he near-permanently presided within the windowless realms of the museum Fred found himself in.

All in all the man was a finer-featured, more delicate version of Fred.

"You said...relative?" Fred finally ventured, after what felt like forever.

The man breathed a sigh of relief at the fact Fred was clearly still in control of his mental faculties. "I knew you were my great-great-great-grandson the moment I saw you on the news. Obviously I couldn't contact you through usual means, given—"

"You're my – is that why you—"

"Come on, Frederick," he cut in, somewhat impatient, "you're smarter than that. How likely do you think it is that you have an unrelated doppelgänger? Of course we're related. Your mother's side of the family has strong genes. We could be twins, almost. You're even named after me, though I go by my middle name these days. Peter." He held out his hand to shake Fred's. Fred didn't respond.

"You're my...great-great-great-grandfather?" he said, double-checking what he'd heard to make sure he hadn't made it up.

"Yes, but let's move past that. You don't seem all that shocked by the fact I don't look a day over twenty-five."

"That isn't the strangest thing I've borne witness to over the last few months."

Peter smiled carefully. "I had a feeling that might be the case. Knowing how the satyr's auctions usually go it was clear something had gone horribly awry this time. I doubted you'd come away from his facility still clouded from the truth of things, despite what you and your group of friends told the media."

Peter waited for Fred to say something. Perhaps he was watching his reaction to the use of words like *satyr* and *auction*.

But when Fred didn't respond Peter continued, "I trusted that you'd follow the trail of the satyr to Berlin, if you knew what he truly was. Alas, that was a lie. He isn't here. But after hearing about what happened in the Highlands I knew I had to see you in person."

"And why the fuck do you think that?"

"Language, Frederick."

"I'm staring at a man who knows the truth about the hell I went through this summer, who looks just like me, who claims to be my great-great-grandfather—"

"Three greats."

"—and you're worried about language?" Fred finished. *Poppy would bloody love him, berating me like this.*

"Manners are important," Peter said, serious. "Though I guess I can forgive you, given the circumstances. But since you haven't said that this is impossible or refuted my claims, and you aren't all that shocked about my appearance, that leads me to suspect you've seen my kind before."

"And how do you suppose that?"

"When you've been around for as long as I have, you become good at reading people. You know I possess immortal blood, don't you? Or certainly suspect it."

Fred nodded. For what point was there in denying anything now? He had thought his life couldn't get any more bizarre. Clearly he was wrong, and clearly Peter had summoned him for a reason.

"Going by my research it seems you're a scientist, just like me," the man announced, a glint of pride in his pale eyes at this fact. "So tell me, Frederick: how do you work out something previously unknown?"

"...experimentation?"

"Exactly. How do you feel about getting a blood transfusion or eight?"

INTERLUDE II

Jonathan always stayed at the swimming pool right up until closing time. Swimming at night was far preferable, after all, when the pool was calm and quiet instead of filled with the screams of young children gone wild under the neglectful eyes of their parents.

It was cold outside – colder than late October usually was in London – and Jonathan hadn't dried his shoulder-length hair after showering. So he allowed a shiver to travel down his spine, huffed in a deep breath of frigid air, then began the short walk home feeling tired and well-exercised.

He never made it further than the corner of the gym before a needle pricked his neck and he was dragged away from the safety of the street lamps.

All that was left behind was Jonathan's bag, full of swimming gear he would never use again.

A Stranger in Her Own Body

POPPY

POPPY AWOKE WITH A START. She always did, whenever Dorian left her side. He didn't know that Poppy was aware of the fact he often disappeared to go prowling in the middle of the night – if he did then Poppy knew he'd never leave again. But though she was deathly curious to know what Dorian did or where he went whenever he left her, Poppy knew she didn't have the right to ask him. She had the sneaking suspicion that all Dorian wanted was some time to be alone.

After all, Poppy wasn't the only one who had found herself permanently shackled to another soul for the rest of her life.

And though she could never tell Dorian how badly his absence unnerved her, and she wished it didn't affect her in the first place, within seconds Poppy began shivering and her heart rate sped up far past normal. She rolled onto her side beneath the duvet, pulled her knees to her chest and willed the pain in her lungs to go away.

Poppy breathed in deeply, deeper still, then deeper still, holding it in for as long as she could before letting out a low whistle of air through her teeth. She had become used to the process of dealing with hyperventilation and, by extension, panic attacks, by now. She was a veteran of poor mental health.

But nothing was helping Poppy King tonight.

"Where are you, Dorian?" she whispered, simply to hear somebody speak. Her skin prickled as beads of sweat began rolling down her spine, itching at her skin like half a dozen tiny claws. Poppy leapt from bed in an effort to dislodge them, deciding that pacing the apartment would be better than lying motionless. But the new apartment Dorian had found for them in Dublin was tiny, and within four strides Poppy had reached the edge of her current prison.

She wanted to go outside.

She knew she shouldn't.

For even though the highly rebellious part of her wanted to go outside simply because Dorian didn't want her to, Poppy had long since learnt her lesson about being contrary to Dorian's wishes when the only thing he wanted was to keep her safe. All it took was one terrifying, traitorous thought of Nick for Poppy's rebellious urges to quickly dissipate to nothing.

Nick, covered in gleaming scales, curling horns protruding from his head, heavy tail sliding along the floor as he took purposeful step after purposeful step towards Poppy. Propane on the air and a silver lighter in Poppy's shaking hand, ready to die a fiery death before Nick could claim her as his own. But Nick hadn't perished in the flames, and instead his desire for Poppy had been ignited further.

And then there was Aisling, who really would kill her the moment she saw her and consume every last drop of blood Poppy held within her. Poppy had no doubt about it.

Those were the two options waiting for her behind the door of the apartment. If she wanted to live then Poppy had no choice but to remain exactly where she was: trapped with her nightmarish memories and Dorian nowhere to be found.

"Calm down, calm down, calm down," she repeated, though it was to no avail. Poppy knew she wouldn't be able to calm herself down on her own. She needed Dorian to be here, even if he didn't know it, to pretend to be asleep beside her. To be a solid, comforting figure who, only in those dark moments, displayed any kind of physical affection towards her.

For when he thought Poppy was asleep Dorian would wrap his arms around her and hold her close. He would snuggle against her neck for no purpose other than to kiss her skin and smell her hair – no ulterior desire for blood present. It was in those small, midnight, forbidden moments that the true extent of Dorian's feelings for Poppy were revealed to her, though it was clear he knew she couldn't reciprocate. How could she? Dorian was the sole reason Poppy was stuck in a nightmare. So she'd been keeping her distance, except in those moments when to keep her distance from Dorian would mean to lose her mind entirely.

Poppy knew who she really needed right now. Wanted. She was panicking enough to forget why she had resisted calling him in the first place.

She grabbed her phone from the bedside dresser and called Andrew.

It was three in the morning, and Poppy was calling from a burner phone Andrew did not have the number for. By all accounts Poppy knew he would not pick up. But even the mere *idea* that he might pick up was enough to slow Poppy's heart, just a little. Just enough that she remembered why she shouldn't call him. She sat back down upon the bed and hovered her finger over the keypad, meaning to hang up.

Andrew picked up the call.

"Hello?" Andrew's achingly familiar voice asked, bright, formal and wide awake. Not asleep at all. And then, after a second of silence, "Poppy?"

The hope in his voice when he said her name was all it took. Poppy began crying in earnest, folding back into a foetal position on the bed to sob down the phone.

"Poppy?! Poppy, what's happening? Are you – what's wrong? Are you in trouble? Are you—"

"I'm okay," Poppy gasped, eyes clenched shut against the tears streaming down her face. Her chest heaved with the effort it took to speak. "I'm – I'm okay, I'm safe, I'm—"

"You don't sound okay."

"Th-that's because I'm not."

"You just said that you were."

Poppy could have laughed if she hadn't been crying so hard. "I'm okay in that I'm safe," she explained between sobs. "Not in d-danger. Andrew, I'm so glad to hear your voice."

It wasn't something Poppy should have said given how they'd left things the month before, and after what Dorian had so obviously insinuated regarding Andrew's feelings towards Poppy, but in that moment she was too relieved to think about the impact her words might have.

There was a pause. "...what does that mean?" Andrew asked, too confused to take Poppy's statement at anything more than face value. "Poppy, please tell me what's going on."

"I just needed to hear your voice," Poppy said, realising that talking to Andrew was finally beginning to calm her down. So she wiped her tears away, hauled in a shuddering breath, then wrapped the duvet around her shoulders before putting the phone on speaker and settling it on the pillow by her head. "I had a nightmare."

"It must have been a pretty bad nightmare."

"Yeah. Why are you awake?"

"Nightmare."

Poppy didn't doubt it. She let out a small, humourless laugh. "I wonder if they'll ever stop."

"Rachelle says it's good to talk about them when you have a nightmare," Andrew said, painfully serious. "She says if you talk about it you make the nightmare seem less real."

"Rachelle is very wise. I suppose she's always been that way. You should listen to her, Andrew. You know she's speaking sense."

"We all miss you. *I* miss you, Poppy." And there it was. The truth from which Poppy could not escape, nor in all honesty *wanted* to escape.

"I know."

Another pause. "...can you tell me where you are? Can I see you?"

"Andrew, I—"

But then Poppy stopped. She had been about to tell Andrew what she *should* tell him. That she couldn't see him. That he couldn't know where she was. If Poppy saw her friends then they weren't safe. But at the rate she was going Poppy would be sure to break down entirely.

She needed to see them. Badly. Desperately.

"Yes, I want to see you, too," she said. "We should try to work something out."

"Really?!" Andrew had clearly not expected Poppy to agree with him; his excitement was palpable. "When? Where? I can leave tomorrow. No, today, it's already three in the morning. Do you want me to tell Rachelle? Or Nate? What about—"

"One thing at a time, Andrew," Poppy laughed, overcome by his enthusiasm. Then she heard the shuffling of footsteps outside the door, and the jingle of keys, and she stiffened. "Look, Andrew, I need to go, but I'll talk to you tomorrow. Okay?"

Even before he spoke Poppy could tell Andrew was

disappointed their call had been cut so short. So was she. "Do you promise?"

"I promise. I'll speak to you tomorrow."

"Poppy—"

Poppy hung up, though it pained her to do so. When Dorian walked in, windswept and dripping wet from the howling rain outside, Poppy knew she needed to talk to him even if it meant cutting Andrew off.

Dorian practically tripped over himself when he looked up and realised Poppy was wide awake, staring at him. "Poppy. I—"

"It doesn't matter where you were," Poppy said, even though in truth it did. But all that mattered now was that he was back. "Jesus Christ, you're soaked. Get changed into something dry."

"Why are you awake?" Dorian asked warily, wincing when he peeled off his jacket and unbuttoned his shirt. Poppy looked away to give him some privacy whilst he changed clothes, even though she could tell Dorian was disappointed that she didn't look.

"I couldn't sleep," Poppy said, which was barely half of the story. "I want to ask you something."

"...and that would be?"

It was now or never. Poppy sucked in a breath just as Dorian finished tugging on a pair of jogging pants. "I want to see my friends. I know you've said so many times that I can't - that it's dangerous and stupid - but I—"

"No, I agree."

"—but I can't - wait, you do?"

Dorian smiled softly as he sat down on the bed beside Poppy, rubbing a towel through his sodden, overgrown hair to dry it off. "I got a message from Patrick last month. He not-so-subtly reminded me that we're not the only two people involved in this. We should touch base with everyone Aisling and Nick would be likely to contact in order to reach *us*. Whether I like that fact or not, it's the sensible thing to do."

Disappointment flooded Poppy when she realised *this* was the reason Dorian was agreeing with her, though it was with some horror that she realised he was correct. Still, it would have meant more to her if Dorian had possessed enough of a heart to believe she needed her friends for the sake of her mental health. Her sanity.

For the sake of love.

Gently – carefully – Dorian touched Poppy's shoulder, and bowled through Poppy's disappointment with a few scant sentences. "I also know you need to see them. You never got a proper goodbye. You never got anything. And I can't...I can't do that to you. Never mind the fact I'd like to see Patrick. I never thought I'd be in a position where I had to say goodbye to him, either." A wry smile. "After all, I didn't plan to be on the run."

The two of them sat together in silence for a few moments, digesting everything that had been said. The rain outside blasted against the window as the wind howled, until Poppy was half-convinced the glass would smash all over their heads.

"Patrick suggested we stay with him and Casey for Christmas," Dorian finally offered, breaking the silence. He sounded more hopeful than he had in a long time. "He has a house off the west coast of Scotland left to him by his grandfather. It's huge; I've been there before. Plenty of space for everyone. Impressive cliffs to one side and a forest around the rest. Remote place. Well protected."

Poppy nodded, not trusting her voice. Because as she listened to Dorian talk she realised that what he'd said earlier – that they needed to talk to everyone who might be contacted by Nick or Aisling – involved more than just their closest friends.

"Poppy? What's wrong?" Dorian asked, when he saw the way she grimaced at nothing. That grimace only grew more twisted when she turned to face him.

"I think I need to give Sampson a call."

HYPOTHESIS

FRED

FRED WINCED WHEN THE NEEDLE WAS removed from his arm, signalling the end of another transfusion of his great-great-great-grandfather's blood into his own body. It was his fourth transfusion in as many weeks.

During those weeks Fred had told Peter all about his experience at the Highlands Adrenaline Sports Facility. Except for Poppy King. He hadn't told Peter about what he'd done to Poppy, though there was something about the way his immortal relative regarded him that told Fred the man was not entirely ignorant to the fact that something had gone on that Fred wasn't telling him about.

What shocked Fred most was how little time it had taken to tell Peter about what had happened to him. The man already knew about monsters, and immortal blood, and human trafficking auctions. There was no need to explain them, nor Fred's resultant numb and stony façade that had built up in response to the trauma to which he'd been subjected.

It was in this way that, after the first transfusion, Peter regaled Fred with the highlights – and lowlights – of his own, very long life.

"So you didn't move away with your daughter – my great-great-grandmother – from Germany during the First World War?" Fred asked, rubbing at his arm after the needle was taken out. It was a large, horrible thing, for Peter had had to upgrade to a thicker and bigger needle with every transfusion. Fred took that as a sign that things were working. That he was growing more impenetrable with every pint of blood he took from his immortal relative.

It hurt like hell.

Peter shook his head. "She left with my wife and most of the rest of my family, though my brother and uncle stayed behind. We were fighting in the war; I didn't know, in fact, that it was incredibly difficult for me to die until I was on the battlefield. Once I worked that out it was easy enough to fake my own death to fade into safety and obscurity."

"So you spent the last hundred years in hiding?" It was something Fred still couldn't wrap his head around, even after weeks of hearing the same stories retold half a dozen times. "Couldn't you have spent a few more years with your family before they worked out something was...wrong?"

"I could have." Peter avoided eye contact as he cleaned the transfusion equipment, handed Fred a plate of biscuits they both knew he wouldn't eat, then sat in a chair opposite Fred with a posture that could only be described as old-fashioned. Peter steepled his fingers together. "I thought about it. Once or twice I found myself jumping on a ship over to England. But then..."

"Then?"

"Then I realised things would be better for my family if I stayed away. Or better for me, maybe. I was used to being on my own. Used to pretending I was a ghost. For me to return to my family would mean returning to who I *was*. And I wasn't that person anymore; I hadn't been since before the war."

"So then..." Fred chose his next words carefully. "Where

were you during the Second World War?" He'd wanted to ask about this for a couple of weeks now, but Peter had danced around the subject. To his surprise his great-great-great-grandfather laughed.

"I wondered when you'd ask about that. There were three of us – that I knew about – during World War Two."

"Three what?"

"Men with blood like mine," Peter said, waving emphatically at himself. "Unsurprisingly we were taken hold of for experiments, but then a handful of monsters in the ranks of the Nazis found out about us. I escaped, but the other two...well, they weren't so lucky."

"And the monsters?" Fred asked, leaning forward with renewed interest. "Are they still around?"

But Peter shook his head. "They were foolish and acted without a plan. They were gunned down again and again and again, too quickly for them to heal. It was all for naught."

"So how did *you* get away?"

"When you have no qualms about breaking your own bones to fit into impossible spaces you find it remarkably easy to escape, Frederick."

The thought made Fred cringe. "Noted."

"You have to get used to pain if you're going to be immortal. It comes with the territory."

Given what Fred had put Poppy through, he didn't doubt it.

"I think after another three transfusions we should give you a break," Peter said, clucking his tongue in satisfaction when he checked Fred's blood pressure.

That meant they were done for the day. The man had made a quick study for Fred; it was clear he liked his personal space. When Fred got to his feet he found that he no longer swayed like he had done when the transfusions first began. Obediently he made his way to the door. "To see if this amount of blood is sufficient to change my circulatory system?"

"If it doesn't we'll try a full cycle again," Peter said, inclining his head as he followed Fred to the door. "I'll see you in a few days."

As Fred wandered his way back to his hotel, shivering against the bitter November wind, he wondered what he should tell his former friends. Would they listen to him, if he told them everything he had learnt? Would *Poppy?* The existence of another soul with immortal blood – and the means to transfer that blood to a living relative – seemed like something he should tell her.

But Fred didn't want to. Not yet. Not until he knew it worked. And even then...

No, Fred decided, resolute. *For now I keep this to myself.*

When he returned to his hotel room there was a stark chill in the air that alerted Fred to the fact the window was open when it hadn't been before. That was how he knew Aisling was waiting for him, though Fred could not have prepared for what she *looked* like waiting for him.

There was no dark-haired, intimidatingly beautiful woman waiting for him. There was only a monster, though said monster was alarmingly no less beautiful than the guise of humanity Aisling had been using up until now.

Where the woman's arms had been were iridescent wings of long, luxuriant feathers the colour of an oil spill. They ended in midnight talons, their sharp edges as long as Fred's hands. Peering at her Fred realised Aisling's skin was almost lilac – too pale and blue-toned to be human. Her legs were scaled and powerful, ending in talons three times the length of the ones that adorned her wings.

Those wings were neatly folded against Aisling's back as she reclined against the open windowsill. Fred couldn't fathom how huge they would be fully spread out.

"It seems you've relocated to Berlin, Frederick," Aisling

drawled. "Any reason why?" Her voice sounded *wrong* to his ears. Garbled and high-pitched, somehow, though in truth the harpy's voice was as low and clear as it had ever been.

It took him a moment to remember how to speak, though because Fred's stunned reaction to Aisling's true appearance was clearly what she had wanted she did not grow impatient. "I can't face going home," he eventually said. "Seeing my parents. Seeing...everyone else." It was true, but it wasn't the reason Fred had remained in Berlin. That was a truth Aisling could never find out. But his excuse seemed to appease her, for which Fred was grateful.

"How's you search going?" she asked.

"A man matching Dorian's description was found in the west end of Berlin. I've been chasing it up."

"To no avail, it seems." Aisling fell easily upon the bed and stretched out her taloned feet over the edge. Her hawk-like gaze followed his every movement as he flinched away from her razor edges.

"It would – it would seem that way," he said, hating that he stuttered. Fred's heart was in his throat, as it had been when Dorian revealed his true form and swore he would kill him. The urge to fight or flee throbbed insistently inside him.

Right now Fred could do neither.

Aisling watched his face pale with growing amusement. "And what of—"

A vibrating from Fred's pocket gave them both pause. At a nod from the harpy he pulled out his phone and checked the screen. It was an unknown number.

"Pick it up," Aisling hissed, when Fred didn't immediately answer.

"It's probably an insurance scam or something," he said, though even as he said it he knew it wasn't true.

"Or it might be Poppy King. Pick it up."

Fred had no doubt Aisling wouldn't waste any time in using her wickedly sharp talons to make him do as she asked, so he chose the safer route and complied without the need for physical coercion.

"...hello?" he murmured, turning from Aisling as soon as he answered the call.

"God, I thought you weren't going to pick up," came the unmistakeable sound of Poppy's voice. "Did you think I was a scam or something? I couldn't imagine having to *text* you to tell you I needed to talk."

Fred found himself grinning despite himself at Poppy's age-old derision towards him. It felt so familiar. So safe. How had he ever hated it? But he was being watched, so Fred schooled his expression as best he could when Aisling shifted on silent wings to observe his face.

"Good to know you aren't dead," he said.

"Funny. How are you?"

"Do you actually want to know how I am, or are you being fake-polite?"

"Well, I *did* want to know how you are but if you're going to be like that—"

"I've been worse," Fred cut in, once more fighting a smile. "What about you? Are you on your own or are you still with the goat?"

A pause. That's how Fred knew that whatever Poppy was about to say wasn't going to be the whole truth. He glanced at Aisling, who was listening attentively with a cocked head. "I'm still with him, yeah," Poppy finally said, in a way that brought up far more questions than it answered. "But I didn't call you to talk about Dorian."

"Why *did* you call me, then?"

"To ask..." Poppy sighed. "Well, the thing is, I'm planning to spend Christmas at Patrick and Casey's place. Andrew, Rachelle and Nate are coming, too. It's some massive cabin on the top of a cliff along the west coast of Scotland. It's absolutely gorgeous, apparently, though stormy as hell."

"Well that's very nice for you."

"Don't be a dick. I'm calling to ask if you want to join us."

It was Fred's turn to pause. "Are you...are you sure? Considering—"

"I haven't suddenly lost my memory, Sampson," Poppy bit out, all snark and impatience that hid something much darker. "It's *because* of what happened that I want you to be with us. I think we all...need this. To clear the air. God knows the last time we met achieved precisely nothing."

"*Say yes*," Aisling mouthed, a calculating look on her face as she spoke. A horrible knot of dread twisted Fred's stomach; if he was going to be the reason all of his friends died he'd rather face Aisling's wrath right then and there, all on his own.

"I'll be there," Fred said, barely aware of the words he said. "And Poppy..."

"Yes?"

The sharp point of one of Aisling's foot-long talons tickled the edge of Fred's neck, her leg stretched out from the bed with languid ease. If he said the wrong thing then he'd bleed out on the floor before managing to warn Poppy of anything.

If Fred could bleed out on the floor. But he wasn't ready to test that yet.

"Yes, Fred?" Poppy repeated, clearly impatient. "The hell is it?"

"It's – it's good to hear from you. Stay safe."

Fred hung up.

"Very good," Aisling crooned, removing her talons from Fred's neck before primly crossing her legs. "I knew I could count on you to do as you're told."

"You can't touch my friends," Fred pleaded. "You said you wanted Poppy and Dorian. You can't touch—"

"And who said I would? You're going to see your friends for Christmas, and you're going to get Poppy nice and drunk, and you're going to find out where she plans to be next."

"I'm going – you're not going to follow me and use this as an opportunity to—"

"Do I look like I have a death wish, Frederick?" Aisling cut in, dark eyes flashing dangerously. She stood up to her full height, then spread her wings until the tips of her feathers brushed either side of the fifteen-foot-long hotel room. "A stormy cliff-side in the middle of winter, when faced with a mountain goat and a god damn monster of the sea, is what one might call an *uneven match-up.*"

Fred considered this. The harpy certainly had a point. "So this is a reconnaissance mission?"

"Exactly. So don't mess this up or I *will* harm your friends. Got it?"

He nodded. Of course he got it. He understood loud and clear the situation he was in.

He had to find a way to convince Poppy to remain as hidden as possible...for as long as possible.

INTERLUDE III

The snow on the ground muffled Jin's footsteps as he rushed down the street as fast as he dared.

Someone had been following him for fifteen minutes.

But Jin was quick on his feet, and it wouldn't be long before he came across the hostel he'd been staying at with his friends whilst they visited Warsaw. *If only I hadn't left my wallet at the train station,* he grumbled, the annoyance he felt at his friends all refusing to come with him to pick it up rapidly transforming into a fear he didn't want to admit to.

Whether Jin admitted to it or not, being followed down foreign streets was scary as hell.

Eventually he couldn't take the pounding of his heart any further. Full of adrenaline, Jin turned on the spot to face up to his stalker. "What the fuck do you—"

He slipped on the snow underfoot, and something that wasn't an arm caught Jin before he hit the ground.

A long, fur-covered tail, with enough strength to wrap around Jin's stomach to prevent him from escaping.

"Get away from me!" he screamed, beside himself with white-hot terror. Through the darkness Jin couldn't see the creature to which the tail belonged. In truth he didn't want to. But no matter how hard he squirmed and clawed at the tail it wouldn't budge; Jin was stuck.

"You shouldn't have gone back for the wallet," a garbled voice laughed. It was inhuman. Unreal.

A monstrously clawed foot the length of Jin's entire arm stepped forward, crunching snow beneath it, and Jin passed out.

When he woke up he was in a cage, and he was alone.

"Help me!" he cried, shaking the iron bars for all the good it would do. "Help me!"

Nobody came.

A STORMY CHRISTMAS

POPPY

"*Poppy!*"

Casey crashed into Poppy's arms before Poppy even had a chance to call out her friend's name.

"Good to see you, too," Poppy said, the words getting lost in the other girl's fiery hair when she nuzzled against her. Poppy meant every word more than she could ever say.

Patrick's house was so remote that Dorian had almost gotten lost three times en route despite the fact he'd been there before. The journey had taken them through deep forest, then a winding, dangerous cliff-side road, then finally a single-track dirt path which led through a further flurry of trees. When they finally arrived – an hour late – Poppy was met with a large, two-storey building constructed of brick, glass and slate tiles surrounded on three sides by trees and one side by a steep, unrelenting cliff-face.

It was just about the most inhospitable location for a house Poppy could have ever imagined. The house itself, by contrast, was warm and bright and welcoming.

And full of all her favourite people.

"Something smells good," Poppy murmured into Casey's ear, not yet willing to let the younger girl go. It was true; filtering into the hallway – which was white with an eclectic mix of paintings and boat paraphernalia adorning the walls, and exposed wooden beams running along the ceiling – were the smells of goose fat, potatoes, oregano, turkey and garlic.

"We've been cooking all day!" Casey exclaimed, pulling back from Poppy a few inches to flash a smile at her. Her face was perfectly made up, as usual, though there was a softness to Casey's look now that suggested she didn't care *quite* as much as she had done before about always wearing a full face of make-up. She was also wearing a ridiculously oversized, green woollen jumper over a dress that was so short the jumper crept well past the hem of its skirt, which was a look the old Cassandra O'Donnell would never have been seen dead in.

Poppy could only assume the jumper was Patrick's.

"*We* including you?" Poppy scoffed. "Should I be concerned?"

Casey flicked Poppy's nose with her thumb and forefinger. "Bitch. Nate and Rachelle are doing most of the cooking, to be fair. It isn't as if Patrick has the best, um, *palate,* for taste-testing."

Poppy tried hard not to think about the reason behind that.

Behind Casey the door to the kitchen creaked open, revealing Patrick and Nate and Rachelle all wearing aprons in various states of ridiculous food mess. Barely a moment later Rachelle bowled through the door and into Poppy and Casey, completing their trio for the first time in what felt like forever.

"Don't ever go that long without seeing as again," Rachelle said, voice full of tears, before covering Poppy's face in kisses. Poppy responded by licking her cheek.

"I get it, I swear," she promised. Then, over Rachelle's shoulder: "Hey Nate, fancy seeing you here."

Nate's mouth broke into a wolfish grin. "Yeah, imagine. Seen any monsters lately?"

"Only this one," Poppy said, indicating towards the front door just as Dorian propped it open with a shoulder, struggling with two overflowing bags within his arms. Poppy had gone absolutely mad picking up presents for her friends from all of the places they'd run to thus far. After all, what was the point of hopping around Europe if she didn't do some shopping?

Dorian huffed his annoyance at being used as a pack horse, though when Poppy caught his eye she could see he was relieved to be here. Almost happy, even through the freezing sleet and wind that had battered his face on the short journey from the car to Patrick's house.

Poppy turned from Dorian to scan the hallway and the kitchen beyond it. "Where's Andrew?" There was a stairwell leading up to a dark first floor, and two doors on Poppy's left which were closed, but Andrew was nowhere to be seen.

"He's out on the veranda – this way," Patrick said, indicating towards the closest door. "Through the glass doors at the end of the living room." Then he moved past the gaggle of girls to strong-arm Dorian into a furious hug. "Dorian, you bastard," he exclaimed, squeezing his best friend just as hard as Casey and Rachelle had held onto Poppy. "Have you forgotten how to smile?"

It hurt her heart to see Dorian drop the shopping bags to desperately return the gesture, for it made Poppy realise just how truly lonely he had been whilst out on the run with her. She had felt so isolated over the last few months – separated from everything and everyone she had ever held dear – but Dorian had been going through exactly the same thing without a single word of complaint.

"Maybe," Dorian replied dryly. "Nothing a glass of whisky can't change. A large one."

"Easily rectified." Patrick took the fallen bags from the floor, brought them into the living room, then waved Dorian through to the kitchen for the promised whisky. Poppy followed them through to wrap her arm's around Nate's neck despite the flour and grease coating his apron.

"I've missed you," she whispered.

Nate gently kissed her hair. "You, too. But you should know…"

Poppy pulled away from him to frown, confused by Nate's sudden hesitance. "Know what?"

"*He's* here. On the veranda with Andrew. Are you really sure about inviting him?"

Poppy nodded in understanding. "It was necessary."

"I don't want to hear it," Rachelle complained from the doorway. "Why on earth do we need Fred here?"

"Yeah, Poppy," Casey chimed in, glancing at Dorian and Patrick behind Poppy busy downing shots of amber liquid before saying, "I get working with him back at the facility but… come on."

Poppy merely smiled in as reassuring a manner as possible, though she didn't feel it. "Just trust me on this, okay? We need everyone together right now."

To her surprise Nate directed his attention to Dorian to see what he thought. Dorian merely shrugged. "Couldn't hurt to have him on board when the alternative is for everyone to die."

"*Dorian!*"

"I thought we were all being honest?" Dorian protested, deftly avoiding Poppy when she grabbed a piping-hot roast potato and threw it at him. Patrick caught it and popped it back into the pan.

"Speaking of potatoes," Patrick said to Rachelle, Nate and Casey, "are you really going to leave all the cooking to me while you natter away?"

The girls squeezed Poppy's hands; Nate ruffled her hair. "Huge, massive catch up once we're done," Rachelle promised.

"Humungous catch up," Casey added sagely.

"We'll pull an all-nighter if we have to," Nate finished.

Poppy could only laugh at their enthusiasm before heading into the living room on her own. The room took up much of the floor space of the entire ground floor of the house, going by the looks of things, and was similarly painted in white with exposed wooden beams just like the hallway. A huge stone fireplace ablaze with a welcoming fire took up most of the south wall, whilst the west wall was made up of a pair of glass doors leading out onto a veranda overlooking the cliffs. A plush velvet curtain in deep crimson was currently pulled across one of the doors.

In the middle of the room was a large corner sofa and two very comfortable-looking matching recliner chairs, all upholstered in chocolate leather but covered in a mis-match of blankets. The floor was hardwood but it, too, was covered in mis-matched rugs of various sizes. Every inch of wall space was covered in seemingly unrelated photos: family photos, fishing photos, sailing photos, Scottish landscapes, sporting events.

Then, across it all, were strings of red and gold and green tinsel, and a fresh pine tree at least eight feet tall stood in the corner furthest from the fireplace. It was decorated in the most gaudily excessive selection of Christmas decorations Poppy had ever seen.

It felt like the room belonged to a doting, enthusiastic grandfather; Poppy wondered for how long the house had been in Patrick's family. In any case she adored it, though it caused a fresh wave of grief over the loss of her own family to hit her.

A few moments later she heard the tell-tale sound of Dorian's footsteps behind her. He touched her shoulder, urging her to turn around. His gaunt face looked troubled even through the ruddy blush three shots of whisky had granted him. "Are you sure you're ready to face him?"

"How many people do I have to reassure?" Poppy huffed, though she tensed beneath Dorian's hand on her shoulder nonetheless. "I can handle Fred."

"I meant Andrew."

"Oh."

Dorian waited patiently for an answer, sipping from a generous glass of whisky Patrick had poured him. From the looks of things it wouldn't be long before both monsters masquerading as men would be completely and utterly wasted.

Eventually Poppy sighed. "It'll only get worse if I delay it." It was true, but that didn't make things any easier. Considering what had been said between Poppy and Andrew the last time they'd seen each other – and what *hadn't* been said – Poppy had no idea what to expect when she finally saw Andrew face-to-face.

"After you, then," Dorian said, waving towards the doors that led onto the veranda. The wind was howling against the glass but thankfully the sleet seemed to have finally abated, for which Poppy was grateful. But she dithered by the door nonetheless, wondering if she had somehow forgotten how to move during the last three seconds.

When Dorian clicked open the handle Poppy scowled. "I could have done that myself."

"Could you?"

She half-heartedly hit his arm, Dorian allowing her to do so with the same benign resignation as he always did. It left Poppy feeling sad. The two of them were in such a state of inertia – unable to move forward together but just as unable to move back – that neither of them knew what to do with each other. Poppy knew fine well that Dorian wanted more than what they had right now, just as she knew that she didn't. But she didn't want things to remain as they *were*, either.

Poppy wanted to be able to stop running. They'd only been doing it for three months and already she was sick to death of it.

Well, at least here was an opportunity for her to stop running from two other personal matters. Poppy stepped over the threshold into the bitterly cold winter air, and prepared herself to come face-to-face with the two people who had so drastically consumed her thoughts for months now.

Andrew and Fred had been in the middle of what could only be described as a very intense staring competition, but when Poppy stumbled out onto the veranda they both swung their attention to her so quickly she almost thought they had whiplash.

Poppy had no idea who to face first.

"Andrew," came Dorian's voice from behind her, absurdly pleasant and conversational. "It's good to see you."

But Andrew did not reply. Both he and Fred maintained their attention on Poppy, and when she felt Dorian's eyes on her, too, she became wildly uncomfortable. They were all waiting for *her* to say something. So Poppy took several steps forward until she reached the edge of the veranda, leaned against the wooden railing separating the house from the cliffs – wind smashing into her face in the process – and forced herself to get it together.

"Hey," Poppy said, turning to face Andrew first with a grin on her face. His doe-brown eyes were wide and achingly familiar as they stared at her, but to Poppy Andrew looked so grown up he was almost a stranger. His brown hair was unusually dishevelled and plastered to his forehead because of the weather; Poppy noted that it was in need of a cut even more than Dorian's was. There was stubble across his jaw where before Andrew had always been clean-shaven. He held himself straighter. He was dressed better than he'd ever dressed before – like an actual adult – in a shirt, fitted trousers and shiny leather boots Poppy had a sneaking suspicion Rachelle had probably helped him buy. It unsettled her to no end that Andrew now looked like a *man*, though in truth he hadn't been a boy for a long time now.

Andrew gulped. At his side Poppy noticed him clench and unclench a fist. But then he said, "Hello," and all the odd tension between them evaporated entirely.

Poppy's forced grin grew genuine. "Did you get taller?"

"No."

"Really? You look taller."

"Maybe you got shorter."

"It wouldn't be the oddest thing to happen to me."

"Why is *he* here?"

Leave it to Andrew to get straight to the point, Poppy sighed, finally giving Frederick Sampson her attention. Out of the corner of her eye she saw Dorian move past her to exchange a very awkward handshake with Andrew.

Fred looked absurdly good, considering everything that had happened thus far, which oddly mirrored how Poppy looked better now than she had in months. As opposed to Dorian and Andrew, Fred seemed to have been taking proper care of himself, shaving his face, cutting his hair and keeping himself well fed. But there was still a haunted, frenzied look in his eyes that Poppy had first seen in all its horror when Fred confronted her in Dorian's facility, in the quiet hours of the morning, knife in hand and—

"King."

"Sampson." His surname was out of Poppy's mouth before she could help it, though she hated when Fred's lips so easily quirked into an almost-smile at the sound of it. Then, to answer Andrew's question: "I asked him to be here. Ash and...and..."

"Nick," Dorian said, saving Poppy from having to put the monster's name in her mouth. Poppy was more grateful for it than she could ever say.

She nodded. "They could use any one of you to try to find me and Dorian. That includes Fred. They don't know what he did, after all. They...well, they think we're friends." Poppy paused, then let out a huge sigh. "And we all need this. So please, Andrew. Put up with him for me."

Poppy could tell Andrew was staring at her, not Fred, though she and Fred currently had their gazes locked on each other, calculating and reassessing the situation between them. But then

Andrew said, "Okay," and Poppy felt as if the stick keeping her forcibly upright finally dissolved.

"God, what do I have to do to get a drink around here?" Poppy laughed, her voice narrowly dancing along the edge of unhinged. "What are you doing drinking beer, Sampson? I thought you were all about the wine."

"I got a taste for it in Berlin."

"*Berlin?*"

"He was looking for you," Andrew said.

"What the fuck for?" It was Dorian who spoke. He'd taken up his usual spot on Poppy's right-hand side, leaning against the bannister with his gaze trained on the edge of the forest which wrapped around the northern part of the house. There was a set to Dorian's shoulders that told Poppy he longed to go in amongst the dense protection of the trees – to shed his human guise and run.

If he didn't do it of his own accord over the next couple of days, Poppy would insist upon it.

She wished she could she be there to see Dorian running wild and carefree again. Poppy had only ever witnessed it once, the day they scaled the cliff behind his facility and she gave into her traitorous desire for him. But she doubted she'd ever experience such a thing as the true Dorian ever again.

The realisation almost broke her heart in two.

Fred scratched his head awkwardly before shivering against the cold. It was only then Poppy realised both he and Andrew were not at all dressed for the weather, suggesting Andrew had come out here to avoid Fred but Fred had followed him anyway. Poppy shouldn't have been surprised; before Fred attacked her Andrew's closest friend aside from Poppy had *been* Fred.

"I needed to talk to you," Fred muttered, more to himself than anyone else. "But you got hold of me in the end, so I guess I shouldn't have bothered looking for you."

Poppy wanted to call bull shit though she couldn't pinpoint why. She locked the feeling in a box to bring up later. "Can we go inside? It's cold out here and I want alcohol."

Dorian held up his now-empty glass. "I second that."

And so the four of them headed back inside, Dorian's hand finding the small of Poppy's back to gently push her through the doorway as if it was the most natural thing in the world. It hurt her that it was so easy for him to treat her like she was precious. Important.

But Poppy shook the thought from her head. Tonight was for friends and alcohol and blowing off some steam, and then planning their next moves against the monsters intent on tracking her and Dorian down.

At this rate, she'd happily put off the honest conversation she needed to have with him for all eternity.

Just Between Friends

FRED

"You're awfully quiet, Dorian."

"That's because I'm not drunk enough for all of this yet."

Patrick snickered, handing Dorian a fresh beer when he gulped down the remains of the half-empty bottle in his hand. Fred had been relieved when the two of them moved on from whisky to something much weaker; he didn't imagine being in the company of two drunk monsters would be all that much fun for him. *Doubtless they'll be back on the hard stuff later,* he mused, sipping upon his own beer as he scanned the array of people in the living room, *though hopefully by that time I'll have long since gone to bed.*

Dorian, Patrick and Casey – who was sitting on Patrick's lap – were relaxing on two leather recliners close to the fire, whilst Poppy and Nate were sprawled on the floor playing dice upon the coffee table. Fred sat on the smaller side of Patrick's massive corner sofa, alone, whilst Andrew sat quietly beside Rachelle on the longer side. Dinner would be ready soon, but everyone had silently agreed that another drink or two before sitting down to eat was an excellent idea.

Andrew was listening hard to what was going on around him without speaking himself, which was usual Andrew behaviour. What was *unusual* was the flush of Andrew's cheeks, the slight sway of his shoulders and the rate at which he was drinking vodka and orange juice. Fred had never seen him so tipsy before.

Clearly it wasn't just Dorian who needed to be drunk to get through the night.

Fred settled further into the sofa and revelled in the warmth of the house. He'd explored the place as soon as he'd arrived, in awe that a house so large could be nestled away in the middle of nowhere, out of sight and out of mind. It was the kind of house Fred thought he would have lived a happily married life in before his life had been turned upside down. Now the mere idea that any woman would be able to tolerate Fred and all his broken, ragged edges was impossible to imagine.

"So you chose not to go sailing after summer, like you planned, because you...want a family?" Rachelle asked Casey and Patrick, disbelief plain as day on her face as she directed the conversation back to the odd couple. "Casey, I never thought you—"

"Oh, I've always wanted kids," Casey cut in, beaming rosy-cheeked at Patrick. She kissed him lightly before saying, "So I figured why wait? And apparently having, um, monster children, extends the life of the human mother by a couple decades—"

"If you survive giving birth."

"*Poppy!*"

"No, she has a point," Patrick said soothingly, responding to Poppy's muttered comment before Dorian could. The satyr folded back into his chair, thoroughly rankled, though he remained silent. "But there's nothing to worry about where *mini-mes* are concerned, given how...flexible...my body is."

"Oh, please stop it," Rachelle cried, just as Nate burst into raucous laughter. Fred himself was tempted to laugh - he'd certainly responded that way when he'd first learnt that Patrick's true form involved tentacles – but then he caught how rigid Poppy had gone.

It was in this way that Fred realised the idea of having monster children was the specific fuel of one of Poppy's numerous nightmares, though he doubted Poppy would ever confide said specifics with him.

Not for the first time that evening Fred felt entirely out of place even though most of the people in the room were his friends. Well, former. And Poppy. Since when had Fred ever considered Poppy his friend? It felt like he had no words to describe her, past or present.

What were they to each other? Was he a villain to Poppy's hero? Were they rivals?

Something else?

"Dammit, Nate!" Poppy raged several minutes later, sliding her hand across the coffee table to knock half a dozen dice to the floor. Clearly Fred had zoned out long enough that she had returned to normal. "How are you so good at this?"

"Never pegged you as a sore loser, Morph," Nate said, good-naturedly clearing the dice from the floor for another round.

"That's because she never used to lose," Fred cut in before he could stop himself.

All at once the atmosphere turned to ice. From his corner by the fire Dorian's hand tensed around his bottle of beer, close to cracking the glass at the mere sound of Fred's voice.

But then Poppy's eyes caught Fred's, and some semblance of understanding crossed between them. She scowled, though now he knew it was all a show. "That's rich coming from you, Sampson. You're the biggest loser of them all."

"Hardly an insult considering the person giving it to me, King."

The tension in the room broke in one fell swoop. If Fred and Poppy had accepted falling back into their old, immature rivalry, then everyone else was happy to play along with their farce.

For tonight, at least.

Nate reset the dice on the table. "This game is all about luck, anyway," he said. "No skill required. So clearly your *luck* ran out, Morph."

Poppy waved emphatically towards Dorian. "I wonder when that happened?"

It was a horrific thing to say – to remind everyone about – but their group of friends laughed, even Andrew. What was left for them to do now except laugh? The situation Fred and his friends had been left in was fucked. There was no other word for it.

"I'm going to take that as a cue to get back on the harder stuff," Dorian grunted, getting out of his chair and making his way towards the door. A moment later Patrick slid Casey off his lap to join him. Before they exited the living room Fred caught the way Dorian and Poppy exchanged the smallest of glances, which was how Fred knew Dorian was making himself and Patrick scarce so she could talk to her friends alone.

Once Patrick and Dorian left for the kitchen – leaving the door ajar – the rest of the group automatically turned to Poppy.

"So..." Nate said, putting the dice away and sitting up from his relaxed sprawl on the floor. There was no point in pretending to play when more important things demanded his attention.

"So..." Poppy echoed back. For a moment she looked dark and serious, but then she shook her head and flashed a grin at Casey. "Check you out living a happily married life with a tentacled—"

"He'll hear you!" Casey cried, all false modesty, casting a glance back at the open door as she moved from the fireplace to settle in between Rachelle and Andrew. Rachelle began absent-mindedly playing with her auburn hair the moment she sat down. "It's impolite to talk about monsters like that, Poppy. You should know that."

"I should know what, exactly? Monster etiquette? Who do you think you're talking to?"

"I thought Dorian would have taught you more about their society and how they interact with humans by now."

"That would involve King being interested in their world, and she isn't," Fred said, knowing his observation was correct. "Why would she want to know anything about monsters given... well, everything?"

"As much as it pains me to agree with him, I'm with Fred on this one," Nate said. Rachelle nodded. "Considering what we've all been through - especially Poppy - why should she care, Casey?"

"Because why *not*?" Casey looked to Andrew for support. He responded with silence and a large glug of his vodka and orange juice. "They can't help that they need to eat us to live; that's just the way things are for them. Monsters have lived for as long as we have, guys. Longer, even. So why aren't you at all interested?"

"Because I don't want to discover I'm one of them," Poppy muttered, barely coherent. She lay down upon the floor, face down, and sighed. "What if I learn more about everything they do...and find out that I'm far more like them than I ever was like all of you?"

Rachelle reached out her foot to nudge Poppy's head. "Is *that* what you're worried about? How would that change anything?"

"If you haven't noticed, Poppy, I'm *with* one of those monsters," Casey pointed out. "And I love him. So does it really matter if it turns out you're closer to them that you are to us? Honestly, why do any of you care?"

"Because it *does* matter!" Fred bit out, growing frustrated. "I get what you're saying, Casey, I really do," he added on hastily, when it looked like she was going to tell him to fuck off, "but that doesn't change the fact that *they eat us.* You don't sleep with your food, do you? So finding out you're more monster than human *matters.*"

Fred would know. He would have rather liked to never know the full extent of the violence to which he was capable. When Poppy turned her head to stare at Fred her vision glazed over, and he knew she was thinking of exactly the same thing. He wanted to look away.

He owed it to her to maintain eye contact and own up to everything that he was.

"You're very quiet, Andrew," Rachelle said, tapping his shoulder in a clear attempt to diffuse the tension in the room. "What's on your mind?" Even Poppy got up from her position languishing on the floor to drag her attention to him, though she avoided his eyes.

Andrew fiddled with his thumbs, intermittently putting one on top of the other over and over again. His empty glass was abandoned on a walnut side table; Andrew kept glancing at it as if he wished it were full again. "I...agree with all of you," he mumbled, speaking faster than he usually did due to the alcohol in his system. "I want to know more. I want to know everything. I want understand. But I wish – I wish I could go back to..."

"Not knowing anything at all."

Poppy had summed it up perfectly with that one statement. And it was true for them all, for not a single one of them would have chosen their current fate over remaining blissfully ignorant for the rest of their lives. Even Casey sobered at the thought. A silence spread over them, punctuated only by the crackling of the fire. Nate fiddled with the bag of dice. Rachelle and Casey both downed their drinks. Poppy looked at anyone but Andrew.

So Fred broke the silence first. "King, whether you like it or not, the trajectory of your life *has* changed. Discovering the truth about monsters wasn't going to make a difference to that. Not knowing more about why you're different would be stupid."

She turned her gaze to Fred, eyes sizzling with what almost looked like betrayal. "I thought you were on *my* side, Sampson?"

"When it comes to learning about their culture and the way they like to live, yeah. A hundred percent. I couldn't give a crap about that. But your blood, on the other hand..."

"Don't even go there," Nate warned.

Fred ignored him. "Poppy, you owe it to yourself to find out why you are the way you are. How could you not want to know?" He waved around emphatically at their friends, knowing he was quite potentially excluded from what he said next. "We're all going to get old, we're all going to die, but you—"

"Have you ever thought that might be exactly why I don't want to know?"

"That's just madness! That's—"

"I need some air," Andrew all but yelled, scrabbling to his feet and rushing for the terrace doors without once looking at anybody. A rush of bitter air swept over the group when he swiftly opened and closed the door, the darkness swallowing Andrew from view within moments.

It was Rachelle's turn to glare at Fred. "That was out of line. Why did you have to bring that up? What purpose does it serve to make everyone so upset, especially Andrew?"

"What purpose would it serve any of us to be *dead?*" Fred threw back. "We can't keep our heads in the sand when it comes to knowing how to keep each other safe. That includes knowing about Poppy's blood."

For a moment it looked as if Poppy was going to finally yell at him - Fred almost wished she would - but instead she silently followed Andrew out onto the terrace. Fred had expected she would; it had always been either her job or his to calm Andrew down. Considering Fred was the reason he was upset, that left the job to Poppy...even if Fred had noticed she'd struggled to look Andrew in the eye all evening.

Fred sagged against the sofa, all the fight drained out of him. "I'm sorry," he mumbled, to nobody in particular.

"We know you are," Casey said, "you always are. But you have to stop yourself from saying these things *before* you hurt people."

"Because heaven forbid Fred *hurt people*," Nate spat, chucking a dice at his head. Fred didn't even try to avoid it, though the wooden cube stung his temple where it hit and threatened to leave a bruise.

If Fred hadn't been full of immortal blood.

"Nate—"

"I deserve it, Rachelle," Fred said, interrupting Rachelle coming to his defence. Even now, after everything that had happened, she wanted to see the best in him. It hurt him to know that he didn't deserve it. He rubbed at his head where Nate hit him. "As much as we need to move past what I did for the sake of, well, all of us not dying, I know what I've done. I know I have to live with that."

Potentially for longer than any of them could ever imagine.

"So then *why*, Fred?" Rachelle asked, voice so soft she could barely be heard over the crackle of flames. "Why did you do it?"

"If you'd witnessed what I'd witnessed I'd defy you *not* to do something similarly insane."

"I could never—"

"You might. You could never know until you're faced with it." Fred didn't know why he said it, but it was true. He looked at Rachelle then Nate then Casey in turn, begging that they deny his claim. They didn't. "What I saw," he continued, "I can't describe. I don't even know what came over me. I wasn't myself, except that I was. I never knew I had that level of violence in me. And I may never have discovered that, if it hadn't..."

"If it hadn't been Poppy," Casey finished for him.

He nodded in resignation. "If it hadn't been Poppy."

DORIAN

"You look like shit."

"Thanks."

"I'm serious. When was the last time you ate?" Dorian flinched; only Patrick could cut to the bone this quickly. He sifted through the kitchen cabinets until he found the bottle of whisky Patrick had opened earlier, swigging straight from the bottle. Patrick's made to complain, paused, then grabbed the bottle to drink from it directly, too. When he was finished he wiped the back of his hand across his mouth. "I think that's all the answer I need. Does Poppy know?"

"Know what?"

"Cut the crap. Does she know you haven't eaten in years? That you're starving?"

"And how do you propose I bring it up? 'Poppy King, I know I already destroyed your life and pulled you away from everything and everyone you hold dear but did you *also* know that your blood isn't enough to stave off my hunger, and that at any moment I might pounce on an unsuspecting member of your kind and slaughter them to pieces?'" Dorian ran a hand through his dishevelled hair, exhausted beyond words. "Somehow I doubt that would go down well."

"There's obviously a better way to word it than that, Dorian," Patrick said, a knowing look on his face as he surveyed his best friend.

Dorian rolled his eyes. "Obviously. But what does it matter? The truth is the truth."

"We both know that you could *make* her understand. Use

that damn voice of yours properly."

At this a torrent of wind slammed against the dark kitchen window. It rattled the glass in its frame. "I don't think even my voice would cut it this time," Dorian mumbled, watching the window for sleet to leave a trail of water on the window. But though the wind was strong it seemed as if the sleet had finally abated once again, for which Dorian was grateful. He cast a glance at Patrick, who was patiently waiting for him to elaborate. "And if it did...that's hardly getting Poppy to understand, is it? That's unfairly influencing her opinion, not making her understand."

"*Oh.*"

"I don't like how that sounds."

"You love her, don't you? It wouldn't be enough for you to keep her obedient and on your side."

"*Of course it wouldn't.*" Dorian cried, losing his composure in one fell swoop. He dug into the counter-top so hard he was in danger of dropping his human guise and cracking the marble. But then Patrick rested a hand on his shoulder and squeezed with almost sickening force. It was enough to make Dorian take several deep breaths, until the colour red stopped flashing across his vision and the urge to revert to his true form abated. He sighed painfully. "Of course I love her, Patrick. After everything we've been through how could I not?"

"Does she love you?"

"I haven't asked."

"*Dorian!*"

"Because I know the answer will be no," Dorian finished explaining, shrugging off Patrick's hand to once more glare out of the window. In the reflection he saw Patrick run his fingernails over month-long stubble; blithely Dorian wondered if he was growing a beard. His facial hair hadn't been this long in years.

"You never know," Patrick said slowly, "it wasn't as if Cass loved me at the start. But she gave me a chance and now look at us! Honestly, Dorian, I've never been happier. And I can tell she loves me – truly, genuinely loves me – despite the way we met. Despite what I am."

"And I'm happy for you. You know I am. But with Poppy... with Poppy it isn't like that. I don't think it ever will be."

"Then at the very least you owe it to yourself to talk to her about your feelings. You're in this together until the end, aren't you?"

"For forever...or until someone kills us."

Patrick chuckled, then handed Dorian the whisky once more. "That's the spirit. Just talk to her, Dorian. No matter the outcome you'll both be the better for it."

Dorian turned from the window to give the living room door his attention; it was open just enough for him to see Andrew run for the terrace, Poppy following closely behind. He couldn't compete with how she cared for Andrew. He could *never* win against that.

But Patrick was right. If Dorian did nothing then nothing would happen. Something had to give, and he knew Poppy wouldn't be the one to make the first move.

Even if it hurt him in the process, Dorian had to talk to Poppy King.

ALMOST A CONFESSION

ANDREW

BLOOD WAS RUSHING INSIDE ANDREW'S EARS when he stepped out onto the expansive wooden veranda of Patrick's house. There was a sizeable overhang, which helped protect Andrew from the weather, but he was thankful nonetheless that the rain and sleet had stopped a few minutes earlier.

In the furthest corner from the terrace doors was a large, swinging wicker bed, chained to the overhang and laden with blankets. It looked like the perfect place to hide from everyone and calm down. So Andrew followed his instincts and crept into the bed, smothering himself in blankets before pushing off the wall to set the bed into a swinging motion.

He closed his eyes.

The rocking helped calm him. Forward, back, forward, back. Again and again, each time the distance getting smaller, until Andrew pushed off the wall to begin the motion all over again. He wanted to do nothing but swing, see nothing but the inside of his eyelids, and hear nothing but the wind howling against the cliff-side whilst the waves battered the rocks down below.

Just as his nerves began to calm and the flush of his skin

abated, the terrace door quickly opened and closed. Andrew knew it was Poppy without looking at her.

"I'm sorry about what happened in there," she said softly, shocking Andrew by easily sliding into the hanging bed with him and snuggling under the covers. He resisted the impulse to flinch away. After all this time, having Poppy so close was almost more than he could bear. But Andrew could bear it even less if she moved away because of him. He desperately wanted her closer. So Andrew opened his eyes and turned to face her, and found Poppy's brow frowning in concern. "Fred really bothers you right now, doesn't he?"

He didn't want to talk about Fred. But Andrew knew Poppy likely wouldn't drop it unless Andrew gave her a straight answer. "How couldn't he bother me? I know you said we should all work together. But..."

"You saw what he did. I know that. I wish we could all go back to when none of this had happened, too."

"That will never happen, will it?"

"Who knows? Considering all the things that have happened so far, would it be so strange to discover we could travel back in time?"

Andrew laughed, which made Poppy laugh. And perhaps it was because he had consumed more alcohol than he had ever drank before, or perhaps it was because of the swinging of the bed, or perhaps it was because Poppy was there – tangibly there – for the first time in months, but Andrew found himself beginning to relax. He let out a low whoosh of breathless air. "How are you, really?" he asked, though he didn't expect Poppy to answer honestly.

"Do you actually want me to give you a real answer?" Poppy asked, once more surprising Andrew. "You must know things are shite, Andrew. Excuse my language."

"You're excused."

Another laugh from Poppy. She turned onto her back to

stare up at the overhang as if she could see through the wood towards the night sky. Now that the rain and sleet had cleared, and the wind was finally beginning to die down, Andrew wondered if the clouds would dissipate at some point in the next few hours to provide them with a beautiful sky for stargazing. For he realised, in that moment, that he would love to stargaze with Poppy.

He'd love to do *everything* with Poppy.

"I'm sorry I couldn't keep in contact," Poppy finally said, breaking the silence in two. She kept her eyes turned upwards. "I could say it was because Dorian said I shouldn't talk to anyone, to keep you all safe. I could say that I didn't call because I didn't know what to say. Both are true, but not the whole truth."

"What does that mean?"

"You know what it means."

"No I don't."

"Back in October, when we all met to talk about everything that happened over summer," Poppy said, so quickly that Andrew realised she must have been thinking about it for far too long, "you asked me if I loved Dorian. Why?"

"If you're asking that does it mean you know the answer?"

"...I think so. But I want to hear it from you."

"Are you sure?"

Poppy cast a furtive glance away. "Not really. I'd like nothing better than to continue running from everything but look where that's gotten me. I might have all the time in the world but nobody *else* does, do they?"

"Don't say that." Andrew hated hearing her say such things. He wanted to wrap his arms around Poppy and somehow protect her from her fate. To keep her safe from everything and everyone who meant her harm.

"But it's true," Poppy insisted, breaking Andrew's wish in

two. "And since it's true – there's no point disagreeing with me, Andrew – then I don't want to run from my friends anymore. I want to be honest with them, and for them to be honest with me. So tell me why you wanted to know if I love Dorian."

"Because *I* love you."

"Oh."

That was hardly the response Andrew had wanted to hear. But when he focused on Poppy's face in the darkness he noticed a blush had spread across her skin that had nothing to do with drinking alcohol. When he dared huddle closer to her Poppy only grew warmer.

"What are you thinking about?" Andrew pressed. He expected Poppy to move away. Instead she also moved closer to Andrew, rolling back onto her side so that their noses were almost touching. She maintained steady eye contact with him, for which Andrew was deeply appreciative even if it caused his brain to short-circuit and his heart to thump at what felt like a mile a minute – two turns of phrase he had never quite understood before but wholly embraced now.

"I was wondering for how long you've loved me," Poppy admitted quietly. "Have you always loved me?"

"I am ninety percent sure that I have."

"What about the other ten percent?"

"The other ten percent I was in denial because I thought you were going to go out with Nate."

A soft smile curved Poppy's lips; when she licked her bottom one Andrew found his gaze helplessly drifting to her mouth. Her smile grew wider when she noticed where Andrew's attention had gone.

"You've never looked at me like that before."

"I always looked at you like this before. You just never noticed."

Poppy slapped his chest. "You're such a liar!"

"I never lie. You just weren't looking."

"I still call bull shit. There have been *so* many times when we've been as close as this and you've done nothing. Either you have balls of steel, Andrew, or—"

Andrew kissed her.

He didn't think about it. Didn't worry about it being the right or the wrong thing to do. He'd spent so much time in the past keeping his feelings for Poppy locked up but now, still reeling in the wake of their near-fatal summer, Andrew understood with perfect clarity that hiding his feelings was pointless.

So he put his hand behind Poppy's neck and pushed her lips to his.

Poppy froze for the briefest of moments. Then all the tension left her body, and she leaned into the kiss, and her hands curled into the front of Andrew's shirt. To his dismay he let out perhaps the most pathetic whimper he'd ever heard. But Poppy ignored it, or found it endearing, because her tongue flicked experimentally against Andrew's teeth until he opened his mouth and let her deepen the kiss.

His hand trembled on the back of her neck. Andrew's *entire* body was shaking, he realised, thrumming with tense, desperate longing. Poppy hooked a foot around Andrew's calf to pull his leg between hers; when she squeezed his thigh Andrew bucked alarmingly against her.

Then Poppy broke their kiss, her breaths coming in heavy gasps. Her eyes were glazed over but they were directed downwards at Andrew's groin. His entire body felt like it was on fire.

"Where did you..." Poppy bit out. "Where on earth did you learn to kiss like *that,* Andrew?"

"From Casey," Andrew replied before he could stop himself. He'd never been a good liar, though he sincerely wished he was just for this specific moment. The last thing he wanted to do was talk about Casey instead of kissing Poppy again.

Poppy met his gaze once more and Andrew saw, to his dismay, that her vision had regained some clarity. He tried not to feel bitterly disappointed when she put an inch of distance between them both. Only an inch, but it felt like a mile.

"Now was this before or *after* you saw her naked, I wonder?" Poppy teased, referring back to when Andrew had admitted at Dorian's facility to accidentally coming across Casey entirely undressed.

"It was a different day!" he panicked. "She saw a girl in my geography class ask me out and when I said no, Casey came over and asked why I'd turned her down. I told her I didn't know what I was supposed to do on a date so she took me on a practice one."

"That sneak!" Poppy exclaimed, glancing back through the glass door of the deck to spy her red-headed friend laughing raucously into a glass of prosecco. "I was the one who suggested that idea. We were supposed to do it together with Rachelle." She paused. "So did Casey go any further than teaching you how to kiss? Surely not...otherwise I'd have heard about it."

Andrew looked away, furtive, as he mumbled, "Well, yes and no."

"And what does that mean?"

His face grew scarlet. "She said she'd go further if I – if I wanted her to. But I was nervous, and I didn't think I'd be able to look at her again for the rest of my life if I said yes, so I said no. Was it a good kiss?"

Poppy looked as if she'd developed whiplash from the sudden question; now it was her turn to blush and look away. "...it was."

"Better than with Dorian?"

"Dorian? What has this got to do with Dorian?"

"Poppy—"

"Why would you want to be compared with an eight-foot-tall goat man, Andrew?"

"Because he's Dorian. And he's...with you."

"I'm not *with* Dorian," Poppy said, grimacing. But her entire frame stiffened slightly, which was how Andrew understood that what she said next wasn't going to be the whole truth. "We have an agreement. A promise to each other. I can't break that."

"Can't you? Because I think..." Andrew considered his next words very carefully. When Poppy reached down to squeeze his hand he took that as the kick he needed to continue. "Poppy, I think he's in love with you, and I think you know that he's in love with you. So if you said you didn't want to be with him then I think Dorian would...let you go."

A pause. "What makes you believe that?"

"Because I don't think he's a bad, um, person. Monster."

Poppy's expression softened. She squeezed Andrew's hand once more, then reached up to touch his face. Andrew was torn between closing his eyes and committing every visual detail of the moment to memory; he decided on the latter. "*You're* a good person, Andrew," she murmured, "to believe that after everything he put us through. But it isn't as simple as asking him to let me go. It's—"

The terrace doors slid open, the sounds of revelry from the living room bowling over what Poppy had been about to say. Dorian stepped out, a smile on his face that even Andrew knew wasn't quite genuine.

"Come on back inside," he said, waving at them to get up. "It's freezing out here and dinner's ready."

Poppy shifted her attention to Dorian, then back to Andrew, then to Dorian again. Andrew desperately wished that she'd tell Dorian that they were, in fact, quite warm, and happy to be alone. His body was still taut and on-edge and very physically aware of Poppy's presence so close to his own.

But Poppy swung out of the hanging bed and, with an apologetic shake of her head, followed Dorian back inside.

Andrew knew he'd never get a plainer answer than the one Poppy had just given him. He knew it, but he couldn't give up. Not like this. Not when he'd only just found the nerve to tell Poppy that he loved her, and knew how it felt to kiss her and have her kiss him back. There had to be a way to push through the defences she had put up to protect herself.

All Andrew could do was be there for Poppy in every way she needed and hope that, one day, it would finally be enough.

One day, before he had no more days left.

NERVES OF FIRE

POPPY

She could still feel Andrew's lips on hers.

Poppy didn't know how she had expected to react to it, but in that moment her heart was threatening to burst from her chest and her cheeks were burning feverishly hot. She knew better than anyone that such a reaction to a kiss didn't *have* to mean anything; physical feelings had so often been fleeting for her in the past.

But this was Andrew. *Andrew,* whom Poppy cared about more than anyone. She couldn't risk everything they already had together just to find out if the excitement she felt – as well as the fledgling flame of desire she was holding – were worth indulging. Developing.

In all honesty, Poppy wasn't sure she was capable of committing to someone for romantic reasons. She'd never been able to do so in the past, after all. And now...

Now she was going to live forever, whilst Andrew would grow old without her. It was cruel to give him even some semblance of hope that they could be more than they currently were to each other.

Poppy was so focused on such thoughts that by the time she knew it everyone had eaten dinner and the conversation had flown by for over an hour without her having a clue what anyone was saying.

"Earth to Poppy," Rachelle teased, waving a hand in front of her face. Poppy didn't even bother pushing it away. Her friend's brow furrowed. "Poppy, are you okay?"

"Huh? I'm fine," Poppy said quickly, convincing precisely no one. Casey was busy lighting an excessive number of candles around the living room much to Andrew's chagrin, insisting that the air needed the smell of cinnamon cookies and pumpkin spice to truly complete the Christmas aesthetic. But she stopped what she was doing when she heard the concern in Rachelle's voice, putting down her silver Zippo lighter on the coffee table before sitting on Poppy's right-hand side.

"No lying," she said firmly. "What were we saying before dinner about keeping things to ourselves, Poppy? We're not doing that anymore. So spill. What's up?"

Out of the corner of her eye Poppy saw Fred and Nate talking with Andrew, though Andrew was keeping his gaze on his hands locked between his knees as if he couldn't face anyone without blabbing about what had transpired out on the terrace. Of course Poppy couldn't tell anyone about what had gone on between them, though she had a sneaking suspicion Dorian had seen more than he would ever admit to. He alone had remained as quiet as Poppy herself over the last hour, clearly disassociating into his own head to get lost in his own troubles.

But it wasn't as if Poppy's melancholia was only focused on what Andrew had told her, what her true feelings towards him were, and how that affected Dorian. Her troubles ran far deeper than that.

And though it was likely because she was drunk on prosecco and vodka, Poppy impulsively grabbed Casey's lighter from the table and clicked a spark into life, holding the flame beneath her palm to lick at her skin. "Son of a bitch," she gasped, cringing at the pain. Rachelle and Casey reached out for her immediately.

"The hell are you doing?!" they cried in unison, bringing everyone else's attention to what was going on. All except Dorian, who remained lost in his own head even as Patrick tried to bring him back into the present.

Perhaps he's too drunk to hear what's going on, Poppy mused, getting used to the burning of the flame until the pain grew dull. *He's been drinking like a fish.*

"Just wait," Poppy said, waving off her friends as they formed a circle around her and tried to snatch the lighter away. "I'm trying to show you what's on my mind." And so, though it was clear none of them wanted to do as she said, they backed down.

Eventually – much later than it would have happened to anyone else – Poppy's skin began to blacken, though the moment she moved the flame to the left the skin she'd been burning began to heal.

Casey, Rachelle and Nate all paled in the face of what they were seeing. Andrew, by contrast, was visibly red and angry. But it was Fred's reaction that grabbed Poppy's attention. He was watching her with keen interest, green eyes bright and calculating, perhaps the only one who truly understood that what Poppy was currently doing was merely an experiment rather than a sign of her losing her mind.

Except Poppy was beginning to think it was already lost.

"I'm not going to die," she eventually said, unnervingly calm even to her own ears. "I'm not going to age. My friends will die, one by one, and then there will just be me." She forced herself to meet Andrew's gaze, willing him to understand. But he was shaking with silent fury, clearly unwilling to accept neither Poppy's words nor her visual display of what was wrong with her.

"You can't live your life like that," he just barely managed to get out. "You can't – you may as well be dead if you live like that."

Nate nodded in agreement. "Andrew's right. Morph, we're

still here. We're in good health, and we're together. Why jump the gun with thinking this way? We can all cross that bridge when we come to it – the way we always have."

"But you don't…you don't understand," Poppy insisted, growing more upset with every passing moment. How could she make them understand? If fire wasn't enough…

Then blood would have to do.

In a moment of true insanity she dropped the lighter and moved past her friends to grab the nearest empty glass on the coffee table. With one quick strike she smashed it to pieces. Thinking about how Dorian had first consumed her blood what felt like a lifetime ago, Poppy picked up the largest shard and dragged it down and along her forearm.

"*For fuck's sake, Poppy!*" Dorian roared as he jumped to his feet, the smell of blood startling him back to life. She stared blankly at him as she continued cutting into her arm, blood falling hot and steady to the floor, but Poppy knew the moment she stopped shredding her arm that the wounds would heal.

She dug the glass in harder, and let out a garbled scream.

Dorian threw her to the ground.

"Let go!" she cried, struggling against his grip. But it was iron – the strength of his true form. Before Poppy's very eyes the lines of his body were rippling in and out of focus. "I'm trying to *show* them, Dorian! They need to see to understand."

"Not like this they don't!"

"But you all…you hate Fred for what he did to me. But *look* at me! Look at how much of a freak I am! If you even manage to cut my skin it heals right up. I'm really not – not human. I'm not —" Poppy's words were lost to sobs. They wracked her chest, more painful than the glass to her forearm had been, as she cried and cried into Dorian's shoulder.

Nobody said a word. Poppy had no idea what she would have wanted them to say, anyway, given how hopeless she felt. How had she come to Patrick's house feeling excited to see her friends? How had Andrew made her heart race like a giddy teenager? How had all of that happened mere hours before *now*, when Poppy was lying on the floor in Dorian's arms, blood covering her skin as she thrashed and wailed?

It didn't take long for Poppy to cry herself out. The mere fact she'd shed tears in front of her friends was enough to sober her up, and she grew slack beneath Dorian.

Dorian's body settled back into focus in tandem with Poppy calming down. Once it was clear all her strength had left her Dorian gently picked Poppy up and placed her on the sofa between Rachelle and Casey, who were both crying harder than Poppy had been. Nate looked like he might be sick. Andrew, to Poppy's horror, got up to help Patrick gather cleaning supplies to wash Poppy's blood from the floor.

But Fred hadn't moved. Perhaps he'd expected Poppy to break down like this from the very first moment she walked into Patrick's house. Perhaps he simply didn't know what he was supposed to do when faced with Poppy's hysteria.

Perhaps he knew she had to get it out of her system.

"Well this evening's gone to shit," Patrick said, before wordlessly passing a bottle of whisky to Poppy. There was barely a quarter of the contents left, demonstrating just how much he and Dorian had been drinking when nobody had been looking. She couldn't blame them. Patrick sat down on the short side of the sofa, pulling Dorian to sit beside him even though it was clear to everyone he didn't want to move from Poppy's side. Everyone else sat by Poppy on the long arm of the sofa or on the floor in front of her, as if her friends could somehow protect her from what might come next.

Patrick cast his gaze over them all. "Poppy, would it help you – would it help everyone – if Dorian and I told you what we knew about immortal blood? Not that we know much, and most of it is likely gossip and myth, but it might help nonetheless."

Poppy didn't feel herself nod, but she must have, for Patrick began speaking. Going by Dorian's expression he couldn't trust himself to utter a single word.

"Immortal humans have been part of our stories for as long as...well, since before Biblical times, I suppose." Patrick scratched his nose, caught Fred's eye, then added, "Or whichever religion you want to pick."

"I'm not Jewish," Fred retorted. "I'm an atheist."

"Oh. Well—"

"Fred's making you feel awkward to be a dick," Rachelle cut in, not looking up from Poppy's arm as she gently washed away the blood covering her friend's skin when Andrew handed her a wet cloth. "All of his family on his mum's side are Jewish. They left Germany during World War One."

"Doesn't change the fact that I'm—"

"Just shut up," Dorian snapped, taking over when it was clear Patrick didn't know how to deal with the interruption. He held Poppy in his gaze, and it was she alone whom he spoke to with his lilting, intoxicating voice when he next opened his mouth. "Our kind have told stories to their children for centuries about immortal blood. About pacts between humans who lived forever, and the creatures who promised their heart to them in return for that life. About the shadows in the night who stole that life for themselves. About wars waged for their blood, and secrets hidden in caves and mountains and deep underwater to stop the knowledge of immortality from spreading."

The words had been for Poppy alone but everyone was nonetheless frozen, transfixed by the sound of Dorian's voice. Poppy hadn't heard the satyr's voice take on its current cadence for a long time. Not since they'd climbed the cliffs behind the outdoor sports centre, and ran off to the trees, and lost themselves in each other by the crashing of a waterfall.

"We all know immortal blood is a real thing," Dorian continued, "but as a species we don't exactly keep good records.

The last reported immortal human was over a hundred years ago, though there were also some rumours floating about back in the forties."

Dorian's eyes watched Rachelle's every move as she cleaned Poppy's blood; it didn't escape her nor Casey's notice that both Dorian and Patrick's pupils had massively dilated in the wake of iron on the air. Casey clutched onto Poppy's thigh – an unspoken concern that something might go wrong – but Poppy minutely shook her head, and Casey relaxed.

"The average lifespan of our kind is a solid hundred years," Dorian said, "or a hundred and fifty if you come from a particularly well-off family with a high quality food supply. So we see more of what humans manage to do in their lifetimes than humans themselves do. The buildings they spring into life. The songs they create. The art. The science." He paused, considering something. "And the destruction, too. But it isn't enough. We all want to see more. Live longer, experience bigger and better things, retain our youth..."

"That doesn't sound any different to humans who want eternal life," Nate said from his position on the floor. Around him everyone bar Poppy nodded.

"Exactly. Except our kind has the means to steal immortality for ourselves, whilst all you can do is wait to be eaten."

"Can immortal humans not make other immortal humans, then?" Casey asked. Poppy stared at her; how had she not thought of such a thing before? If there was a way to *create* immortal humans then—

"If it had happened already then, trust me, monsters would know about it," Dorian said, ripping Poppy's newborn dream in two. "It would mean more monsters could consume immortal blood. There'd be a damn business built around it."

"I wouldn't be so sure."

It was Fred who had spoken. Everyone turned to stare at him, though in Dorian's case it was more of a glare.

"And why is that?" he demanded.

Fred shrugged. "If there's one thing humans excel at it's lying and keeping secrets. It stands to reason humans could be keeping the secret of their own immortality from your kind."

"Well then I guess we'll never know."

"I guess not."

Fred and Dorian continued to glare at each other until Rachelle piped up to say, "So there's been no...no rumours of anyone possessing immortal blood after World War One? Not until Poppy?"

"Not that I know of. But then again" – Dorian laughed bitterly – "I'm hardly in the secret-keeping upper echelons of society."

"You're just a farmer," Poppy mumbled before she could stop herself. Everyone stared at her.

"What did you just say?" Patrick asked, defensive on behalf of his friend.

Poppy shrugged helplessly. "It's not an insult from *me*. Nick said that. He asked why I would want to be with a farmer when I could be with the one who...pays the farmer. Given that he also expected me to give birth to giant lizard-ox children I didn't pay what he said much attention at the time."

"He said *what?*" Andrew demanded, getting up from the floor as if he was willing to punch Nick right there and then. But Nate pulled him back down with a wan smile.

"I don't think we want to get into that," he said, risking a smile at Poppy. She returned it only to placate him.

"That would certainly explain why King didn't like the idea of Casey and Patrick—"

"*Fred!*"

"Do none of you have any tact whatsoever?" Dorian complained. "I'd rather you didn't make light of what Nick said, all things considered."

"It isn't like we know *anything* he said to Poppy," Fred continued, bulldozing forward. "She hasn't told us what went on before you both set the facility on fire."

"And she doesn't have to," Rachelle warned him, finally satisfied with her clean-up job. But Poppy's dress was soaked through with blood, likely ruined forever. She squeezed her hand. "Why don't you go change, Poppy? Do you want me to—"

"No, I'll go alone," Poppy cut in, getting up and moving to the door without daring to look at anyone. Except for Dorian. Despite how he'd thrown her to the floor, and defended her, and explained what he knew about immortal blood for her, Poppy felt a distance between the two of them that she wished wasn't there. She wasn't stupid enough to believe it was only her fault; Dorian was being careful with her just as much as Poppy was putting up a wall with *him.*

When it had just been the two of them, and Poppy had missed her friends, that distance had been okay. But now she was beginning to fully realise the extent of her new reality: Dorian was the only one she couldn't afford to be distant from. He was the only one who truly *did* understand what she was going through. After so much overwhelming time with her friends all she wanted to do was lie in bed with Dorian and pretend that everything was okay.

One look at Dorian, whose cool gaze cut to the dark glass of the terrace doors, and Poppy knew she wouldn't get that. Dorian would go to the woods and drop his human form. He needed it. Poppy could feel it in her bones.

They had come here to keep their friends in the loop in order to keep them safe. And though Poppy felt better having her friends in her life - it had been so lonely without them - it was only now fully beginning to sink in that keeping them around was selfish. After Aisling and Nick were dealt with, if such a thing were possible, Poppy now knew she and Dorian had to consider fully cutting themselves off from the people they loved.

If tonight had proven anything, none of them would ever truly understand what forever meant.

AN ACTUAL CONFESSION

DORIAN

Despite the fact Patrick had told him to talk to Poppy – and considering all that had transpired that evening – the moment everyone went to bed Dorian crept outside and shed his human form. Well, Poppy had been in the shower, washing blood off her skin, but in all honesty Dorian hadn't known how he was supposed to face her.

So he went outside and forgot all his worries along with his human skin, instead.

The forest surrounding the house had been itching at the back of Dorian's mind ever since he and Poppy had driven through it earlier that day, begging for him to get lost beneath the dark and lonely expanse of pine trees. As he bounded towards the forest, gaining strength and speed with every step, Dorian thought about what exactly he was supposed to say to Poppy when he got back from his midnight excursion, for he knew she would in all likelihood wait up for him. It felt like everything had changed now that she'd all but broken down in front of her friends.

Everything is fine. It's fine. You just have to tell her how you feel. Tell her that the monster responsible for ruining her life, torturing her and slaughtering her friends is desperately in love with her. What could possibly go wrong?

Dorian knew the answer to that was *everything.*

It didn't take long for Dorian to become accustomed to his true height – nor the fact his horns snagged on the branches looming above him – and within seconds he was bolting through the trees darting this way and that, barely making a sound as he moved. The frozen earth that drummed beneath the flat expanse of his hooves provided great leverage for him to jump higher, then higher and higher still, until Dorian could almost scale the height of a tree in a single bound.

And so it was that he propelled himself from one trunk to the next, daring himself to see how long he could remain off the ground before having to succumb to gravity. It had always been one of Dorian's favourite things to do, when he was younger and there had been nobody around. Just like scaling a cliff without any idea of when he'd reach the top.

This was Dorian at his best. Full of adrenaline and challenging himself to push his body past its previous limits. This was what made him feel invincible. With Poppy's blood running through him Dorian had never felt closer to that true, impossible pinnacle of perfection.

Nothing could stop him. In this position he was the only predator and everything else was prey.

Dorian knew the alcohol in his system was responsible for some of his confidence. It was dulling the edges of his incessant hunger, and numbing his frustration about the turn his life had taken over the last few months. It was easy to forget about all those things on his own, in the dark, the wind whistling past his pointed ears, when the only company for miles around were trees.

But it had to end, just as everything did.

When the air grew still and silent around him, announcing

that the wind had finally died down, Dorian forced himself to turn around and head back to Patrick's house.

He had no idea for how long he'd been out. But by the time he trudged through the edge of the trees – the muscles in his legs stiff and tired after his jaunt in the forest – the night sky had completely cleared of clouds. Thousands of stars spanned above Dorian. He'd never been one for looking at the sky like this before, appreciating every twinkle and marvelling every flash, but now Dorian wondered why that was. The sky was startling in its beauty. It never ended.

It would continue on forever, like he would.

Dorian remained in his true form even when he reached the edge of Patrick's house. He lingered outside, not willing to shake back into his human guise and return to the warmth and shelter the house afforded. It was in this way that he noticed a movement that his human eyes would have missed, in the darkness to his right, sitting on the edge of the cliffs in front of the veranda.

Poppy, huddled under several blankets. Even from here Dorian could tell she was shivering.

"You should be inside," Dorian said, closing the distance between them on silent feet. When Poppy turned she did not look surprised to see Dorian in his true form. She looked up, craning her neck as she gave him a knowing smile that left him feeling raw and ragged.

"I figured you were in the forest. I wanted to go with you."

"You wanted me to carry you around like that scene in *Twilight*?"

"You saw *Twilight*?"

"Everyone's seen *Twilight*, Poppy. Get it together."

"Point taken. I guess it wouldn't have been very freeing if you had to carry me," she relented, shoulders sagging as she spoke. "I hope you had a nice time."

"...I did."

"I wish I could do what you can do. I miss using my body like that."

"It's been a while since you've last climbed. Either of us, really. We should rectify that soon. Maybe you'll feel more like yourself if we do something stupidly physical and reckless."

At this Poppy's smile grew less sad, and there was a glint in her eye that Dorian adored more than anything. "I think I'd like that."

When she motioned for Dorian to sit beside her he elegantly folded his long legs and allowed Poppy to sling one of her blankets around his shoulders, though in truth he didn't need it. The cold had never bothered him in his real skin. But he liked the idea that Poppy was taking care of him, so he snuggled a little deeper into the cover.

"How long were you out here waiting for me?" he asked, after several minutes of not-entirely-painful silence passed between them.

Poppy knocked into his shoulder. They were both behaving far too well considering what had occurred earlier that evening, but for the life of him Dorian didn't know what to do *or* say other than pretend like everything was all right. "A while," Poppy said. "It's fine though. I've enjoyed watching the stars." So Dorian watched Poppy watch the dark sky, all the while a knot filling his stomach that had been building for months now. It had only grown larger when he witnessed Andrew kiss her on the terrace. "You know," Poppy continued, blissfully unaware of Dorian's internal torment, "looking up at the sky before I always felt so small. So insignificant. But now...now I like that feeling. It's comforting somehow."

"I know what you mean."

"They really do go on forever, don't they? The stars I mean. I could spend forever counting them and I would never even scratch the surface. Well," Poppy chuckled, shaking her head, "I do have forever, I guess. I don't imagine it would make for much fun though."

"I'll be there, too," Dorian said gently. "As time goes by. When everyone else is gone. When we get to the end of the road – however long it takes, or if we never reach at all – I'll be there with you, Poppy. You can count on it."

"I know I can. That's what makes it so sad."

Dorian knew Poppy was now watching *him*, not the stars, but he also knew that if he returned eye contact he would lose the courage to say everything he needed to say. So he kept his gaze trained on the stars, whistled in a breath, and said, "I love you. I know that you know that. I know you can't reciprocate. But I just...I had to say it out loud."

Poppy said nothing. She didn't need to, for the truth was Dorian really *had* just needed to say it out loud. To clear the air – to know that there was no way either of them could deny the way things were between them. It scratched the itch Dorian had felt during that final night back at his facility, when deep in his bones he'd known that something was wrong when Poppy gave herself up fully to him. He'd wanted her to be that way for *him*, but Poppy had done it to save her friends.

She would never be his.

It was therefore to Dorian's surprise when he glanced at Poppy and realised she was crying.

Immediately he turned to face her, sloughing the blankets from both of them to grab at her shoulders. His claws bit in enough to cut Poppy's skin, but neither of them seemed to care. "Why are you crying?"

Poppy rubbed the back of her hand over her eyes. "It's – it's nothing. Well. It isn't nothing. But I just...I don't know what to do. I'm sorry I can't reciprocate your feelings, Dorian."

"You don't have to be sorry. After everything we've been through, and everything I did to you, I could never expect you to feel the same way about me. I just had to tell you. So please, don't cry."

Poppy cried.

Dorian gnashed his teeth together, shaking his horned head as if that might force some sense into him. He was making her cry. He loved Poppy King and he was making her cry.

Part of him was happy that, at the very least, she cared enough about him *to* cry.

"Could you..." Dorian began, deftly sweeping Poppy into his arms to sit her on his lap before his better senses could tell him not to touch her. She was so small, staring up at him with shoulders shivering from the cold, skin pale and hair tangled and windswept, but despite her tears the look in Poppy's grey eyes was molten. "Could you *pretend* that you do? Just for tonight."

She scrunched her nose. "You want me to...what?"

"Pretend that you love me."

"But I...Dorian." Poppy raised herself up on her knees to trace her hands up Dorian's arms, his neck, around the base of his horns and along the length of his ears. He stifled a moan, though they both knew perfectly well Poppy was aware what her touch on his ears would do. "I don't think I've ever been *in love* with someone before," she whispered, voice unsure where her actions were steady. "So how can I pretend?"

"You did an excellent job pretending everything was fine back at my facility. For a while, at least." Dorian's arms wrapped around Poppy, holding her up until her face was level with his own. He could feel her breath on his lips, hot where the air around them was frigid.

Poppy gulped. "What would pretending I love you achieve?"

"Nothing. Nothing at all. Yet even so..."

"Even so?"

"It would mean everything." Dorian's mouth captured hers, hungry and desperate. He'd longed to kiss her for months now; to separate the distance between them that drinking Poppy's blood hadn't been able to quell. She eagerly responded, tongue sliding over Dorian's sharp canines before whimpering in a way that told Dorian he wasn't the only one who was desperate. "Say it," he urged. Begged.

There was barely a pause – barely a lie – before Poppy said, "I love you."

Dorian didn't care for words after that.

INTERLUDE IV

One of the best things about studying abroad was that the weather was much better than in England. The streets were safer, too; Jennifer would never have dared to go jogging through the twilit streets of east London, especially when there was nobody around.

It was only April and already the temperature was in the low twenties. "Best decision I ever made," Jennifer said, pausing from her jog to take a selfie and send it to her sister. Said sister promptly messaged back telling her to fuck off.

Giggling, Jennifer slid her phone back into the pocket of her bike shorts and began running again. But before she could turn her music back on a noise from a side street to her left gave her pause.

"...is someone there?" Jennifer asked, voice full of the practised uncertainty most women who were raised in east London felt. "Hello?"

Nobody responded.

Glancing around Jennifer worked out her quickest route to a main street, feeling stupid but nonetheless giving into her fear that she needed the safety of other people around her.

Perhaps Barcelona isn't as safe as I thought, Jennifer mused, breathing a sigh of relief when she came across a cobbled street full of little restaurants abuzz with people. Or maybe I'm being paranoid.

Either way, Jennifer knew she'd start her daily jog a little earlier next time.

Just in case.

HUNGER

DORIAN

"THANK GOD FOR BARCELONA IN THE SPRING! I was getting fed up of the cold; I felt like I'd never be warm again. What about you, Dorian? Dorian?"

Dorian flinched when he realised Poppy was watching him, suspicion darkening her pale eyes. He forced himself to process what she'd just asked. "Yes, it definitely makes a change from Scotland," he said. "And Ireland, and Germany, and the Netherlands, and—"

"I get the picture. I know we have to keep moving. Still...it would be nice to stay here for a while." Poppy held a hand over her eyes to protect them from the sun, a wistful sigh escaping her lips as she relished in the warmth spreading across her skin. Dorian only too eagerly agreed. Barcelona was one of his favourite places in the entire world. It had been his father's favourite place, too, and in fact was the first city in which Dorian had ever held an auction.

Since Christmas an easy game of pretend had begun between Dorian and Poppy as they continued travelling across Europe. They pretended to be together, and pretended to be happy, and pretended that absolutely nothing was wrong. Dorian hadn't gone out at night roaming alone, and Poppy's nightmares had finally begun to subside. But just as he knew that no nightmares didn't mean Poppy wasn't still deeply disturbed be the turn her life had taken, Dorian knew that not stalking potential prey didn't mean he wasn't still hungry.

He was well past starving. It was agony to stand in the middle of La Rambla, thousands of humans milling around him with limbs and organs and the fluttering pulse of an animal that was *prey.* Dorian held onto Poppy's hand a little too tightly and threaded them away from the main street before his true form broke through and reared its ugly head.

"Dorian?" Poppy asked, concern causing her to jog along with Dorian's loping strides instead of digging her heels in to get him to turn around.

"Sorry," he muttered, not stopping until they came across a dark and empty side street barely wide enough to fit the two of them. "I was just thinking."

"Do you want to think out loud?"

When Dorian let go of her hand Poppy crossed her arms over her chest. She was almost as pale as the little white sundress she was wearing; the freckles sprayed across her cheeks were stark in comparison. *Some warmth and sunshine is what she needs,* Dorian mused, even though he knew his primary reason for wanting to stay in Barcelona was incredibly selfish. Heaving in a breath he tumbled into what he'd prepared to tell Poppy from the very moment they set foot in the city.

"Barcelona has experienced a high number of strange attacks and disappearances lately," Dorian said. Strictly speaking this *was* the reason he wanted to be here: to use the attacks as a means to hide himself doing the very same thing. For if Dorian was going to kill a human, Barcelona was the place to do it.

He just couldn't tell Poppy that.

A shudder ran down Poppy's spine. She huddled a little

closer to Dorian as if she were suddenly freezing. "What do you mean to do about it?"

"I don't mean to do anything," he said, stroking Poppy's hair almost absent-mindedly. "But it may be worth investigating whether that means someone else is setting up auctions in my stead."

In truth Dorian already had a reasonable notion that it was Nick. It made sense after what Nick had told him on the phone back in November, and the Richardson family also had a mansion in Barcelona. This made the city a dangerous place to be but, then again, the Richardsons had estates all over the world. It was simply that this *particular* mansion in Barcelona was the only one Dorian himself had ever visited, so he was wary of it.

Given that Nick knew that, Dorian was hopeful that the Richardson heir would never imagine Dorian to be so stupid as to bring Poppy into a city that he so often frequented.

Poppy sobered at the notion of a new auction. She looked up at Dorian as she chewed the inside of her cheek, clearly trying to work out what to say. "You told me before that auctions were the most efficient way for monsters to eat," Poppy eventually settled on. Her voice was barely audible even with her right next to him; Dorian had to strain to hear her. "The stealthiest way. The safest way. And I get it, I do," she added hastily when Dorian made to interrupt her. "But that doesn't mean I'm not glad you're not the one organising them. I just couldn't..."

"I know."

"It's just—"

"I know, Poppy."

"Do you?" There was a desperate edge to her voice that Dorian was only too eager to assuage. "Do you really mean that?"

Gently, so gently, he lifted his hands to Poppy's cheeks and cradled her face. The feel of her skin beneath his fingertips filled him with guilt, for he knew what he was about to do next. "How could I do something like that when you're right here, beside me? I'm done with being a monster...irony intended." Dorian inflected his voice with every ounce of charm and persuasion he had, even though back at Christmas he had sworn to Patrick he would never use the gifts he was born with on Poppy again. But Dorian was starving. Walking through the crowds of humans all around them was torture. One day soon - too soon - he was going to break.

Just this once, he was willing to manipulate Poppy into letting down her guard long enough for him to eat.

INTERLUDE V

Jennifer had changed her jogging route no fewer than four times in the past two weeks.

Each and every time she felt sure she was being followed.

The paranoia was too strong for her to ignore. There were footsteps that would stop and start whenever she turned to search for their origin. There were shadows where there shouldn't be shadows – unless there was something there, hiding behind the corner waiting for her.

Even worse, the shadows seemed to ripple and warp whenever they got close enough.

"It's in your head," Jennifer said aloud, carefully taking out her earbuds, placing them in her pocket and then double-checking that her location was being tracked on her phone. She hadn't told anyone about her worries when out jogging yet; after all, what could her friends and family do about it, back in London? And the friends she'd made here in Barcelona would tell her not to worry so much. This wasn't London, after all.

Jennifer had long since passed believing that. Something was out there, following her.

She was terrified to find out what it was.

When Jennifer turned onto a narrow side street that would reconnect her to a busier part of the neighbourhood a dog began barking in earnest. She yelped as loudly as the dog did, terrified out of her mind, before understanding what it was that she was hearing.

A dog. Just a dog.

As she ran down the street, her pace quickening with every step, the dog's barking grew more incessant. Louder. Higher-pitched. It filled Jennifer's head, ringing inside her ears and warning her, somehow, that she should be careful.

But then the barking stopped.

Knowing she should ignore it – it was just a dog, after all, and it had probably been barking at a stray cat – Jennifer nevertheless found herself changing direction to follow where the barking had come from. When she turned onto the side street parallel to the one she'd been running down she held a hand to her mouth and forced back a sob.

A black-and-tan dog lay on the ground, its neck snapped clean in two.

"Holy f-fuck," Jennifer bit out between tears, legs shaking under the weight of her terror. She fled at a breakneck pace.

There was something out to get her, and Jennifer felt more certain than ever that she would not be able to outrun her fate.

EXPERIMENTATION

FRED

F~RED~ TAPPED HIS FOOT AGAINST THE PAVEMENT, impatient beyond belief. *She's late,* he huffed. *The bloody witch can fly and she's still late.*

Two months had passed since Fred last saw Aisling. She had been in touch, of course, through texts and phone calls, but it seemed very much as if she was inclined to stay indoors and sheltered during the winter months. Fred reasoned this was because she was an overgrown bird. But now it was early May, and the sun was shining and hot in Barcelona.

Fred knew Poppy was here; he'd spied her and Dorian a handful of times in the most crowded tourist areas of the city. They didn't know he was tailing them. Or, at least, they hadn't *said* anything about him being there.

So Fred was nervous. Poppy was here, and Fred knew where she was staying, and now he was about to meet Aisling. He had to find a way to prevent her from getting hold of Poppy without ending his own life in the process.

He clenched and un-clenched the small razor blade he had taken to carrying wherever he went. The cold steel bit into his flesh after a not-insignificant amount of resistance. He healed almost immediately, even though he cut himself again and again and again. The pain didn't register any more. Fred didn't even wince.

Back in Berlin Peter would be celebrating his success.

"You know," an annoyingly familiar voice said, "you could have called to find out where I was."

Fred stilled. "Why would I interact with you any more than I need to?" he demanded of Aisling when he turned around to face her. She was striking to behold – even Fred could acknowledge that – in a daring red dress and an oversized floppy hat upon her head, her long hair braided down her back and her lips painted scarlet. More than a few pairs of eyes were drawn to her appearance.

Aisling pouted her perfect lips. "Oh, Frederick, can't we lose all this antagonism? You're so much more handsome without it."

"What did you mean I could have called?" Fred asked, choosing to ignore the comment. "That implies you knew how long I was standing here."

She shrugged, then pointed to a tall clock tower on her left. "Perhaps I was watching from the top of that tower to see how long you would bother waiting for me. Half an hour is impressive."

Fred squeezed his hand around the razor blade in his pocket instead of allowing his impatience to show on his face. In truth his heart was pounding. Aisling had become no less terrifying to Fred despite his increased exposure to her over the last few months. Whenever he locked eyes on hers he wondered how he had ever thought she could be human. For there was nothing but predatory calculation in Aisling's gaze; Fred was food to her. A plaything at best.

A slow and painful death at worst.

"Tell me what you know," Aisling said, clearly bored of

Fred's silence. With a commanding pull on his arm she led him towards a sprawling outdoor coffee shop, ordering them both an espresso the moment they sat down. Fred didn't even like espresso. He'd always ordered lattes loaded with caramel syrup even though both Poppy and Rachelle had mocked him for it. But once more he said nothing. Aisling tapped her lacquered fingernails on the table impatiently. "Well?"

"She's here. Poppy. And Dorian, too."

Aisling purred approvingly. "I had a feeling they were. Do you know where they are?"

Fred nodded. "I've been tailing them for days. So what's the plan?"

Aisling held his gaze for a few moments, then flashed a brilliant smile when a waiter brought out their coffee. He grew noticeably red beneath her attention. Once the man was gone she returned her eyes to Fred. "The beach. It's open to the air and the sand will impede Poppy's ability to run. Dorian will be at a severe disadvantage; he'll never get the power he needs to land a kick from the sand."

"I thought as much," Fred murmured, because he had. There was barely anything else to think of these days aside from what Aisling planned to do, and how Fred might be able to stop her. "But wouldn't that draw some...unwanted attention?"

At this Aisling laughed. "Are you worried about me, Fred? How refreshing! I'll attack at night, of course, when the beach is empty."

Fred frowned. "How are you getting Poppy to the beach at *night*?"

"That's for you to work out. What's the point of dividing up this job if you don't do your part?"

Fred knew he couldn't disagree. "Why are you in Barcelona in the first place?" he asked, pretending to take a sip of espresso to appease Aisling. "If you didn't already know that Poppy and Dorian were here, I mean?"

"As it happens I enjoy the architecture in the city. Though that isn't why I'm here." She regarded Fred critically, then said, "Nick is hosting his first auction in the city in a few days."

"...Nick is?"

"Someone had to step in and take over from that treacherous satyr," she snapped. It was clear Aisling was just as furious now as she had been months ago at Dorian's betrayal. "He plans a far flashier affair than the goat ever put on. A formal affair. Though I imagine some of the clientèle will prefer to wear their...birthday suits, as it were."

A drop of cold sweat ran down Fred's spine. His brain was working furiously to come up with a plan. There was no way Fred could help Poppy – or, reluctantly, Dorian – if he took them to a beach for Aisling to take them out from the sky. A busy auction, however...

"Would it not be easier for you to take Poppy from the auction?" Fred suggested, willing both his voice and his face to remain even. "Dorian won't be able to get within a hundred miles of the thing. Everyone wants him dead. And nobody but you knows what Poppy looks like. And Nick, but if he's running the entire auction he can't possibly be everywhere all at once."

Aisling considered this. There was a glint of pride in her eyes, as if Fred coming up with a better plan on her behalf had been all her doing. "True, but if you somehow managed to trick Poppy into coming to such an event without Nick getting wind of it his cronies will still be around and on high alert for her. He has far more resources than I do."

"Let me try, anyway," Fred insisted. "You're far less likely to draw attention to yourself this way. Have you seen the beaches here at night? There are *tons* of people still around."

Neither of them spoke for a few moments, Aisling considering all that Fred had said. "If this fails then you're dead, Frederick," she said, finishing off her coffee before rising to her feet. "You know that, right?"

"Painfully so." He cut his hand with the razor blade once more; Fred allowed his flesh to heal around it simply to feel the pain of yanking it out of his skin.

"The auction, then. Remember to dress up."

Then Aisling was gone, swift on her heels and with so many eyes upon her Fred wondered if the woman had ever known what it felt like to be invisible.

Fred sat for a while on his own before paying the waiter when the man came out to see if Aisling was still there, disappointment plain as day on his face when he discovered she'd already left. Once the waiter's back was turned Fred poured his untouched espresso onto the broad paving stones beneath him. Despite the lack of caffeine his entire body was jittery; he had too much energy. Fred wanted to punch something or get into a fight, but he knew it wouldn't be enough.

He wanted to feel something break.

Fred looked at the clock tower Aisling had said she was watching him from. It was definitely too tall for him. *Not too tall for Poppy, though,* he thought. But then it hit him. Why did it have to be too tall for him? There had been a reason Poppy could scale dizzying heights without any safety gear, and now that same reason coursed through Fred's body.

Not giving himself enough time to think he threaded through the crowd towards the clock tower. But when he reached the base of the building Fred realised it was smooth and unclimbable; Aisling had only reached the top because she could fly. The building next to it, however, was rough and full of cracks that Fred could use to climb its surface.

So he did.

It was easily done from a narrow, empty side street coming off the courtyard. Sweating profusely against the harsh Barcelona sun, Fred relished in the burning of his muscles as he ascended the building, thinking of nothing but where his hands and feet were going and propelling himself up, up, up.

When he reached the top, however, it was far too soon. He had climbed too quickly. Too efficiently. Thoroughly dissatisfied, Fred walked over to the edge of the building and surveyed the next rooftop. There was an eight foot drop separating him from it.

"You can jump that, Fred," he said, though his heart was threatening to stutter to a stop in sheer terror. "It's no problem at all."

It was only then, as he paused in anticipation of his daredevil jump, that Fred noticed the tell-tale figure of Poppy, queuing for an ice cream at a nearby shop far down below him. *Alone.*

Where's Dorian? Fred wondered. From his vantage point he saw two otherwise anonymous figures tailing Poppy through the crowd. Fred would have missed them if Aisling's words weren't still ringing in his ears.

Nick was hosting an auction in a few days. Here, in Barcelona. And he was after Poppy.

Did the men following Poppy work for him?

Protectiveness overcoming his fear, Fred leapt from the roof to the next building.

And came crashing down to the ground.

Missing the roof by the span of his hand, Fred tumbled against the rough stone surface of the building and landed in a cracked and broken heap a mere second later, the wind thoroughly knocked out of him.

Dully Fred realised that he wasn't dead because he could still think and breathe and see. Through the miracle of human disinterest nobody had noticed his fall, for which Fred was grateful. It took him an agonisingly long time to shuffle into a sitting position; he'd broken both of his legs. But there was no blood, only bruising, and as Fred concentrated on breathing in and out – his ribs were broken, too, going by how painful each shuttering breath was – he actively felt his body beginning to heal.

A minute later and the bruising disappeared. Gingerly Fred got to his feet. Every inch of his body ached but he was in one piece. He was unbroken. He was unmarked.

He was *alive.*

Riding on the biggest adrenaline rush of his life, Fred bolted through the crowd to find Poppy.

HER LONELINESS IS KILLING HER

POPPY

IT WAS LONELY, LIVING A GAME of pretend with Dorian. They'd been in Barcelona for three weeks and, after several months of having Dorian present in both body and mind beside her, Poppy only felt worse about their relationship than she had done before Christmas, especially when he went off on his own.

Unlike the previous apartments and obscure houses Dorian had rented across Europe he'd decided to book an expensive hotel for their stay in Barcelona. This involved him having to take care when going through the hotel lobby to ensure he wasn't recognised, but he said it was worth it to have plenty of guests and security present to keep Poppy safe.

Poppy was pleased to stay somewhere large and bright, with a swimming pool, a spa and a gym at her beck and call. Of course she was. But whenever Poppy decided to stay at the hotel to use these facilities Dorian would go off on his own to investigate the attacks plaguing the city. Of course Poppy had wanted to go with him on these excursions, though she knew it was in her best interests to remain safe within the confines of the hotel.

Aside from that Dorian was with her all the time. Together the two of them had explored most every inch of Barcelona, for which Poppy was grateful. They'd visited every Gaudí structure of note. They'd dined late into the night at the Spanish Village. They'd spent long afternoons at the beach or browsing second-hand bookshops nestled down quaint, cobbled side-streets even though, a year ago, Poppy had never been much of a reader. So Poppy knew she shouldn't take it to heart that, sometimes, Dorian needed to do things on his own.

Yet take it to heart was exactly what she did.

It wasn't that Poppy didn't *trust* what Dorian had told her. That there might be an auction occurring soon, and that it would explain the strange disappearances happening in the city, but that the city being so busy – giving them decent cover to take a breath and relax after the last six months of running all over Europe – made it worth remaining in Barcelona. No, Poppy believed all that.

It was only that she also believed there was more to the story than what Dorian was telling her.

Something was going on with him – something Dorian was keeping from her – and Poppy was desperate to work out what it was. Desperate, but also afraid. For the shadows beneath Dorian's eyes had turned dark as bruises lately. He struggled to maintain attention on anything for longer than a few seconds at a time. He was always distracted.

Poppy didn't like what any of that suggested.

So today, when Poppy convinced Dorian she was happy to remain by the pool and relax for a few hours on her own so he could do some investigating, she instead began to follow him.

"He'll understand even if he sees me," she lied to herself, backing behind a corner to stop Dorian from noticing her an hour into following him. He'd walked into Park Güell. Readjusting her dress when one of its thin straps slipped off her shoulder, Poppy headed into the park after him. "I have a right to be worried..."

After their night together at Christmas Poppy and Dorian had re-established the physical relationship they'd begun back at his facility last summer. He drank her blood every week, because Poppy wanted him to, and she held his hand when out walking together, because Dorian wanted her to, and they spent far more time in bed together than was perhaps healthy, because they both wanted to. But there had never been anything *healthy* about their relationship to begin with.

And now Dorian was in love with Poppy, and she was letting him. She was lonely, starved for both physical and emotional closeness, so she gladly took everything Dorian gave her.

She knew it wasn't fair on him.

For what felt like the millionth time Poppy had to remind herself that Dorian was a victim of circumstance just as much as she was. He might have been her own personal villain once upon a time, but he wasn't a villain in the grand scheme of things. No, he was a victim, and he was trying to cope as best he could.

What does he want in the park? Poppy mused, giggling softly when a parakeet flying overhead swooped down and just barely grazed her shoulder. She adjusted the strap of her dress once more and made a mental note to sew them shorter when she returned to the hotel. *We've been here twice already.* But if people had been going missing from the park then it made sense for Dorian to return. *Or maybe he just wants to be alone for a while, without me.*

It made Poppy uncomfortable that, though Dorian had turned Poppy's life upside down and learned basically everything there was to know about her, she knew comparatively nothing about him. Had he been a largely solitary person before meeting Poppy? Did Dorian value being alone? Aside from his work, what had he liked to do to pass the time? Where had he grown up? What had his parents been like? Had his only friends been Patrick, Nick and Steven? Poppy had forced Dorian into killing one of them, and another wanted to kill *him*. Did that leave Dorian with Patrick and nobody else?

He kept so much to himself, and Poppy had never cared to ask. Because if she did then that meant she had to commit to learning about the world of monsters. At Christmas Poppy said to her friends that she didn't want to know anything about the world he inhabited. But she'd been lying; of course she'd wanted to know. But Poppy also knew herself. The moment she committed to learning about Dorian's world, so new and strange and exciting to her, she would never want to stop learning.

And Poppy wasn't ready for that.

Just a little longer. She wanted for just a little longer to be the Poppy King she had so far grown up to be. To be human, a normal, mortal being – even if she was the furthest thing from it – before her life changed forever.

Poppy watched as Dorian approached an ice cream stand, bought what looked like a double vanilla cone, then continued on his way. The idea of him eating ice cream was funny to her, though Poppy supposed he was doing it to blend into the crowd. Not that Dorian ever really blended in. He was too tall and good-looking to avoid attention, even in his very boring ensemble of a white T-shirt and navy shorts, aviator sunglasses and a week's worth of stubble along his jaw. Poppy had been asking him to shave it for days because it itched her face when they kissed.

Luckily the attention he was drawing now was all from admirers who were incredibly unlikely to see past Dorian's handsome face to the fact he was a wanted criminal.

I want ice cream, Poppy thought, trying to distract herself from the twist of desire that always caught her in its grasp whenever she looked at Dorian for too long. With some effort she resisted the urge to copy exactly what Dorian had done for fear that he would notice her. But Poppy was growing bored of tailing him on her own with nobody to talk to, so before she could think too much about it Poppy pulled out her phone and called Andrew.

On the second ring he picked up. "Poppy? I thought you were calling me later."

"Well I can hang up if that's what you want," Poppy said, dead-pan, knowing the comment would horrify Andrew. After what had transpired at Christmas she made a point to talk to Andrew on the phone at least once a week to ensure no awkward distance spread between them. She didn't bring up what happened out on Patrick's veranda, and neither did he. They were happy just to talk and remain exactly as they were.

For now. Poppy knew it couldn't last.

As expected Andrew squeaked out a noise of protest. "No, I – I also want to talk to you now! I just, one minute, I just need to take my break early."

There was a fumbling on the other line as Andrew sorted himself out. He and Nate had both taken up part-time jobs at the local climbing centre recently to keep busy, which Poppy thought was a great idea. It was Andrew's first job, after all, and she was more grateful than she could ever say for Nate helping him get the position. Andrew was great at the job, of course; Poppy had never doubted his abilities for a moment. He was absurdly good with kids, and even better with adults who were nervous about their first time climbing. He'd just needed some help to pass the interview.

"Okay," Andrew said after a couple of minutes, "I'm ready. How are you?"

"Oh, I'm just stalking Dorian through Park Güell," Poppy said in what she hoped was a laid-back manner. "As you do."

"Does he know you're following him?"

"No, Andrew, of course he doesn't know I'm following him. What would be the point in that?"

"What's the point in following him in the first place, then?"

"Good point. I don't know yet."

"Has he done anything strange lately?" Andrew asked, which was a fair question.

"No stranger than usual. He - he - damn." Poppy felt like slapping herself. In talking to Andrew she'd grown so distracted she'd lost sight of Dorian.

"What happened?" Andrew asked, voice hitching in concern. "Is everything all right?"

"I'm fine," Poppy sighed. "Don't worry. It's just that my reconnaissance mission has failed. I can't see Dorian any more."

"Well why don't you do something else instead?" Andrew suggested. "Maybe you'll find him if you stop looking for him. Or you could go back to the swimming pool at the hotel. I wish I was at a pool in Barcelona."

Andrew had been making it increasingly obvious with every phone call that he wanted to come out and join Poppy. She wished he would, all things considered, but at the same time she was afraid that it would push them out of the happy middle ground that they had currently carved out for themselves. Over the phone she and Andrew were safe. They could be friends. There were no physical interactions between them that could confuse Poppy's feelings and—

"Poppy?"

She shook herself back into the present. How many times had she been lost in her own head these last few months? "Sorry, Andrew," she said, making her way out of the park onto the bustling streets surrounding it. "You're right. If I can't find Dorian then I should do something else until I see him again."

"Why don't you ask him what's going on?"

"As if he'd tell me."

"I thought he told you everything?"

"Well he isn't lying to me, at least," Poppy said, spying an ice cream shop on the edge of a paved courtyard that looked too good to walk past. A large clock tower overlooked it, providing a welcome beam of shade for what looked to be a group of very sunburnt English tourists. "But I feel like he's hiding things by omission."

"What's do you mean?" Andrew asked, sounding as confused as Poppy's head felt.

"It means he's deliberately talking or doing things he knows will distract me from whatever it is he doesn't want me to ask about."

"That sounds really convoluted."

"It is. It – wait a moment, Andrew, is that...Fred?"

As Andrew asked Poppy to repeat her question Poppy zeroed in on a flash of sandy blonde hair headed straight towards her that was definitely familiar. "Andrew, I'll...call you later." Poppy hung up before Andrew could say goodbye. For Poppy's eyes hadn't been deceived; the blonde hair *was* familiar.

Just what was Frederick Sampson doing in Barcelona?

FRUSTRATION

NATE

"How many times are you going to sigh, Andrew?" Nate asked, double-checking the carabiner and pulling the rope taut to prepare himself for supporting Rachelle as she began her ascent of the climbing wall. She had taken to regularly climbing at the end of Nate and Andrew's shifts, forming an easy and maintainable routine for the three of them to hang out.

She hadn't intended to come climbing today but Nate had insisted she do so, anyway. All afternoon Andrew had been distracted and, for lack of a better word, sad.

Nate was determined to find out why.

Andrew crossed his arms protectively over his chest. "I have *not* been sighing."

"Yes you have."

"No I haven't."

"I thought you never lied, Andrew?" Rachelle laughed, dangling from the rope instead of choosing to climb. She rotated one hundred and eighty degrees then gently kicked off the wall to spin the other way so she was facing both Nate and Andrew.

"Spill," Nate insisted, forcing Andrew to hold his gaze. "You know we won't leave you alone until you tell us what's up."

For a moment it looked like Andrew was going to try and deny it. But then he sighed – *again* – and muttered, "Fine. Poppy called me."

"I thought the two of you talked every week?" Rachelle asked, confused. "So what happened?"

"I don't know. She was following Dorian. She said there wasn't something quite right about the way he's been behaving but then she lost him and I told her to go do something else so she went to get an ice cream then I think she saw someone and I swear I heard her say Fred's name. And then she hung up."

Both Nate and Rachelle were more than used to Andrew's information dumping by now, so they took a few seconds to absorb everything he said. Nate slackened the rope in his hands to allow Rachelle to touch the ground once more. "Poppy following Dorian is new," he admitted, "though given that he, you know, ran a murder camp, I suppose I can't blame her for following him to see if something is wrong."

"And Fred went to Berlin to look for Poppy months ago," Rachelle chimed in. "As annoying as it is, him maybe being in Barcelona isn't that unusual. Besides...he's always been obsessed with Poppy." Her face darkened at the thought. "I just never realised *how* bad he had it until last summer. Looking back all the signs had been there from the beginning."

"But that's the problem!" Andrew burst out. "The two of them – Dorian and Fred – they've ruined Poppy's life. They're not...not healthy for her. So why do they get to be in Barcelona with her but whenever I ask to go she—"

"*Ahh*," Nate said, understanding dawning on him all at once. "You're jealous."

Rachelle's face softened. "Andrew, it's all right to be jealous, you know."

But Andrew shook his head and slumped onto the floor even

though he knew they weren't supposed to sit right below the climbing walls. "No it isn't. It's unfair on Poppy. I'm supposed to be supporting her but all I'm feeling is...this. I'm useless."

"That's to be expected."

"What's that supposed to mean?"

"This is just the way things work where Poppy is concerned. If you're intent on liking her then it's part of the job." Andrew stared at Nate as if he were speaking a foreign language, so Nate continued, "Andrew, you know I was crazy about her. I played it casual because casual was all Poppy wanted. I was happy with that – or, at least, I could lie convincingly enough to myself that I was fine with it. But I always wanted something more than what she gave me. I also knew that, if I told Poppy what I wanted, things between us would end and we'd go straight back to being only friends."

"...so what should I do? Tell me what I'm supposed to do."

"The reality is, Andrew, you have three options," Nate said, holding up three fingers of his right hand. "Number one: you bring up your feelings to Poppy and risk that she might cut you off completely. The upside being that she might respond the way you want."

Andrew grimaced. "That doesn't sound right. At least not right now. What are the other two options?"

"Two: you continue as you are now, knowing you want more but also knowing what you *have* still gives you some kind of happiness. And three: you accept that Poppy will never want more from you, move on and get on with your life."

"*Those* are my options?!" Andrew cried, beside himself. He ran his hands through his hair – Nate took note that he needed to drag Andrew to a barber's to get it cut soon – and gnashed his teeth. "They're all terrible."

"Unfortunately I agree with Nate," Rachelle said, not unkindly. She tapped Andrew on the shoulder to get him back to his feet, then together with Nate wandered over to sit at a vacant table so they weren't hogging the climbing wall. "Especially now that Poppy's perspective on her life has changed. Andrew, as much as you love her I don't realistically think you're going to get the answer from her that you want. Look at how much distance she put between me and her at Dorian's facility!" Rachelle laughed bitterly but without malice. "You know, back then I was *so* jealous of you for getting closer to Poppy when she was clearly pushing me and everyone else away. So I guess it's all a matter of perspective, because to me you're already closer to Poppy than anyone else. Well, apart from Dorian, maybe. Can't you be happy with that?"

"But she doesn't love Dorian."

"True, and she might never love him. But the promise she made to him isn't something she's planning to break. So stop trying to compete with it."

"But that isn't fair!" Andrew protested. His cheeks were growing red as he spun himself further down a jealous spiral; it was painful for Nate to watch him struggle to deal with an emotion he had thus-far been unequipped to deal with. "She didn't have a choice! He forced her into that. He—"

"Poppy was the one who went back to him instead of leaving with all of us," Nate interrupted softly. "It isn't all on Dorian anymore. And what he did at the facility to everyone...he did what was in his nature to do." It was something he'd had to come to terms with himself, though it had taken him months to process it. "There's no point wasting energy hating him. He was just doing this job. And it seems like Poppy's long since accepted that. In the end he could have killed us *all*, Poppy included, if he'd wanted to. He didn't. I know this isn't what you want to hear, Andrew, but that's just the way things are."

This only seemed to further upset Andrew. With a scowl he got up and stormed away from Nate and Rachelle, grabbing his bag from the staff room before wordlessly leaving the climbing centre. Nate had been his ride home; that Andrew was willing to either walk five miles or take the bus, which he hated, spoke volumes about how upset he was.

Nate felt for him. He really did. The guy had been in love with Poppy long before Nate had ever been in a physical relationship with her. It had been obvious to everyone but Poppy herself. *And Fred,* he reasoned, though that was because Fred hadn't wanted to imagine anyone having positive feelings for her. But in his own twisted way Fred – like all the rest of them – was just another person clinging onto an impossible relationship with Poppy King.

Of the three options Nate had given Andrew he had long since decided to pick option number two: accept the way his relationship currently was with Poppy and be happy that he had it. But he couldn't shake the feeling that everything was coming to an end, especially after her breakdown at Christmas. Poppy was disappearing from his life – from all their lives – and there wasn't anything he, Rachelle, or even Andrew could do about it.

Rachelle gave him a wan smile, then indicated towards the climbing wall with a nod of her head. Neither of them had anything else they could do right now. Nothing they *wanted* to do. Or, at least, nothing that would make a difference to their current situation.

So they climbed.

An Unlikely Duo

POPPY

"Why the hell are you here, Sampson?" Poppy demanded, storming up to Fred the moment the crowd parted enough for her to do so. He was more tanned than she'd ever seen him before, and his hair was bleached slightly paler than normal by the sun, but it was still the same Fred she'd had the misfortune of knowing for seven years. "Are you following me?"

Fred didn't miss a beat before saying, "Yes, but not intentionally. Not today, anyway."

"What's that supposed to mean?"

"It means – dammit, King, come with me." He grabbed Poppy's hand and pulled her away from the crowd, towards the clock tower, then down an abandoned alleyway on its right.

The moment they came to a stop Poppy yanked her hand back as if she'd been burned. She gave Fred her most withering scowl. "What the hell is going on? Why are you following me?"

"Not so loud," Fred urged, cutting a furtive glance behind Poppy out towards the busy courtyard. "You were being followed."

"Yeah, by you."

"No, by men I'm pretty sure must work for Nick."

Poppy's blood turned to ice. "You sure?" she mouthed, obediently quietening down in the face of a threat far more unpleasant than Fred. She edged over to the side of the building to cast her gaze across the crowd. Sure enough, when Poppy narrowed her gaze and scanned the crowd she spotted a couple of men appearing to look for someone. They were dressed in white linen shirts and jeans, effortlessly blending into the crowd; Poppy would never have spotted them had Fred not told her to look for them. "How did you know that they're looking for *me*?"

"I may have been on top of the building you're currently standing beside, watching them tailing you."

Poppy craned her head up. The building was tall. Too tall for someone like Fred, with all his love of ropes and safety protocols, to scale. "Bull shit you were up there."

"I was. But that's beside the point."

"What *is* the point, Sampson?"

"The point is that we need to lose your tail."

"What were you doing following me?" she asked again, returning to the other pressing topic of conversation as the two of them slid down the alleyway and ended up on a wide, busy street, parallel with the courtyard. "Because you better have a damn good reason for it."

Fred spared Poppy a glance over his shoulder. He was walking so quickly and with such intent she almost had to jog to keep up. "Well, you know how I was looking for you in Berlin?"

"Yeah. What of it?"

"Aisling sent me."

Poppy froze to the spot; Fred walked alone for several paces before he realised she was no longer following him. He waved for her to join him, impatience clear as day on his face. "Walk and talk, King. Walk and talk."

Poppy hated that what Fred said made sense, though she wasn't about to put her dislike of the man over her own safety just to piss him off. She continued walking. "How did that come about?" she demanded. "Explain every damn detail. Leave nothing out."

So that was exactly what Fred did. As he loped his way down bustling streets and abandoned streets in equal measure with Poppy in tow, constantly checking around them to see if Nick's cronies were following, Fred recounted how Aisling had cornered him at home and demanded he follow Poppy and Dorian, memorise their schedule, and set up a situation in which Aisling could steal Poppy away to drain her blood. And get revenge on Dorian in the process, if possible. She didn't have to hear Fred explain that he did as he was told in order to protect their friends, because that much was obvious, but still he explained it anyway.

"So..." Poppy murmured, when Fred had finished talking, "just what was your plan then? To hand us over? I don't really see you dying on my behalf, Sampson."

Fred twitched but didn't respond to the jibe. Instead he said, "I haven't got to the point where I have a fleshed-out plan. I was trying to find a way to tell you about what was going on first. And, well...now you know."

"So what now?"

"First we have to make sure you're definitely not still being followed. What are you doing out on your own, anyway? That was stupid."

Poppy almost punched Fred in the face but settled on punching his bicep, instead. He didn't even flinch. "I was tailing Dorian."

"Can I comment on the irony of that or—"

"Say a word, Sampson, and I really will punch you in the face."

"That might be worth it."

"I swear to—"

"Over here," Fred cut in, grabbing Poppy and pulling her under the awning of a packed restaurant before she could finish her threat. Poppy's back slammed against a rough stone wall, Fred pressed against her chest. He was close. Much too close. *Has he always been this tall? This broad?* Then Poppy remembered when Fred had grabbed her arm and cut her open. Bowled her to the floor and kept her there, slicing into her again and again and—

"S-step back, Fred," Poppy whispered, splaying her fingers across his chest to force some distance between them. Her heart was racing on a dangerous volume of adrenaline. This was all too much; the last thing she needed was Frederick Sampson this close to her, after everything that had happened between them. She might have been able to put on a brave face in front of everyone at Christmas, and when they worked together to escape the facility, but being alone with Fred for the first time in months was more than enough to shatter all Poppy's previous bravado. If he didn't step away soon Poppy was likely to start shaking and, god forbid it, crying.

But Fred didn't step away.

He rested his forehead on Poppy's, no trace of humour in his green eyes nor the set of his mouth. "They're not far behind us," he said, practically tripping over the words in his urgency to get them out. "I don't think they know you're with anyone; they're just scanning the area. If they think they're looking for a woman all on her own then they may walk right by us if we…"

"If we *what*, Fred?" Poppy urged, knowing that whatever Fred's answer was, she wasn't going to like it.

Fred said nothing for a moment. Two. He bit his lip, a frown shadowing his brow. Then he said, "Fuck it. Sorry in advance."

And then he kissed her.

Poppy was not prepared for this turn of events. She blamed her stunned reaction for why she let the kiss happen. Why she found herself threading her hand through Fred's hair and opening her mouth to let his tongue in. Why her hips bucked against his when he slid an arm around her waist. Why Fred pressed a leg between hers, and Poppy squeezed it as if she wanted nothing more than for it to be there.

It was impossible to ignore the erection Fred was nursing. Poppy would have been disgusted if she wasn't so overwhelmed.

Around them folk tittered at their overt display of affection, and she was aware that people were going out of their way to avoid looking at them. Fred's awful plan was working.

A very long minute later Poppy came back to her senses and pushed him away. Fred was breathing hard; Poppy realised she was, too. With difficulty she cast her gaze down at his crotch then back to his face.

He winced. "Don't think about it."

"I can't think of anything I'd like to think about *less.*"

"It's just a physical reaction—"

"You don't have to explain fucking biology to me, Fred. Are they gone?"

Fred placed his arms on either side of Poppy's head to box her in against the wall, out of sight. It was meant to be protective but all it did was remind her of Fred backing her against the fridge in Dorian's facility, knife in hand. So many emotions – so many chemicals – were coursing through her brain that Poppy couldn't stand it.

After several seconds of scanning the crowd over his shoulder Fred sighed in relief, shoulders sagging as he did so. "They're gone. For now. But you're not safe out on the streets, Poppy. We need to get you into a hotel or something."

Out of the corner of her eye Poppy noticed a very, very expensive-looking hotel with a Gaudí -inspired façade. "That'll do," she said, when Fred followed her gaze to see where she was looking.

"That's way too expensive for me to afford!"

"Who said anything about you paying, Sampson?" Poppy bit out. Shoving him well out of the way she pulled out her purse from the bag she had slung over her shoulder. "I have one of Dorian's many fake credit cards."

Fred dared to smile. "It would only be fair for Dorian to pay for it. It's his fault you were out on your own, after all."

"My thoughts exactly. So fuck off so I can go check myself in."

"Hell if you're going by yourself!" Fred protested, catching Poppy's arm as she barged past him and made a beeline for the hotel. "Poppy, we *literally* just escaped you being noticed by those guys. You need some back-up, at least until you call Dorian and have him pick you up. And something tells me you don't want to call him right this fucking second."

Poppy hated that Fred was right. Even though calling Dorian would be the right thing to do – it was the *only* right thing to do – Poppy didn't want to do it. With all the reluctance of someone who had just been informed they had to eat a slug she allowed Fred to follow her into the hotel.

"Fine," she muttered, "but you're buying the booze."

"Deal."

INTERLUDE VI

Though she had stopped jogging altogether for the last week, and had been sure to get a taxi home from work whenever she could, tonight Jennifer had been convinced to let off some steam by clubbing until the small hours of the morning. Now, drunk and filled with false confidence, Jennifer was making her way home through the dark and lonely streets of suburban Barcelona, thinking about the chips and cheese she'd cook the moment she got in. Her stomach grumbled merely thinking about it.

The alcohol had made her placid enough to forget about her fears over whatever was stalking her. The dog with the broken neck had been horrific, sure, but there was no reason to believe that it hadn't been the work of a sick, psychotic human being, who was probably high or wasted for all Jennifer knew. There hadn't been any sign of said psycho when she found the dog but that didn't mean they hadn't been around. And who was to say Jennifer was their target? It wasn't as if they'd gone after her once they murdered the dog.

It was all in her head. It had to be.

Until she stepped onto a street a mere five minutes from her apartment and met a nightmare.

At first Jennifer couldn't work out what she was looking at. The shadowy figure was tall. Impossibly tall for a human. A network of horns curled up and around its head; the lovely shapes they made reminded her, in that moment, of a winter tree bereft of leaves.

But then the figure rushed forward on furred, bandied legs, hooves – hooves! – click-clacking on the pavement as they galloped.

Jennifer didn't have time to scream. The figure, the monster, snapped one of those legs out and kicked her squarely in the face. She fell with a crash onto her back, blood pouring over her eyes and into her mouth. Jennifer couldn't even feel pain, only dull, ringing blackness.

As her vision dimmed and blurred Jennifer made one final effort to blink. To see. The monster knelt by her side, its inhumanly glacial blue eyes intent on hers. There was something sad about them. She thought, briefly, that in a twisted way the creature was beautiful. Like something out of a fairy tale.

Then it bared its fangs, let out a snarl, and ripped out her throat.

Caught in a Trap

Dorian

Dorian was barely aware of what he was doing as he ripped into the unfortunate woman's stomach, entire body shaking in sheer relief as her entrails slid down his throat.

She had been one of three potential targets Dorian had been tracking. After he'd killed the dog to stop her from realising she was being followed he knew the woman had to die; there was too much evidence left behind if he let her be.

When he kicked her to the ground there had been a moment when Dorian met her eyes, and he thought for one heart-rending moment of Poppy. She was of an age with his victim. The same height and build. The same ash brown hair. But any guilt Dorian might have felt was extinguished almost as soon as it surfaced.

The woman tasted divine. Nothing could compare to the taste of human flesh.

Nothing.

"Oh, but isn't this just the best thing I've seen all week."

Dorian froze. He knew that voice. Had feared that voice for

months.

Aisling.

It was very late. The streets in this part of the city were empty, so when Dorian turned to face her Aisling had no qualms about dropping her human disguise to stretch her wings out. They blocked the moon, casting Dorian in foreboding darkness.

This was bad. All he could do was stare at the harpy, blood drip, drip, dripping down his face.

This was very, very bad.

"No words for me, Dorian?" Aisling sneered, looking down her haughty nose at Dorian crouching over a pile of blood and bones and organs. "I thought you'd have *something* to say, given our last encounter. *And our history*! Have we not been friends for years?"

"You were never my friend," Dorian spat out. "I was a tool to you. You found my job amusing."

"Maybe so, but at least I never betrayed you. Do you have no regret at all for what you did to Stephen? He, at least, was your friend."

If Dorian's stomach wasn't currently full of warm, delicious, life-affirming meat, it would have turned. "*Of course* I regret killing him."

"So why kill him at all? Why not give up the human?"

"You know why."

"So you choose your precious Poppy King over your own kin, even now?"

"She isn't like—"

"If you say she isn't like other humans, Dorian, I'm afraid I'm going to have to stop you right there," Aisling cut in, disgusted by the notion. She rolled her shoulders back, feathers shaking as she did so, then said, "It shouldn't matter if she's different or not. She isn't one of us. She's food. A delicacy, to be fair, but food all the same."

"I'd be very careful what you say right now," Dorian warned, a low growl starting in the back of the throat as he slowly rose to his full height. With the added height of his horns he was almost three feet taller than Aisling; he bared his teeth and let the growl become a full-on snarl.

But Aisling was not so easily intimidated. "I'm just going to straight-up tell you what I'm going to do instead of choosing my words carefully," she hissed, all traces of amusement gone from her face. "I'm going to get my hands on Poppy – you can be sure of it – and when I do, before I drink the final drops of her blood, I'll tell her all about what you did tonight. I'm going to watch as she absorbs the truth that you mercilessly killed one of her kind without her knowing, then laugh as the life slowly drains from her eyes. Only then will I come back and kill you, to put you out of your misery."

In an instant Dorian darted out to grab her. But the narrow street had him boxed in; the harpy had the upper hand. Aisling leapt upwards to catch a breeze, wings billowing just out of reach of Dorian's claws, before she furiously flapped away to safety.

Aisling was gone before Dorian could howl an insult after her.

Leaving Dorian alone with the full reality of what he'd done.

He could do nothing but return to the body he'd been dismembering. There was no point in wasting a single morsel of it, after all. And though he should have felt terrible – and deathly afraid – Dorian felt nothing but calm. He was level and lucid, in a way he hadn't been in months. It confirmed everything he had always suspected.

Poppy's blood would keep him alive forever, but the flesh of her kin would allow him to *live*.

Yet eventually Dorian was done, and the full extent of what Aisling had said crashed over him like a tidal wave. Poppy was alone. He'd messaged her earlier to remain in the hotel for the evening because he'd be back late. Dorian had believed she was safe there, but Aisling had known where Dorian was. She'd appeared in her true form with no regard for anyone catching sight of her.

If she happened to know where Poppy was, what was stopping Aisling from going after her right now?

Dorian wasted no more time in rushing back to the hotel. Behind him he left nothing but bones stripped bare of even a single scrap of flesh. The local dogs would find little to dine on when the sun rose.

But when Dorian barged into their hotel room Poppy was nowhere to be seen. The pool was closed, as were the spa and gym, so he checked the restaurant and then the bar in case she was having a very, very late drink alone.

Poppy wasn't there.

Feeling sick, Dorian bolted back up to their room in case Poppy had magically appeared there in the time it had taken him to go downstairs, but of course she was nowhere to be found.

"Where *are* you, Poppy?" Dorian yowled, collapsing against the railing of the little balcony attached to their room. He pulled out his phone; Poppy had seen his message to stay at the hotel, but she'd never replied. Dorian had literally nothing to go on pertaining to her whereabouts. He had been so consumed by his own hunger that he'd failed at the one thing he had sworn to do: protect Poppy. Dorian was nothing but a monster brought down to his most base instincts, at the expense of all else he held dear.

If Poppy was gone it was his fault and his alone. Dorian's only consolation was that, if Aisling got her way, he didn't have much of his own life left in which to hate himself for it.

An Overdue Confession

FRED

Poppy hung by the window, pulling back the curtain every minute or so to fretfully scan her eyes across the street outside. They'd spent all evening downstairs in the bar to remain safely anonymous so were only now finding themselves alone in the gigantic room Poppy had paid for using Dorian's credit card.

"This is...nice," Fred offered, when he could no longer handle the silence growing between them. "Check out the size of that shower! You could fit half our club in there. Well, what's left of it."

"Reminding me of the fucking nightmare we went through last summer isn't exactly the best distraction, Sampson."

"You're right. But you need a distraction. They don't know we came in here, okay? We'd have seen them downstairs if they had. If you keep obsessing over it then you won't get any sleep." Outside the window the sun had long since set; it would be a long night if neither of them at least *tried* to sleep.

When Poppy finally turned to face Fred it was clear she'd rather remain awake for three days solid than fall unconscious when there were men - monsters - prowling around outside, looking for her.

He shifted guiltily on the spot. "I'm sorry for kissing you earlier." It was the first time he'd brought it up all evening. But now that they were alone and the alcohol they'd been drinking in the bar had loosened his tongue Fred found it impossible *not* to talk about it.

Poppy rolled her eyes before returning her attention to the window. "No you're not."

"The hell does that mean?"

"It worked. We escaped. Why would you be sorry for that?"

"Oh." Had Fred really been the only one bothered by what had occurred between them? It was true he'd kissed Poppy to hide her from view, but that didn't excuse the way he'd reacted to said kiss, nor the way his heart rate escalated when Poppy responded to his tongue slipping into her mouth, their bodies pressed together and—

"I'm going to check out this massive shower for myself," Poppy said, cutting through Fred's disturbing daydream in one fell swoop. She gave Fred a wide berth on her way to the bathroom.

The resounding sound of the door locking behind her filled his ears.

"*Idiot,*" Fred bit out, collapsing onto the gargantuan bed – that they would have to *share* – with his head between his hands. He'd not thought any of this through. How was Fred supposed to spend the night in such close quarters with Poppy King considering everything that had happened between them? Everything he'd seen? Everything he'd experienced?

Everything he'd done?

When Poppy finally let herself out of the bathroom Fred was quick to mutter, "I'm gonna have a shower, too," not looking at Poppy as he escaped into the steam. He couldn't face her. Not when Fred didn't know what to say nor what Poppy might say back to him. For all he knew she planned on saying *nothing* to him now they were alone, and that was worse.

"*Get it together,*" he chastised as he washed his hair. Fred was far too occupied by his own thoughts to enjoy the luxurious shower, nor the products provided for him to use. He felt almost blind as he went through the motions of cleaning himself, though this meant he was finished much faster than he'd intended.

On the wall were two brass hooks; a cotton bathrobe hung from one of them. Reasoning Poppy must be wearing the other one – and not wishing to get back into his clothes after spending a full day under the sun wearing them – Fred shrugged into the robe and tied it tight around his waist.

When he emerged from the bathroom Fred found that Poppy had returned to sitting on the seat built beneath the window. True to his assumption Poppy was in the other bathrobe, though it had slipped off one of her shoulders in a way Fred found himself thinking was *dangerous*. Her hair was still soaking wet; clearly she hadn't even bothered towel-drying it.

Poppy fitfully scanned the dark outside for a sign that anyone was spying on them. Every few seconds she looked at her phone, which she was fidgeting with in her hands, before finally sighing and throwing the device to the floor. It skittered across the hardwood to land at Fred's feet.

"...did you get in touch with Dorian?" he asked, picking up Poppy's phone and gently placing it on top of her bag and discarded clothes, piled haphazardly on a handsomely carved armchair by the mini-bar.

She shook her head. "He told me to stay in the hotel – that he wouldn't be back until late. Hell if I'm dealing with that tonight. I bet he won't even come back until morning."

"Something tells me that's the alcohol talking. You—"

"Are you honestly criticising me *now*, Fred? And telling me what to do? Right bloody now?"

"Clearly being your vice-president has fundamentally changed my brain," he said. "I can't help it." He didn't want to keep standing so Fred ultimately decided to perch on the end of the bed, a few feet away from Poppy sitting by the window. For a moment he considered asking if she wanted the television turned on simply for a distraction. But then – surprising even himself – Fred murmured, "We need to talk."

"About what?" Poppy demanded, not missing a beat.

"About...I don't know. Everything."

She spared him a raised eyebrow. "And what if I don't want to?"

"Well what if *I* do?"

"Since when have I ever given you what you want?" But, despite saying this, Poppy finally pulled the curtains closed over the window and turned to give Fred her full attention. All evening in the bar downstairs she had been very obviously doing everything in her power to do the exact opposite; the effect of her pale eyes now locked on Fred's was alarming.

Dully he realised that he'd never had Poppy's full attention. Not once in all the time he'd known her, bar the night he'd tried to end her life.

"King," Fred coughed, trying to push the invasive thought to the side even though it was related to what he was about to say, "it's obvious you haven't spoken to anyone about what you've gone through. *Are* going through. Given you were tailing Dorian earlier it hardly seems likely that you're being honest with him about what's going on in your head, either."

"Stop—"

"And hell if you've been avoiding having to face up to Andrew after he confessed to you at Christmas," Fred interrupted, though he hadn't planned on bringing Andrew up at all. He'd wanted to talk about last summer. Why was he talking about Poppy's romantic life? "We *all* know what went on between you. The only difference between me and everyone else is that I was still awake when you crept outside and slept with Dorian straight after Andrew confessed to you."

At this Poppy got to her feet, face growing pale rather than red with fury. When she raised a shaking finger to point at Fred her robe slipped further off her shoulder. Fred wished it would stop distracting him. "How *dare—*"

"And you may as well throw a blanket over Rachelle and Nate and Casey's heads, for all that you're keeping them in the dark," Fred continued, knowing now that he was rambling into a ravine he'd never get himself back out of. But he couldn't stop now that he'd started. Fred stood up from the bed to face Poppy, closing the distance between them until all he'd have to do was lean forwards to touch her hand to his chest. "You haven't spoken to a single person about what *you* went through last summer, even though everyone else has. You can't keep that all to yourself. You—"

"Just what do you want me to say, Fred? What the *hell* do you want from me?"

"...why didn't you just show me your arm?"

"W-what?" Poppy stuttered, as if she was unsure what she'd heard. But Fred could tell from the way she froze, from the look on her face, from the way her arm lowered back down to her side, that Poppy had heard him perfectly well. And even though every single one of those things was a sign that Fred should back away and drop the subject, instead he reached out to grab Poppy's forearm the very way he'd done so the night that changed his life forever.

Poppy yelped and stumbled backwards. "This isn't fucking funny, Fred."

"I'm not – no, Poppy, I'm not" – Fred pulled his hand back and ran it through his hair, feeling like an idiot – "I didn't mean it like that. I don't want to hurt you. I don't – *didn't* – want to hurt you back then. Or now."

"Except that you did. You *did,* Fred. I know what I said back at Christmas to everyone. That nobody could really hate you for what you did, because how could any of us know what we'd do when faced with what you discovered?"

"Poppy—"

"Because nobody knew," she cut in. Poppy was trembling. Her eyes were shining, too bright, but Fred knew better than anyone that she'd rather be dead than cry in front of him. "Nobody had ever known," Poppy continued, squaring up to Fred despite her trembling and the fact he loomed over her. "But then Dorian found out and stole my secret for himself, and then it wasn't mine to tell anymore. You can't possibly understand what that's like – to have a part of you taken control of like that. And I thought" – Poppy laughed bitterly – "*you know, when I graduate I might just show Rachelle what happens when I cut myself, and god it'll be hilarious when she freaks out.* But I never had the chance to get that far. Me revealing my secret to anyone because I *wanted* to never got to be more than a thought. But even if Dorian took it from me it was still my biggest, darkest secret, not his. And if keeping it locked inside me saved as many members of our club as I could manage then god damn was I going to stay silent. I watched Craig freaking Hunt being *eaten alive* and still I kept silent."

Neither of them said a word. Poppy's eyes were burning coals, daring Fred to argue with her even though every other part of her body seemed nothing but vulnerable and frightened. "So why did *you* have to know, Fred? Why did *you*" – Poppy slammed her hands against Fred's chest, hard enough that he took a step back – "have to know what was going on with me?" When Fred said nothing Poppy pushed him again, then again and again, until the back of his knees hit the bed and he had nowhere else to go. "Tell me why!"

"*Because I wanted to matter to you!*"

It hadn't been what Fred intended to say, nor was it a conclusion he'd ever wanted Poppy to become aware of. But as he said it Fred realised it was so painfully true that he'd been a fool not to admit to it before.

"Last summer," he said, when Poppy stilled with her hands over his chest, ready to push him again if he didn't give her the answers she deserved, "Rachelle told me I was obsessed with you. She said that whenever *you* insulted me it was in the moment. You never thought about me when I wasn't around. But when *I* insulted you it was clear I'd been stewing over it for ages. Over *you.* I hated that she said that. It was true and I hated it."

Poppy slapped him. Fred brought a hand to his cheek, massaging the burn in his skin she left behind. "You didn't want to see my arm because of some childish vendetta between us, Fred," she said, before slapping him across the other cheek. It felt so good to have her physically respond to everything Fred had done that he almost sighed. "I don't believe that! Nobody does what *you* did because—"

"Who said it was childish, Poppy? There was nothing childish about how much I hated you. How much I *despised* the way everyone listened to you; how they fell under your spell. You could tell someone to jump off a bridge and drown and they'd do it!"

"But I'd never do that!"

"I know, but you had that power in your hands and just – you did fucking *nothing* with it. You didn't care about anything. Or anyone, really. There were no consequences for you. Only impulses and in-the-moment sensations. That was all you were, and I hated it."

Poppy slapped him again. Fred realised he was crying but he didn't care.

"Is that really all you thought of me?" Poppy asked. Through his tears Fred could see that he'd struck a nerve he'd thought Poppy didn't possess. She was offended. She was upset.

She was *disappointed.*

"You know," she continued, when Fred didn't say anything,

"I always respected you. You'll say that's bull shit, but I did. You act as if I wasn't aware of my own faults but you couldn't be further from the truth. I knew fine well what I was lacking. Why else would you think I was fine working with *you* to run our club together? Having you in my *group of friends* – the people I spent all my time with? I didn't like you, Fred, but I respected and I trusted you. But in return you – you—"

Fred fell to his knees. He had no willpower left to stand in front of Poppy King when every word she spoke cut through him like the knife he'd used to hurt her. His hands found themselves grasping at her robe, staring up at Poppy as if she might grant Fred the mercy of a quick death. *Do I want to die?* he wondered, though he knew that wasn't true. If it were true then Fred would never have taken Peter's offer of immortality.

But wanting to die and acknowledging that *Poppy* was allowed to kill him were two different things.

Fred's grip on Poppy's robe finally pulled it off her other shoulder, leaving her chest exposed. Poppy looked down at herself, then Fred, as shamelessly unselfconscious as she had been the night he watched her and Dorian sleep together over a security camera. Then she ripped the robe off and tossed it to the floor.

"I can still feel that knife in my flesh," Poppy bit out in a terse whisper. She took Fred's hands in her own, dragging them over her thighs and up her stomach. "You cut into my arms. My legs. My stomach and my chest." Fred found his hands guided over Poppy's breasts, unable to do anything but watch. Poppy was crying now, too; he could hear it in her voice even as his gaze was transfixed on where his hands were roaming. "Then you flipped me over to slice open my back. You killed me ten times that night. So how could I believe you saying that you didn't want to hurt me? That it was all because you were *jealous* of me?"

Poppy's chest was heaving with every breath she took. When she let go of Fred's hands he found them sliding down to her hips; his fingertips gripped onto her for dear life, holding Poppy in place before him as if Fred might cease to exist without her.

"I'm sorry," he said, so quietly Fred wasn't entirely sure he hadn't simply *thought* the words instead of speaking them. He placed a kiss against Poppy's stomach. "I'm sorry." Another kiss, several inches lower. "I'm sorry." When his mouth lowered again Poppy's hand threaded through Fred's hair to drag his head back.

She stared down at him, expression twisted and confused through her tears. "What are you doing, Fred?"

"I don't know."

He pulled against Poppy's grip to kiss between her thighs, and she didn't stop him. She didn't stop him when Fred urged her legs apart, nor when his tongue found his way inside her. Now Poppy was trembling for a reason completely separate from fear, and Fred discovered that having her like this was greater than any hatred he'd ever held for Poppy in the past.

With a grunt Fred slid his shoulders beneath Poppy's thighs and stood up. She yelped, grabbing onto his hair for dear life as he turned around to throw her on the bed. "The fuck are you doing, Samp—"

"I might not be eight feet tall, or a satyr, or have a dick the size of a rolling pin" – Poppy mouthed *fuck you* at him – "but I think I know enough to get you off, King." Fred laughed humourlessly, the sound fluttering off Poppy's hipbone. "I think I know more about you than I know about myself."

To his gratification Poppy sounded breathless when she said, "Where are you going with this?"

Fred undid the sash of his robe, eyes on Poppy's as he pulled the garment off and discarded it on the floor with her own. "I can't change what I did to you. The pain I caused. But I *can* overwrite that pain...or try to. And I can give you a distraction from that damn window so you can actually get some sleep. Or no sleep at all, if you'd rather."

He almost laughed when Poppy quirked an eyebrow. She propped herself up on her elbows, staring Fred down as if challenging him to look away.

He didn't look away.

"My favourite nights are the ones I'm too busy to sleep through."

"Oh, I'm aware."

"How would you know that?"

"You're not as quiet as you think you are at house parties, King."

"*Sampson!*"

Fred crawled over Poppy to laugh against her lips. "You have no idea how jealous I was, back then. Christ, *I* had no idea I was jealous."

"So...what is this?" Poppy asked, resisting the urge to move beneath Fred's weight pressing against her. He was dying for her to touch him. Had been dying for it for years. "Is this a completely fucked-up confession of love or...?"

"Hell no," Fred spat out. Gently he stroked Poppy's face, slid his fingers over her jaw, then found them curling around her throat. She let him do so. It gave Fred permission to apply the smallest amount of pressure, and then a little more. "This is me telling you I want to fuck you so badly it hurts. I don't love you."

"Oh thank god," Poppy choked around his fingers, laughing in a careless way that reminded Fred of a time gone by when she hadn't been trying to save thirty people from certain death.

"But I *do* want us to be equals. Or...something. I don't want us to keep competing. I want us to be on the same side. I— *haah!*"

Poppy slid her hand down Fred's side and landed on his painful erection. She squeezed until he moaned. Driven to distraction his fingers loosened around her throat. "We were always equals," Poppy said, when she regained her breath. "You were the only one who never saw that. Talk about an inferiority complex!"

For a few moments of slick silence Fred allowed Poppy's hand to move against him, his breath caught in his throat as he tried to comprehend what was going on. But then she paused, and Fred's hazy vision came back into focus. "You aren't doing this as some convoluted revenge against Dorian, are you?" he asked, curiosity getting the better of him. At this point he was past caring *why* Poppy was actually naked beneath him, only that it was happening.

Poppy laughed bitterly. "Trust me, I don't want anyone to find out this happened. So are you going to show me you aren't shit in bed? Or is that just another thing Frederick Sampson can't do right?"

Fred's grip tightened on Poppy's neck once more. The garbled cry that left her throat was too much for him to bear; Fred sealed her lips with his to keep the sound all for himself. When he pressed his body against Poppy's she eagerly responded in kind.

"One night," he breathed, before he lost his senses entirely.

Minutely Poppy nodded. "One night, then you can fuck off."

He might have laughed. Instead Fred kissed her.

INTERLUDE VII

"I can't wait until this auction is over and I can go back to sleeping, you know, at night," Sam complained, grunting as he helped Carlos heave a body onto their unmarked white truck. The auction was in five days which they both knew was absolutely going to drag. Despite their best interests – as well as everyone else working for Nick across the continent – it had proven incredibly difficult to source top-of-the-line humans for the event. And they were still short on numbers, which Sam and Carlos knew meant several more sleepless nights to come.

"At least after tomorrow we won't be tailing this Poppy girl," Carlos said, when Sam started the van and they began driving to the underground storage rooms they'd been using to hide and maintain the stock of humans for the auction. "Kris still has eyes on her in that hotel, yeah?"

Sam nodded, checking left and right before driving straight ahead. "He's in the hotel opposite. Lucky fucker. Though I suppose after those humans got away from him last week he was happy for an easy job. Seems like this Poppy King and her friend have turned in for the night."

"Do you think it's worth grabbing her now?"

"Nah, let's wait 'til morning. Think of the scene it would cause if we took her straight out of the hotel. Besides, if I don't get at least a couple hours of shut-eye I'm going to fall asleep at the damn wheel."

"You have a point." So Carlos took out his phone, fired off a message to Nick that they'd take the girl in the morning once she

left the hotel, then turned on the radio until he found a classic rock station. "What do you think is so special about her, anyway?" he asked after a minute or two. "Poppy King, I mean."

"Knowing Nick's horny ass I'd say he wants to sleep with her."

"That's a hell of a lot of effort to go to for a fuck."

"In his true form."

"Ah." Carlos frowned. "I thought he pretty much destroyed any human he tried to do that with?"

"So clearly something's different about this one. You know he doesn't like to talk about his family line getting older with nobody to replace them. Nick's getting antsy about it."

"Still..." They turned onto a narrow street a few minutes from Poppy King's hotel. Sam killed the engine, and they both reclined their seats to grab some sleep whilst they still could. "She must be special."

"I'd call her doomed." Then Sam lowered his baseball cap over his eyes, signalling the end of their conversation.

In the morning they'd find out exactly what Poppy King was, one way or the other.

WHEN POPPY KING'S LUCK RUNS OUT

POPPY

FRED LOOKED YOUNGER WHEN HE WAS SLEEPING. Poppy supposed it was because he wasn't scowling. But he looked tired, still, and there were haunted edges to his face that hadn't been there before their time in Dorian's facility. For some things could never be unseen.

Some things could never be undone.

But they could move past those things. Whether through healthy means or otherwise Poppy knew that in this regard she and Fred were alike: if they never moved on they would be stuck forever in the past, and would in all likelihood descend into madness.

Poppy was gratified, then, that as she watched Fred sleeping she felt nothing. Their night together had been the catharsis she needed – that Fred had clearly needed, too – but Poppy hadn't suddenly developed romantic or even vaguely soft feelings for her old nemesis. Granted things would be different between them. That was a given, after everything.

But they hadn't fucked things up. After all, the worst thing Poppy King could ever imagine was falling for Frederick Sampson.

She was quite certain he felt the same way.

"You're still here."

Poppy startled at the sound of Fred's voice, all at once realising that he was wide awake and staring straight at her. A self-conscious blush spread across her face, and she rushed from where she sat on the bed to throw on her shoes. "Where else did you expect me to be?" she said, hating that Fred had surprised her.

Fred made no move to get up. "I figured you'd run off as soon as I fell asleep or something. That's totally your style."

"Fuck you, Sampson."

"You already did."

"Don't make me regret this or I swear to god—"

"*Do* you regret it?" Fred finally sat up, spine perfectly straight against the pillows as he held his hands in his lap. He looked for all intents and purposes as if he were giving Poppy an interview - aside from the mess that was his hair and the fact he was completely naked.

She considered telling him she did simply to piss him off. But instead Poppy sighed. "No. Happy now?"

"As happy as I'll ever be."

"So miserable, then."

Fred chuckled. "Exactly. But you really should go, Poppy. Get out of Barcelona today. You aren't safe here."

"But what about Aisling?" Poppy asked, hovering by the door. She was torn between following the itching in her skin that told her to do exactly what Fred wanted her to do - run - and make sure Fred himself would be safe. The fact Poppy was actually concerned for him was disgusting. "What about what she needs you to do?"

"I'll handle her."

"Fred—"

"Don't tell me you're worried about me, King," Fred drawled. He raised his arms to rest his hands behind his head, clearly beyond pleased with this turn of events. "I have more tricks up my sleeve than you realise. So *don't* worry about me. Which should be easy for you, considering..."

"God, is this what we do now, act together in a weird parody of the way we were before?"

Fred shrugged. "Things could be worse."

"Yeah, and Aisling could tear you to shreds the moment she realises you have no plans of bringing me to that damn auction."

"And *I'm* telling you that I'm a grown-ass man capable of making his own decisions. I can handle it. So respond to one of Dorian's damn hundred phone calls and get the fuck out of Barcelona. I mean it, Poppy."

Poppy wanted to argue. Of course she did; she never backed away from a challenge. To leave Fred alone against Aisling was condemning him to die. What had been the point of saving him back in Dorian's facility only for Fred to die, now, in her place? But it was clear by the set of his face that Fred was done arguing. And he *was* an adult, after all. He could make decisions. Even if they were stupid.

Even if it was a decision Poppy King herself would have made.

"Well," she said quickly, adjusting her bag over her shoulder before reaching for the door handle. For a moment Fred twitched as if he meant to get out of bed and—

And what? Poppy thought. *Hug me? He's stark fucking naked, for god's sake. And Fred.*

To her relief Fred did nothing.

"Let me know how things go on," Poppy ended up saying, instead of good-bye.

Fred rolled his eyes. "As if I'll do that. Bye, Poppy. Don't let me see you again."

So Poppy left. She glanced around furtively when she left the hotel to amble out onto the street. The sun had barely risen, and hadn't quite hit the pavement yet, but despite that the day promised to be warm. Poppy found herself suppressing a shiver, anyway. She knew it had nothing to do with the weather.

Dutifully Poppy pulled out her phone, wincing when she looked at the screen. Fred hadn't been exaggerating – Dorian had called Poppy no fewer than a hundred times. Guilt clawed at her stomach, which she realised in that moment was pitifully empty. She was starving; when had she last eaten? She decided to pick up some breakfast from a bakery on her way back to the hotel.

Dorian picked up Poppy's call before the first ring had even finished. "Where are you?!" he cried out, beside himself with worry. Poppy's guilt grew exponentially; Dorian hadn't deserved her silence all night.

"I'm okay, Dorian," she soothed, spying a promising bakery beside the nearest Metro station. "I'm fine. I ran into Fred."

"...Fred. As in Sampson, Frederick?"

"I don't know any other Freds."

"At the hotel?"

"Er, no, I...went for a walk."

"To where?!" Dorian demanded. "Where are you?"

"I'm safe. I swear it."

A long, shuddering silence met Poppy's reassurance. She could tell Dorian was trying hard to hold in his temper. Which was saying something; Poppy knew he was well within his rights to absolutely lose his shit, considering what she'd just put him through. But then Dorian gulped, and Poppy realised that his worry over whether she was safe had overwritten his anger.

"I guess a longer explanation can come later," he said softly. But his voice was trembling. "Where are you? I'll come get you."

"I'm three Metro stops away from the hotel so just wait for me. I'm popping into a bakery first; I'll be about thirty minutes."

"Are you sure nobody's following you?"

"The street is practically deserted, Dorian," Poppy said, grimacing at the thought of explaining exactly *why* she'd been out all night in the first place. Dorian really was going to explode when he heard. "It's too early for anyone to be out. And I'll be careful."

"You better. And Poppy..."

"And Poppy what?" she echoed, when Dorian didn't elaborate.

She could practically see him shake his head as he said, "Never mind. See you in half an hour." Dorian hung up.

Poppy felt a sense of clarity as she walked towards the bakery. A plethora of unhealthy baked goods was exactly what she needed to consume before facing Dorian. She looked left before crossing the road, then right, slightly annoyed to see that the bakery was due to open its doors in five minutes. *So I'll be thirty-five minutes instead of thirty,* Poppy thought, feeling a little guilty.

Considering how terrified Dorian had sounded – she could only imagine how it felt when he returned to their hotel room and discovered Poppy was gone – being late to meet him by even five minutes felt cruel. Especially considering what Poppy hadn't told him over the phone about how she'd been followed the previous day. So Poppy turned from the bakery, choosing to forgo breakfast in favour of meeting Dorian early.

Just as a car rolled to a stop in front of her, threw open its doors, and a pair of strong, burly arms pulled her inside.

"*What the—*" Poppy gasped, before a hand covered her mouth and swallowed the rest of her words. Roughly she was thrown into the back of the car; with a click of the lock the door closed and the vehicle sped away. Poppy recognised the driver first, then with a twist of her head saw that she recognised the man who had grabbed her, too: the men who'd been following her.

Deep, unrelenting dread filled Poppy to her core. *No, no, no, no, no,* she cried, kicking out against her captor when he fought Poppy for her bag. But she was helpless against the sheer size and strength of the man; with a grunt he snapped the strap off her bag, rolled down the window and tossed it out onto the road.

The sense of inevitability that had been creeping beneath Poppy's skin from the very moment Nick announced last summer that she was his began to overwhelm her. Poppy gagged on it, chest heaving in her attempt to breathe air into her lungs. She knew perfectly well what was waiting for her when the car stopped.

This was everything Dorian had been protecting Poppy from. She should never have been curious about what he was up to. She should never have left her hotel room. And Poppy hadn't even warned Dorian about the fact she'd been followed the day before. She'd told him she was safe. She'd lied to Dorian, to keep him from being angry at her. To keep him from making her feel worse than she already did.

Poppy King was doomed, and she had nobody to blame but herself.

Unbridled Panic

DORIAN

"She's *late*."

Now was not the time for Poppy to be late. Dorian's heart felt like it might burst as he paced back and forth in front of the hotel, no longer caring who might recognise him. Aisling's words seeped like poison into his blood. A promise. A curse. Had she gotten hold of Poppy already?

No, Dorian decided, desperately shaking his head. *She only came out to mock me last night. It seemed like she had a plan in place; to take Poppy so quickly after taunting me just isn't Aisling's style. So then...*

Dorian couldn't bear thinking of the alternative. He was overreacting. He had to be. Poppy was only thirty minutes late.

Dorian was calling Andrew before he quite knew what he was doing, whilst at the same time making his way towards the closest Metro station even though he knew it made more sense to remain at the hotel. Because if Poppy showed up and Dorian wasn't there, what was stopping her from leaving the hotel to look for *him*?

Except Poppy wasn't picking up her phone, and it wasn't

going straight to voicemail, either. No, it was ringing out, which meant she wasn't stuck on the Metro delayed somewhere underground. Something *above* ground was keeping her, preventing her from answering.

Which meant something was wrong, and Dorian couldn't waste a single moment standing passive and unmoving in front of the hotel.

"Andrew, thank God," Dorian bit out, seven rings later when Andrew finally picked up. He turned left towards the main street where the Metro was located, scanning the busy crowd of morning commuters as he did so. There was no sign of Poppy.

Down the phone Andrew yawned loudly. "Dor-Dorian? What is it? It's so early."

Dorian glanced at the time, then cursed when he remembered Scotland was one hour behind Barcelona. But he didn't have time for niceties. "When did you last hear from Poppy?"

Even over a phone line Dorian knew Andrew had been jolted into full consciousness by the question. "She called me yesterday afternoon," he said. "But then she cut me off when she saw Fred."

"Fred. Shit, yeah, she mentioned that." Dorian was frazzled; how could he have forgotten that vital piece of information already? "Andrew, can you send me Fred's number? I need to get hold of him."

"Sure, I – hold on, I'll text it. What's going on? Is Poppy okay? Is she—"

"There's no time for this now," Dorian interrupted, checking his phone screen to ensure the text from Andrew came through. "I'll fill you in later. Thanks, Andrew."

Dorian wasted no time in calling Fred the moment he hung up on Andrew. "Pick up, pick up..." Dorian muttered, not quite believing the fact he was willingly calling Frederick Sampson. But he didn't pick up, even when Dorian called a second, third and forth time. Scowling, Dorian paused outside the Metro station to send Fred a text informing him who was calling and to pick up the bloody phone.

Dorian barely had time to avoid eye contact with an attractive woman passing by when his phone began ringing. "Why the fuck would I have picked up a call from an unknown number?" Fred demanded immediately, when Dorian answered the call. "What do you want?"

"Is Poppy with you?" Dorian said, ignoring Fred's jibe.

"No. She left over an hour ago. She isn't with you?"

"*No.* Do you know...do you know where she might have gone?"

There was a pause. It was all Dorian needed to hear – or, rather, *not* hear – to know that Poppy had not been entirely truthful about what she'd been up to when they were talking on the phone earlier. "Tell me what you know, Sampson," Dorian growled, "or so help me—"

"Meet me by Barcelona Cathedral," Fred said, which was not what Dorian had expected him to say at all. "I think...fuck, I think this could be really bad."

This time it was Fred who hung up before Dorian could ask for more details.

All the colour left his face. Something was horribly wrong. Dorian had indulged his basest urges, leaving Poppy alone and unprotected, and something had gone wrong.

Dorian wasn't aware of his journey to the Gothic Quarter of the city. All he knew was that one minute he was stepping onto the Metro and the next he was ambling around the cathedral, scanning for Fred through a throng of tourists.

When Dorian finally spied Fred he noted that the tan on his skin suggested the man had been living in warm, foreign countries just as long as Dorian and Poppy had. *Has he been following us all this time without me noticing?* Dorian wondered, furious with himself when he remembered that Fred had been looking for Poppy in Berlin back in autumn. *Have I been so focused on avoiding Nick that I became blinded to anyone else hunting us? First Aisling, now—*

"No more delays, Sampson," Dorian spat out the moment he stormed up to Fred and leaned well into his personal space. But Fred didn't flinch away from Dorian's intimidation; instead, he squared up to him and maintained forceful, steady eye contact.

"There were a couple men tailing Poppy yesterday. You may have noticed, if you weren't off doing your own thing so much that Poppy felt the need to tail *you*."

Dorian choked on his next breath. He scratched at his throat, swaying dangerously as he took in every word Fred had spoken. This was it. This was everything Dorian had feared.

"What...what was she doing with you yesterday?" Dorian gasped, torn between panic and rage in the face of Frederick Sampson of all people telling Dorian that he had failed. "Were you following us?"

Fred had the audacity to roll his eyes. "You really think that matters right now? Besides, Poppy wouldn't be in trouble like this if she hadn't been following after you like a detective in a fucking YA novel, arsehole."

Dorian just barely the urge to punch Fred in the face. "Did she say why she was following me?"

"Because she was worried about you. Not that you deserve it, after everything you've done to her. But she knew something was wrong. So what have you been up to, leaving her alone when you promised to protect her?"

Of course Fred had hit the nail on the head. Dorian turned from him, disgusted, wanting nothing more than to walk away from the man who had once tried to kill Poppy King admonishing *him* for how he'd ruined her life. But Dorian knew he couldn't. He needed everyone he could get on his side right now. For if Nick was the one who had taken Poppy - and

Dorian was now all but certain he was – then it would be impossible to retrieve her on his own.

So Dorian swallowed his pride, pinched the bridge of his nose, and muttered, "Will you help me get her back?"

He expected a snide remark. An insult. Instead, Fred said, "Of course. I'll do anything you need me to." A beat of silence fell between them, then Fred asked, "It was Nick, wasn't it?"

Dorian nodded. "The Richardson family have a mansion here."

"Yeah, and he's organising an auction to be held in the city in a few days. Why the fuck did you even bring Poppy here if you knew Nick had a *mansion* here?"

"He's *what*?!" Dorian cried, bug-eyed. "Where did you hear that?"

"That's irrelevant," Fred replied, his voice infuriatingly calm where Dorian sounded as if he might lose himself entirely. Fred crossed his arms over his chest, glancing left and right to ensure nobody was listening, then said, "So how do we save her? If we assume she's been taken to Nick's estate, then we...break her out?"

It wasn't as if Dorian had a better plan. "It would be our best bet. At worst we find out she isn't there." They both knew this wasn't the *worst* thing that would happen if things went awry, but neither Dorian nor Fred bothered giving voice to this.

"If it's a mansion I can only assume it's massive. At Christmas you and Patrick kept talking about Nick as if he's a bloody prince."

"He may as well be." Dorian's gaze grew unfocused as he remembered the layout of the mansion, ensured it was all still there in his brain, then indicated for Fred to follow him as Dorian stalked away from the cathedral. "I remember the mansion well enough for us to search it; I visited it once."

Fred scoffed. "And you think that means you remember it?"

"Who do you think designed the floor plans for the Highlands Adrenaline Sports Facility?" Dorian bit back, as they made their way to an internet café. "I'm a licensed architect."

"Okay, well I could hardly fucking know that, could I? King never told me."

"That's because she doesn't know." The two of them sat down in front of a computer, Fred wordlessly observing as Dorian pulled up an internet search for car rental in Barcelona. After a moment Dorian added, bitterly, "She's never been interested in actually getting to know me."

"The two of you are completely fucked, you do know that, right?"

"Shut up, Sampson."

"What's the car for?"

"Getaway."

"I can't drive."

"Neither can I."

"Then how—"

"We won't be saving her alone," Dorian explained, pulling out his phone to bring up Patrick's number. "Casey can drive, and Patrick has a...particular...set of skills we need."

Fred made a face. "I get the picture. So what does that leave me and you to do?"

"I'm the distraction." Dorian bit his tongue, thinking hard. He *had* to be the distraction, otherwise the plan would fail. But if he was the distraction, that left the most vital part of the rescue mission squarely in Fred's hands.

"...I don't like what your silence is insinuating, Dorian," Fred murmured. "If you're the distraction then what do you need *me* to do?"

For another moment or two Dorian stared at the computer screen, watching as the details of one of his many credit cards was accepted by the car rental website. But then he turned his attention to Fred, fought back the churning of his stomach, and said, "How good at climbing are you really, Sampson?"

THE DEVIL IN YELLOW SCALES

POPPY

POPPY KNEW THERE WAS LITTLE POINT in struggling when she was dragged out of the car and roughly pushed down an ornate gravel driveway that curved around both sides of the most ostentatious, pale-stoned house she'd ever seen. *House doesn't cut it,* she mused, desperately trying to take in every inch of the expansive gardens that encircled the estate. *This place is practically a castle.*

Poppy had been driven through two steep, wrought-iron gates built into equally high, smooth-sided walls, so any hope of escape from the place she had would not be found the way she'd come. She could only hope the walls did not encircle the entire property.

Before she was brought inside Poppy thought she could hear the sound of waves, but then she was thrust through a set of carved oak doors and the sound was swallowed entirely. Her footsteps slapped against marble; when she fought against the grip of the man holding her those footsteps became a slide along the floor.

"If Nick demands my presence he can damn well see to my kidnap personally," Poppy growled, trying in vain to wrench free from her impassive captor. If she were a smarter woman she might have decided against goading Nichola Richardson into facing her, but Poppy had never been sensible. She also knew, in her heart and in her gut, that if she faced him with anything less than the breathless gusto she'd demonstrated back at the Highlands Adrenaline Sport Facility then she would undoubtedly lose.

Even though Poppy rather wished she'd never have to face Nick again.

But just as she'd known – the moment Dorian told her the fire hadn't been enough to kill him – that it was inevitable for her to face Nick again, Poppy knew now that she wasn't going to get away with avoiding him for the rest of her life, however long or short that life may end up being.

Poppy barely took in a single detail of the expansive house as she was dragged though it, other than the fact it was cool and airy against her flushed skin. It was only when she was pushed inside a room, the doors ominously locked behind her, that Poppy realised her mistake in not committing to memory every step she took to get there. This *wasn't* Dorian's facility, after all; she didn't have months to memorise it. She had seconds, and she'd squandered them.

Still, all Poppy could do now was rectify that mistake by analysing her new prison for a means to escape.

There was an enormous four-poster bed situated in the middle of the room, twice as large as the beds Poppy had seen in many of the Scottish castles her parents are taken her to during her childhood. Red velvet curtains were tied to each of the posts, revealing an elaborately woven bedspread in reds and purples and white. The bed sat atop a plush rug that took up half of the hardwood floorspace of the gigantic room, in a deeper red than the bed.

Opposite the bed there was a stone fireplace, which was out

of use given the time of year. Further along the wall there was an ornate vanity unit, with a silvered mirror inlaid across it. Poppy turned from her reflection before she could make eye contact with herself. There was a door to the right of the vanity; upon opening it Poppy discovered that it led to an empty walk-in wardrobe that contained *another* door. Behind this door was a small bathroom complete with a brass, claw-foot bath, but little else of interest. Poppy returned to the room proper to scope more of it out.

Along much of the available wall space were enormous paintings, most of them portraits. Walking around the room Poppy could see the similarities between the subjects of the paintings; even without the gold-plated annotations beneath each frame she could tell they were all part of the Richardson family. Here was a woman with Nick's aquiline nose. Here was a man with his raven-black, Hollywood-style hair. Here were two young brothers with the promise of his broad shoulders, his easy brown eyes. Even as children they towered over their mother. She alone in the portrait looked completely at odds with the rest of the paintings, thin and sickly-looking even through the eyes of whomever had painted her.

If she made it into the Richardson family portraits then she must have been special, Poppy mused, forcing herself to turn from the paintings even though a perverse part of her wished to look at that woman for ever and ever and wonder if that was meant to be her fate.

Except Poppy wouldn't die. She was certain, in the pit of her stomach, that the woman hadn't lived much longer after her tragic portrait was painted.

A couple of the paintings *weren't* family portraits. In fact, Poppy herself recognised them; when she searched her brain she realised she'd seen them in Berlin. She'd gone with her parents the Christmas after she'd gone with her friends. When Fred wanted to visit the museums Poppy had laughed in his face, saying that going to museums wasn't something to do in the summer. Even though, in truth, she'd wanted to visit them, Poppy had been too wrapped up in having fun with everyone to do something so austere as to visit a museum. So she waited until she went with her parents, months later, to traipse through the halls of the Pergamonmuseum.

She wondered if the museum or the house she'd found herself captive in held the originals.

Thinking of Fred bothered Poppy somehow, though it annoyed her that it bothered her. Dorian would be in touch with him soon. There was no version of the present, after all, where Dorian didn't chase every lead he could think of the moment Poppy failed to meet him. She'd gone over it all in the car on the way to the Richardson estate. Poppy imagined it would go something like this: Dorian would panic, and then he would call Andrew, who would tell him that Poppy had seen Fred, then Dorian would remember that Poppy herself had told him she'd been with Fred. He'd get his number from Andrew. He would call him.

And then what? Fred would tell Dorian about the men who were following her. He'd know she was following him, and that she'd lied to him, and then they'd plan how to save her. Given how Poppy and Fred had cleared the air between them she had no doubt Fred would insist on being involved.

Just like she'd saved him from Dorian's facility, even after what he'd done.

But Poppy didn't want anyone else put in danger just to save her. She was reasonably certain both Fred and Dorian would agree to leave Andrew out of things, and by extension Rachelle and Nate. *But what about Casey?* Poppy worried, turning from the wall of paintings to chew her thumb. *Dorian will contact Patrick, there's no doubt about it.* And Patrick would bring Casey with him on the next available flight.

So that meant, at most, four people were formulating a plan to rescue Poppy – providing they knew where she was. Part of her knew Dorian must have been aware Nick had a mansion in

Barcelona, which meant he likely had a good idea about where she was. And if all of her suppositions were miraculously true, then...

All Poppy had to do was get out of the building before anything permanent and irreversible happened to her.

To the east, bringing the only source of light into the dark room, was a narrow floor-to-ceiling window adorned with red curtains so dark they were almost black. The pane of glass was unmarred and unopenable, but right at the top was a much smaller window with a handle attached, clearly intended to air out the room. Currently it was closed.

But I can reach it.

So what if the drop on the other side would break Poppy's bones? In seconds she would heal from her injuries, and then she could run, run, run to safety. All she had to do was climb one of the curtains, open the window, and force herself out.

Once, Poppy had tried climbing silk scarves at a circus skills class with Rachelle. Rachelle had been good at it but Poppy lacked the patience to bother learning how to balance her way up the cloth. But now, with adrenaline coursing through her, she knew she had nothing left to lose. Steeling herself for a couple of falls before she got the hang of it, Poppy took a deep breath and ran for the left-hand curtain.

She clawed up the material as soon as her hands found purchase, not daring to give herself a single inch with which to slip. Poppy's muscles were made for this kind of unforgiving task. She could master it, no problem. The velvet beneath Poppy's hands gave her a grip the silk back at the circus skills class hadn't. Before Poppy knew it she was halfway up the curtains. Two thirds.

The latch on the upper window was almost within reach when something too large to be a hand wrapped itself around Poppy's waist and tossed her mercilessly to the floor.

Poppy screamed. Of course she did. But even through her

own voice and the ringing in her ears that met her jarring reconnection with the floor, Poppy heard his voice.

"I heard you called for me."

A voice from her nightmares, garbled and monstrous as if the throat that bore the words wasn't suited to human speech, but with an edge of familiarity that set Poppy's nerves on edge more than anything.

A hand *had* grabbed her off the curtain. The real, true, entirely inhuman hand of Nichola Richardson, six-inch claws and all.

"I have to say, it was interesting watching you foolishly try to escape the moment you thought you were alone," Nick taunted, though Poppy was so blinded by her fear – and the suddenness of her fall – that her eyes couldn't even focus on him. No, all she could see was black and blue and red. But she could hear the scrape of his horns on the hardwood on either side of her head, leaving no inch of her free to try and wriggle away.

Even so Poppy struggled against Nick's vice-like grip on her waist, even when the edge of his claws bit into her flesh and threatened to open up her veins. Had Poppy been a normal human they long since would have.

"It seems not a moment is wasted with you, Poppy King," Nick growled, the words hot and frantic against Poppy's ear, "so I would be wise to do the same." She felt him inhale a breath, maw opened wide, and—

Poppy pulled up her legs to kick Nick as hard as she could in the chest. It wasn't enough to move him – not even an inch – but it distracted Nick enough that Poppy could scratch her hands across his face, digging in when she met his eyes. Nick snarled, his grip loosening on Poppy's waist just enough for her to push off his claws to escape between his horns.

But Poppy didn't make it very far. No sooner had she scrabbled onto her knees than Nick grabbed her ankle and locked her in place. Poppy screamed again at the feel of his scales against her skin – though she realised, blithely, that she hadn't *stopped* screaming ever since Nick entered the room – and tried her damnedest not to hyperventilate into unconsciousness.

Breathe, breathe, she chastised, desperately trying to blink vision back into her eyes even though what she would see was a nightmare. *Just breathe. He won't kill you. He said last year he didn't want to kill you. He—*

"What's going on in that head of yours?" Nick demurred, sounding more amused than pissed off that Poppy had attacked him. "You should be living in the moment, Poppy." With a careless flick he yanked her back onto the floor, holding her down with the weight of an immense, razor-clawed foot so he could loom over her.

Poppy had screamed herself out. All she could do was stare up at him.

Nick's golden scales gleamed in the sunlight beginning to slant in through the tall window, making his enormous, reptilian body appear encased in armour. His huge horns curved down to fine points that jutted out beneath ox-like ears. There were still some human features to his face, but this close up all Poppy could see was the animalistic set of his nose, his brows, his *snarl.*

His teeth.

Beneath Poppy's horrified, undivided attention those teeth broke into a grin. "There you are. Even last year you spent so long in your own head. I guess I can't blame you, given what you were going through."

She spat at him. "Go to hell."

"Poppy, you're already there." Slowly, very slowly, Nick wiped her spit from his cheek with the palm of his hand then licked it clean with an alarmingly thick, forked tongue. His slitted pupils dilated and contracted in quick succession. Nick increased the pressure of his weight on Poppy's chest for a moment, crushing the air from her lungs, before removing his foot to bend down over her once more.

"D-don't – don't touch me," she stammered, hating that she was stammering. Hating that tears were streaming down her face, and her throat was constricting around every breath she forced down, and her heart was beating so fast Poppy thought it would explode. She wished it would. When Nick's tongue traced the line of her artery in her neck she especially wished it. "Please," she begged. "*Please* don't do this."

This gave Nick pause. His face hovered over Poppy's, a careful non-expression painting his features, before he lowered his gaze to take in the rest of her body. It settled on Poppy's right thigh, left hopelessly exposed beneath the tattered remains of her sundress. "Pleading doesn't suit you," Nick murmured, licking his lips. "Either scream or enjoy it."

Then he sunk his teeth into her thigh.

A wordless yowl was ripped from Poppy's throat. Her nails scrabbled at Nick's horns, uselessly trying to force him away as he broke through her flesh and drank. His eyes never left hers, ensuring Poppy bore witness to the exact moment her blood slipped down Nick's throat.

His eyes were *all* pupil now, dark and soulless but shining. Nick sliced his teeth free from Poppy's thigh, not at all gently, to gaze in bloody wonder at her. "You are so special, Poppy King," he said, before returning to drain her of all that made her so.

But Nick was drinking too fast. It was a sensation Poppy was achingly familiar with. Had come to *enjoy,* when Dorian was responsible for it. *Scream or enjoy it, he said. Enjoy it. How could he know I ever enjoyed it?*

Enjoying it was the furthest thing from Poppy's mind now. Her vision grew familiarly hazy; her wrists slackened and she stopped trying to claw at Nick's horns. When her head sagged against the floor, completely resigned, Nick pulled himself up and away from the gaping wound in Poppy's thigh once more.

"You're supposed to tell me when I've taken too much," he

muttered, a frown shadowing his immense brow as he swept Poppy into his arms and laid her down upon the four-poster bed. Dimly she thought he was almost as gentle as Dorian had been, after he'd first drank her blood.

Almost.

Poppy barely registered Nick smoothing her hair out of her eyes with the edge of a claw, still in his true form even as he did something so painfully human. "Sleep," he urged. "We'll continue this when you've recovered."

Just like the ghost of a nightmare, the room grew black, Poppy's eyes closed, and she wished she'd never again wake up.

RADIO SILENCE

ANDREW

ANDREW WAS SLEEPING OVER AT NATE'S. He'd stayed over for the last two nights, unable to remain at home, alone, with nobody to talk to about Poppy or what may or may not be going on with her a thousand miles away.

"Andrew, stop pacing."

"Yeah, Andrew, it won't solve anything."

"Sitting won't solve anything, either."

"That true," Nate said carefully, "but you're making Rachelle nervous. So sit down."

Andrew regarded Rachelle in surprise. She was sitting on Nate's bed, curled around an oversized cushion, and to Andrew's eyes didn't look nervous at all. "How does pacing make you nervous? Aren't you nervous *already*? No one will tell us what's going on with Poppy and—"

"Of course that makes me nervous," Rachelle snapped. Andrew flinched; she never lost her temper. "But your – your – your *visual* panic is making me worse. You're not the only one who cares about her, Andrew. You're not the only one who's furious at being left in the dark."

Andrew could see, then, that Rachelle was speaking the truth. Even though he was often oblivious to what other people were feeling there could be no mistaking the slight shaking of Rachelle's shoulders now that he was looking for it, nor how pale she was.

Ashamed, Andrew sat down beside her.

"Well, what information do we actually have?" Nate asked nobody in particular, taking up the role of group team leader as he so often had done over the last few months. He spun in his desk chair to face both Rachelle and Andrew, laptop blaring anime theme songs from his lap. "We have Poppy hanging up on Andrew because she saw Fred. And then we have Dorian calling Andrew to ask when he'd last heard from Poppy, then asking for Fred's number. Ever since neither Poppy, Dorian nor Fred have responded to texts or calls."

"And Casey and Patrick aren't responding, either," Rachelle added on, nodding sagely. "Which means something very, very bad has happened, and they don't want us to get involved."

"But we have to!" Andrew cried, beside himself. "We can't stay here. We can—"

"What can we really do, Andrew?" Nate said, grimacing. Andrew wanted to shake him for all the good it would do. Why wasn't he losing his mind just as badly as he was? "Think about it: they're probably not telling us to protect us. Poppy would never forgive them if they did something that might endanger us. You must know that."

"Poppy doesn't get to decide what someone does or doesn't do when the cost of doing nothing is *losing* her."

"When did you get so obstinate?" Nate sighed, rubbing a hand over his face. Andrew took it as an insult, at first, but when Nate flashed him a smile he realised that his friend meant it as a compliment.

"He's always been obstinate," Rachelle said. She reached out from behind her oversized cushion to stroke Andrew's arm. "It's just that, before, Andrew's decisions weren't based on...you know, life or death." She laughed ruefully. "In any case there's nothing we can do about it except hope for the best and focus on something else."

"And speaking of something else," Nate said, cutting over Andrew's imminent protest, "I have some interesting information. Fresh from the Dark Web."

Rachelle made a face. "The Dark Web?"

"Yeah, Robin suggested it."

"Oh..."

"After asking me how you were for the hundredth time."

"You know why I can't call him," Rachelle said quietly. Andrew would have felt sorrier for the destruction of her fledgling relationship with Robin if their current situation hadn't been so pressing. Especially because it had genuinely seemed like Rachelle and Robin cared for each other. Were right for each other.

Once we know Poppy is okay then Nate and I can help her fix things with Robin, Andrew decided, impatient that the topic of conversation had been waylaid in the first place. All he wanted to do was board a flight to Barcelona as soon as possible and work out what was going on with Poppy for himself. But Andrew equally knew he'd be lying if he said that he wasn't interested in whatever it was Nate had to tell them.

"What did you find?" Andrew pressed, when Rachelle continued to blush and say nothing at all.

Nate spun his laptop around to face them; both Andrew and Rachelle leaned forward to see what he was showing them. "Barcelona seems to be having a much higher concentration of strange disappearances off the street than the other places we've been looking at over the last couple of weeks," Nate said. He touched his laptop screen to play a video. "And there's this."

At first Andrew wasn't sure what he was seeing. The footage was dark and grainy – taken on a phone at night, to be sure – but even the poor quality of the video wasn't enough to explain away the odd visuals that Nate had presented to them. If Andrew didn't know any better, he would have sworn that the camera had caught the swishing of a large, reptilian tail, and claws larger than a human face shining bright in the darkness.

"The video is from two martial artists who were accosted on the way back from a competition," Nate explained. "It's been taken down across social media, of course. Folk on the Dark Web have been trying to find flaws in the footage to prove that it's fake. Fabricated. But they can't. The person who posted the video says it was a monster who attacked them."

"*Monster?*"

Nate smiled grimly. "A monster. Thing is, though, the martial artists got away. I mean, obviously they did – otherwise we wouldn't have this video."

"So why isn't this video *everywhere?*" Rachelle asked, on her behalf and Andrew both. "Why has it been taken off social media and stuff? It seems like the perfect content for people to dissect."

"Exactly."

"Explain things with your words, Nate," she chastised, sighing into her cushion. "We're not all as criminally online as you are."

"I'd take offence to that if it weren't true."

"Can you please get to the point?" Andrew pressed, too impatient to pretend to be interested in something he couldn't understand. He fell off the bed to kneel in front of Nate and his laptop, emphatically pointing at the video. "Why isn't this everywhere?"

"Well, usually people would dismiss it as a marketing ploy for a film or something," Nate said, "but since it keeps getting taken down that points to something quite sinister. Why can't you both see it yet? The monsters have their own in places of pretty fucking high responsibility."

Andrew digested this slowly. If monsters were in control of what was posted online, then...

"So they control the media, or at least stuff that would reveal what they are," Rachelle said, voicing Andrew's thoughts before he had formed them. She tucked an errant strand of hair behind her ear before saying, "Which implies they control a whole lot more."

Nate gave her a thumbs up. "Bingo."

"But what does this mean? If there have been more attacks in Barcelona, and the monsters responsible are doing their best to conceal it...*oh.*" Rachelle gasped. "You think the next auction is in Barcelona, don't you?"

"That's exactly what I'm thinking." A feral grin spread across Nate's face. "And I found something else on the Dark Web. Rumours of a secret, high-society event in Barcelona. Black tie thing. There was mention of an *auction.* One of the guys who was paid off to book the venue in secret blabbed about it; he's dead now, of course."

"Which means...?"

"Which means I think *we* should go to Barcelona."

At this Rachelle frowned. "Wait, I thought you said we shouldn't go there? To leave whatever's going on with Poppy to Dorian and Fred and—"

"I do think that," Nate said. He held up a hand to stop Andrew protesting again. "If we could do something about it then we all know Dorian would have contacted us. But this is *our* investigation. We're doing this for ourselves, and for our club, and for everyone who died." Nate gulped. "And if it so happens to bring us into the same city as Poppy, well..."

Andrew rushed forward and hugged him fiercely. He was barely aware he'd done it, but every fibre of his body was so deeply appreciative of this man that Andrew would have happily kissed him. "Then we go. Let's go *now.*"

Nate patted his back, let out a conspirational chuckle, then said, "I already booked the tickets. We leave in three hours."

A Hint at Things to Come

POPPY

"Won't you eat, Poppy? You're going to have to keep your strength up if you're—"

"There's no end to that sentence I want to hear."

Nick laughed heartily. "Oh, so you're speaking to me now? I'd say that's an improvement. Sit down."

Two days had passed since Nick drained Poppy of half the blood in her body. Fifty-one hours. She'd counted. If she'd lost this much blood at the same time last year then it would have taken Poppy at least a week to recover back to full health. Now, because of Dorian and, in a twisted way, Fred's vicious attack, Poppy was completely fine.

Poppy made no move to sit down at the table laden with every breakfast food imaginable that Nick had prepared for her. For her, since he of course had no need to eat anything presented before him. So far she'd ignored any and all food delivered to her room and had refused to emerge from the ridiculous four-poster bed except to use the bathroom. But Nick had left Poppy no leeway to refuse his summons this time – if the gun-clad, six-foot-four security guard who had come to fetch her was anything to go by.

She scanned the room she was in. It appeared to be a study, with a gigantic desk and a dozen bookcases lining three of the walls. The polished table covered in food was set into the alcove of an expansive, curved window, sunshine spilling through to limn every dish, glass and varnished surface in gold. Nick himself was reclining in an expensive leather chair at the head of the table, sipping an espresso and perusing a newspaper. Along with his immaculately styled raven hair, loose linen shirt and grey slacks, he looked for all the world like an old-time Mafia boss.

Given his status within his own people, Poppy wondered whether he *was* the monster equivalent of a Mafia boss.

Nick cast a critical glance at Poppy – not quite impatient, but close enough to a warning that she decided sitting down was a better option than testing the edges of his tolerance towards disobedience. For though the marks had now disappeared from her thigh, Poppy could still feel Nick's teeth sunk deep into her flesh. She had no desire whatsoever to repeat the experience.

The moment she sat down Nick asked, "What were you doing wandering the streets of Barcelona on your own, anyway? It truly was very stupid of you." When Poppy's only response was to glare at him and grip the table with shaking knuckles Nick merrily continued, "Do you know how long I waited for Dorian to leave your side? I imagine something terrible must have happened to split the two of you apart. Or something... inevitable."

Poppy hated the smug look on Nick's face. The easy way he reclined into his chair. As if he knew something Poppy *should* know but simply didn't. Going by the calculating look in his eyes Poppy having no answer to his question only served to confirm this. Nick was clearly filing away that information and was analysing it – working out how to use it to his advantage. Just how had Poppy missed the shrewd nature of the man masquerading as a monster before her? She had dismissed him, along with Aisling and Stephen, last summer. She had been so tied up in her position with Dorian, and her fear of him, and her fascination of him, that she had pushed the far more dangerous threat out of her mind.

Casey's words from Christmas echoed in her ears. Wasn't Poppy interested in learning about monster culture? What separated them, really, from men? She hadn't wanted to know – not then. She'd wanted to distance herself as much as possible. But now, faced with having to deal with a monster who wasn't Dorian, who clearly knew far more about what was going *on* with Dorian than she did...

Poppy regretted ever being so obstinate. Information was power, which only grew more evident as she watched Nick size her up even as she did the same to him. She'd *had* the opportunity to obtain the information she needed, every single day she spent with Dorian. But Poppy had never asked him about a single thing. She was going into this interaction with Nick blind and it was all her fault.

"Eat," Nick insisted again, pushing Poppy's empty plate towards her. And despite the casual, easygoing way he was sitting, and the charming smile on his face, and the wonderful sunshine warming his skin that made him look almost harmless, Poppy knew she was helpless to do anything but comply.

She had no doubt Nick had zero qualms about forcing her to eat if she didn't. He'd likely enjoy it.

"Let me tell you a few things I think will interest you while you eat," Nick said, when Poppy finally selected a couple of pastries, a roll and sausage, and a small bowl of sliced mangoes. "We were hardly in a position to have a civil discussion the other day, after all. The fault for that of course lies with me; I apologise for getting so excited."

Poppy could do nothing but stare at him. Nick sounded, for all the world, sincere. *Clearly he's an excellent liar,* she thought, sullenly biting into a mango that tasted even brighter than the sunshine streaming through the window. *He can't possibly be 'sorry' for what he did to me.* But when it became clear that Nick was waiting for a verbal response from her, Poppy swallowed down the mango and muttered, "Would could you possibly say that would be of interest to me?"

"God, you're an awful liar, Poppy King. You were that morning back at the facility before you burned it to the ground, and you are now. Why not admit the truth for once?"

A rebuttal was on the tip of her tongue; Poppy was desperate to let it loose. Instead she took a bite of a Danish pastry and minutely nodded her head for Nick to continue. Getting into a petty fight was not the kind of thing she currently had the energy for...especially not with a monster whose intentions were to keep her locked up as his own personal slave.

A slow, satisfied smile crept up Nick's face. In that moment Poppy realised their entire interaction was playing out exactly as he wanted it to, and she hadn't been smart enough to see it. "That's what I thought," Nick said, primly folding his newspaper and lowering his coffee to grant her his full attention. He interlaced his fingers upon the table. "So this is how I see things, Poppy." Poppy wished he'd stop saying her name, as if he knew her. "Since you and I and Dorian will be living for a very, very, *very* long time, I feel it would be prudent to let you in on a few things. It wouldn't serve to have the mother of my children remain so ignorant of the world she's being brought into, after all."

"I'm not going to be the mother of your damn children," Poppy spat, wiping her mouth with the back of her hand as if even saying the words disgusted her.

Nick's smile only grew wider. "We'll see. But onto the crux of the matter at hand: your species doesn't know it, but your position at the top of the food chain is over. I know, I know, we already eat you, so in truth you were never at the top at all. But your time pulling the strings on everything that happens on this planet is figuratively on its knees. Monsters across the world are growing impatient with having to live in the shadows, relying on auctions and stalking the streets at night in order to avoid becoming known. There's only so much people like myself and, yes, Dorian, can do to stop the inevitable. A nightmare will descend upon this planet soon, Poppy King. I wonder if you would be interested in being on the side of those who wish to stop it?"

Poppy had been so genuinely engrossed in what Nick was saying without interruption that it took her a few seconds to realise he was asking her a question, never mind what the content of the question actually was. "Of course I'd want to stop it," she bit out testily, swallowing down a mouthful of pastry with a glass of orange juice. "Why would you even have to ask?"

"Even if it means working and living by *my* side?"

"Like hell are you on the same side as me."

"And if I said I was?"

"I'd say you're a filthy liar."

"Not something I've ever been accused of." Nick shrugged. "Ask Dorian about it. I've always been honest about my goals and intentions. Haven't I always been honest with *you* every time we speak?"

Poppy could hardly believe what she was hearing. "You call masquerading as a harmless human whilst knowing me and my entire club was doomed to die *honest?*" Her grip tightened on the silver knife in her hand, though what a butter knife could do against Nick was piteously little. "You laughed along with my friends – made them think you were *their* friend – when all that time you were—"

"This sounds like ground you've trod with Dorian already. I can tell even by the way you're saying it that you're tired of it." With a huff Nick stood up, walked around the table and leant against it when he reached Poppy's side. Her body reacted on instinct, jerking back so violently Poppy almost toppled out of her chair. But Nick didn't laugh at her; rather, all his previous easy-going humour left his face. "So I hid what I was, because I had to. That doesn't change that I was still being *me*, Poppy."

Poppy hated that Nick actually sounded honest. So even though she was still shaking, and her brain was yelling at her to run, run, run away, she forced herself to return to where she'd originally been sitting to face him properly. "Even if that's true, why the hell should I accept you?"

"Because it's clear all the satyr has done is tiptoe around you in order to keep you *safe* and *happy*."

"Oh, and that's so wrong?"

"Are you either of those things?" Nick asked. Poppy flinched at how easily he'd hit the proverbial nail on the head. "Has he not been lying to you?"

"...I'm sure he has his reasons."

"I don't doubt it. But here's the thing, Poppy: you need someone who will challenge you. Who won't soften the truth or take any of your crap. Who'll give as good as they get."

"And you think that's you?"

"I'm arrogant enough to think so, yes."

"Have you ever thought that maybe, just maybe, you aren't my type?" A moment of silence passed between them, then Nick reached out a slow hand to touch Poppy's face. This time Poppy *did* fall out of her chair, banging her knees on the floor before she skittered out of reach. "Don't - don't touch me," she cried, hating how scared she was.

To her surprise Nick lowered his hand and stayed exactly where he was. His gaze softened. "I don't want to scare you."

It terrified Poppy to know that he meant it. But still, she said: "I find that hard to believe, given everything that's happened so far."

"You didn't let me finish. I don't want to scare you, but I have no desire to cut my claws, so to speak. I am what I am.

Dorian hasn't been doing you any favours by trying to appease to your human nature; I'm sure you're beginning to work that out for yourself. It's only going to end in tears between the two of you."

"Don't talk about him as if you know him!"

"Know him?" Nick barked out an incredulous laugh, a vicious sound that propelled Poppy to stand back up in a vain attempt to hold her ground, even though she knew, in her heart, that she was going to lose this argument. "Poppy, do you honestly think you know Dorian better than I do? My family has worked with his family since long before he was born. You've spent – what – a year with him? During which time you've actively rejected what he is, where he's from and what he does. To me that sounds like you've been living with a stranger."

"That's not true," Poppy said, even though it sounded like it was. "I know him. I know what I'm doing with him."

"Do you really? Tell me then, Poppy, why things are different with him than they could be with me? Dorian kidnapped and murdered half your club. He intended to kill you, too, but instead kept you prisoner and forced you into a twisted game to choose who out of your friends would live. Even to *me* that's another level of dark. And yet *I'm* the monster to you?"

"Because it's – it *is* different," Poppy insisted. She hated how stupid her answer was. She wanted to say it was because Dorian regretted what he'd done to Poppy. That it wasn't the sum of who he really was. That he truly loved her. But admitting to that out loud – to Nick, no less – was more than Poppy could bear. Yet it was in her own head, at that moment, that the reality of her situation with the satyr truly hit home. *Dorian's in love with me,* Poppy thought. *He's in love with me, and I can't love him back. For all the reasons Nick said and more. I can't be by his side the way he wants me to be, or even pretend to be. To do so would be cruel.*

She thought of Andrew, and his confession, and Poppy grew

afraid. To be by anyone's side when she didn't know if she wholeheartedly loved them the way they *wanted* her to love them wasn't something Poppy could do. Did that really mean leaving *Andrew* behind, forever?

A knock on the door interrupted whatever Nick had been about to say to break the long, tense silence Poppy had let stretch out between them. She had a suspicion he had been about to gloat over his obvious win against her. "What is it?" he called out, running both his hands through his hair in obvious irritation.

A pause. "Sir, you have a guest."

"Tell them to leave. I'm busy."

"I think...I think you'll want to see him."

A frown shadowed Nick's brow. In that moment Poppy knew who was at the door. Part of her rejoiced; another part of her despaired. She wished for him to leave before she could ruin him more than she already had.

"Who is it?"

"It's Mr Kapros."

Poppy had expected Nick to grow angry at hearing Dorian's name. Instead his entire demeanour brightened. "I guess we better get you back to your room then, Poppy," Nick said, striding past her to open the door. "I'm sure we can continue this interesting discussion over dinner. Or tomorrow, or the next day, or the next. We only have forever, after all."

If Dorian – and everyone else likely helping him – had anything to do with it, Poppy knew that Nick's words would imminently be proven false.

The Villain Becomes the Hero

FRED

They didn't have much time. Fred knew Dorian could only stall Nick for so long, then eventually he'd simply have him kicked out...or killed. Fred had to break Poppy out as quickly as he could.

"For how long can you hold your breath, Fred?" Patrick asked, as they waded into the sea at the closest accessible shoreline to the Richardson mansion. Even with a particularly fast speedboat it was at least five minutes away – and they didn't have a boat. No, they had nothing at all.

In any case Frederick Sampson could only hold his breath for three minutes.

Patrick stretched his burly arms over his head until his spine cracked. He sighed in satisfaction. He, alone, seemed calm and focused. Fred was busy thinking of every part of the plan that could go wrong. Casey, who was responsible for driving Dorian to and from the mansion, was naturally beside herself with worry.

And Dorian was so furious – with himself, with Nick, with Fred, with Poppy – that when Fred and Patrick bid him good luck he looked ready to snap them both into two.

But now it was just the two of them, staring out at the sea with nothing but the clothes on their back.

"Erm..." Fred murmured, peering over at the Richardson mansion, in the distance, then back at Patrick. The man's dark hair whipped over his eyes as he returned the look.

"What?"

"What happens now?"

At this Patrick grinned. "What happens now is that I dive into the sea, and you dive in after me, and then you try not to die of fright. Got it?"

"I—wait!" But Patrick didn't wait; with all the grace of an Olympic swimmer he cut beneath the waves, leaving Fred all of two seconds to take a breath, collect his thoughts and crash out after him.

At first Fred had no idea what was going on. Salt stung his eyes as he pushed himself through the water. The current was strong, forcing him back to shore. But then the strong and supple glide of something entirely inhuman across Fred's stomach caught his attention, and before he knew it an impossibly large, black, iridescent tentacle had him in its thrall.

Then the tentacle hurtled itself and Fred through the sea.

Fred clung on for dear life, unable to tell what was up or down, left or right. But he was aware of more tentacles around him propelling them forwards, regardless of the fact he'd screamed out all his air and was sure to die.

Just as thought the blood vessels in his eyes were about to pop, Fred broke through the surface and heaved in a breath of air. Daggers in his lungs had never felt so good. It took him a few moments to realise Patrick was laughing at him.

"F-fuck you," Fred cursed, his entire body shaking as the sea monstrosity brought them both to the base of the cliffside that would be his next challenge. Taking a proper look at him Fred saw that some semblance of Patrick's human body remained until his torso – where it blended seamlessly into the tentacles Fred would no doubt have nightmares about for the rest of his life – though his skin was glistening with slime and his hair was long and ropey, like seaweed.

Patrick's eyes gleamed red.

"You okay to climb?" Patrick asked, still laughing as he loosened his grip on Fred to allow him to slide onto a rock to steady his shaking limbs. "You don't look too good."

"Who's fault do you think *that* is?"

"I had orders from Dorian to make the journey as unpleasant as possible."

"That – that – screw this," Fred spat, pure spite forcing him up the cliff despite the way his muscles protested. For now was not the time to glower over the way Fred was being treated; now was the time to save Poppy.

If the goat wanted to put him through the wringer even now, in the middle of a rescue mission, then Fred would make him pay for it later.

"Do you remember where Cass is parked, if Poppy's in no state to climb down here?" Patrick yelled up at Fred, his voice almost lost to the waves despite the fact Fred was barely ten feet above him. He spared a hand for a moment to give the tentacled monster a thumbs up.

And then it was nothing but the cliff and Fred. A scant three days ago he'd been wishing for a more adventurous climb to test his new blood. A challenging climb. An impossible one.

He couldn't get much more impossible than this.

DORIAN

"I never expected you would literally waltz in here, Kapros," Nick said as he led Dorian down an airy corridor towards his office. Dorian was gratified to see that his memory of the Richardson mansion was so far proving correct. "You've got guts, I'll grant you that."

"You said you wanted to talk to me."

"Six months ago."

Dorian raised an eyebrow. "Does that mean you don't want to?"

"That means I should punch you in the face for waiting so long," Nick joked easily, before leading Dorian into his office. A table by the window was laden with food – human food – leaving Dorian with no doubt that Nick had only just been with Poppy. But she was nowhere to be seen now; Dorian couldn't even smell her. That was a good sign his hunch that Poppy would be on the other side of the mansion from Nick's office was correct.

He could only hope Fred made it inside with enough time to help break Poppy free...if he survived the climb to reach the estate in the first place. The cliff-facing wall was the only side of the building where the windows were left open to air the mansion out, because it was deemed unimpeachable. *Granted, I doubt they ever imagined someone might break in by scaling a cliff,* Dorian mused, sitting down when Nick proffered him a seat. *If all goes well today they'll have no choice but to address the glaring flaw in their security.*

"So I'm here," Dorian said, when Nick made no move to begin their conversation. "Let's talk."

"No begging me to release Poppy King?" Nick asked incredulously. He picked up a small cup of still-steaming espresso from the table, sipping from it surprisingly delicately for someone of his size.

"Will you release Poppy King?"

"No."

"But you *do* have her."

"You knew that already."

Dorian stopped himself from gulping down a breath just in time. In truth he couldn't have been sure until now; it could have been Aisling. That Nick himself didn't seem to think it reasonable that anyone else could have kidnapped Poppy was, in this one and only instance, reassuring. "Why did you say you wanted to work with me, six months ago?" Dorian asked.

When Nick caught his eye Dorian knew he had to be very, very careful. Though he had on the air of a casual, easy-going man, Dorian was only too well aware that Nick was anything but. "Either you have something up your sleeve, Kapros," Nick began, "or you're finally coming to your senses. Given the fact that you and I will be living for a long, long time, you'll forgive me for hoping that it's the latter."

There was nothing he could to stop his skin growing pale. Dorian could barely contain the jitters that ran through his hands. *He's drank from Poppy already. He's drank from her. Has he done anything else? Has he—*

Nick's throaty chuckle rumbled in the air. "No need to be so horrified, Dorian. I haven't done what you're thinking...yet. I'm nothing if not a gentleman, and the lady in question was hardly in a state to consent after I took her blood. You knew this was inevitable. Just take it on the chin and move on."

"Move on." Dorian could hardly speak. All that was keeping him level and speaking was the acute knowledge that, in this space, in this room, with Poppy's blood flowing in both of their veins, Nichola Richardson could rip Dorian to shreds in a matter of seconds if he desired it. "Just like that, I move on?"

"If you want to leave this room alive, that is."

"...fine." Dorian was anything *but* fine. He wanted to slice

Nick's throat open – right across the dull scar that was the only proof the fire last year had ever hurt him. "So I move on. What's next?"

If Nick knew what was going through Dorian's head, he didn't let it bother him. He downed his coffee before saying, "I'm holding an auction tomorrow; doubtless you know about it now."

"What of it?"

"It's been hell to organise. I've hated every minute of it. Join me in organising all future events."

It was flattering, all things considered, but Dorian didn't want to hear it. "I'm out of business, sorry. You and Aisling made sure of it."

"And I can just as easily get you back *into* business. I need your expertise."

"My face is known all over Europe. How could I be of any use to you?"

Nick laughed, easy and arrogant. "The police are easily bribed. It would be worth it to have you on my team. You must have known how difficult it would be to fill the gap you left in the market. For all my talk disparaging your career – your place in the food chain – before all this mess, I can admit when I'm wrong. You've thoroughly humbled all of us who rely upon your services. And we *do* rely on them, if we're to maintain the balance you know fine well we need to protect."

Dorian knew it. His father had known it, after all, and instilled that knowledge in Dorian himself. His mother had deemed a shift in the balance of things inevitable, which had been why she didn't want her husband and then her son work in the field of the dead. Better to live away from it all, picking lost humans off the faces of mountains like sheep, than live right in the centre of the drama when everything came crumbling down around them.

With every passing day Dorian believed his mother had been

right all along.

"...I've lost my stomach for it," Dorian finally said, which was true. But he knew it was easy to say that now that he was full of human flesh and bone. He was more himself now than he had been in the last half a year, and he hated himself for it. Hated what it would mean for Poppy when she found out what he'd done.

She could never find out what he'd done.

Nick watched him with an inscrutable expression. "Tell me what's going on with you, Dorian. Has she really affected you this completely?"

"If you'd spent all the time I have with *her* then you'd be changed, too," Dorian muttered.

"Oh, I plan to." Nick's mouth slid into a self-satisfied smirk. "You know fine well my interest in Poppy was genuine *before* I knew about her blood. She's interesting. Fierce. Impulsive. I can see why you love her so much."

Dorian wanted to shake the mere notion of Poppy King from Nick's head. But he couldn't – not if he wished to live. And he knew, now, because of Nick and because of Aisling and because of what he himself had done, that trying to keep Poppy hidden and safe had been a mistake. For running wasn't winning. Running was simply putting off the inevitable.

He could see that now.

"Perhaps you need more time to think about things," Nick said slowly, glancing down at his watch before returning his attention to Dorian. "There's plenty yet to organise for the auction, since I can't seem to rely on anyone to do as good a job as you. You're welcome to attend, of course. So give what I've said a think. You should be on my side, Dorian. You know you should."

Dorian couldn't trust himself to speak, so he said nothing.

As Nick led Dorian out of his office, right up to the grand

front doors, then even further down the driveway to the front gates, Dorian kept breathing through his nose and begged himself not to give the game away. Had enough time passed? Had Fred found Poppy? Were they free? Nick didn't seem aware of a disturbance. Was that a good thing or a bad thing?

"I'll see you tomorrow, Dorian," Nick said, closing the gate between them with an air of finality. He sounded so sure of himself that Dorian didn't know whether it was inevitable that he *would* do exactly as Nick expected him to.

Dorian settled on nodding. "We'll see. "

"I'm sure we will."

As Dorian made his way back to Casey and the waiting car it was all he could do not to vomit. *Get her out, Sampson,* he begged, close to tears. *Get her out before Nick truly does get everything he wants.*

FRED

Fred shuddered when he dropped down through the open window, his limbs dead and aching and crying out for help. But he had no time to be in pain or to recover; he had a job to do.

Rolling to his feet Fred began stalking down the hallway, desperately trying to remember everything that Dorian had told him. *West wing, west wing, he said it was the west wing.* Orienting himself Fred bolted to the left as soon as he was able to.

"*Fuck...*" he breathed, when he ducked through an open door simply to have a moment's respite. He wasn't cut out for such sneaky heroism. It was then he noticed the room he had brazenly rushed into was some kind of weapons store or armoury; directly in front of him was a wall cabinet full of semi-automatic pistols. *Okay, maybe I'm not terrible at this after all,* Fred thought, walking straight up to the cabinet and stealing one of the guns with the confidence of a man who had worked with guns all his life. In truth Fred had next to no experience with firearms. But his dad, at least, had taken him hunting once or twice, so Fred knew enough to check if the gun was loaded and riffle through a drawer beneath the cabinet to find an appropriate box of ammo before jumping out of the room.

West wing, west wing, Fred repeated once more, a shiver running down his spine at the feel of cool metal in his hands. It felt absurdly *right* for him to be holding a loaded weapon, though Fred couldn't work out why. He pressed on down the corridor, then took another left and then a right, growing ever more frantic as the seconds passed by.

Then, when he reached a crossroads – the mansion truly was gargantuan – Fred had to make a choice. Left, right, or straight ahead. He had no idea which was right.

He went left.

When he came across a tall door some instinct in Fred told him it was the right one. But when he ran over to it and tried the handle the door was locked.

"*Damn it,*" Fred cursed, before placing the side of his head against the door. "Poppy? Poppy, are you in there?"

"...hello?" came Poppy's muffled voice a moment later. "...Fred, is that you?"

Fred minutely punched a fist into the air. "It is! The door's locked. Is there any other way out on your side?"

"A window, but it doesn't have a latch. I could climb to the little one above it but I'll break my legs falling out the other side."

"Heaven forbid I carry you," Fred joked before he could stop himself. He looked to his left; a window overlooked the estate, in the direction of Casey and the waiting car. If Fred exited through that window, and helped Poppy out of hers...

"Get to your little window," Fred urged Poppy. Then, before he could think better of it, he shot the window twice. The first bullet cracked the glass; the second bullet shattered it to pieces.

"*The hell was that?!*" a voice roared, echoing down the corridor from somewhere far away. Not Nick's voice, but Fred imagined he wasn't the only monster likely lurking within the house.

Or they could be a man with a gun, Fred reasoned, which was equally as unappealing to him right now. Not wishing to waste another second he bounded over the broken glass, over the window frame, and followed the smooth stone edge of the mansion until he spied Poppy struggling her way out of perhaps the smallest window space she could possibly have squeezed through.

Her eyes went wide when they saw Fred. "Catch!" she yelled, crashing through the air and barely landing in Fred's arms when he rushed to meet her. He fell to his knees, air thoroughly knocked out of him. "You need to work out," Poppy said, rubbing a stitch out of her side as they both got to their feet. Her gaze found the sliver of metal Fred had hastily tucked into the waistband of his shorts. "Is that a *gun?*"

"Later," he promised, bounding in the direction of freedom without another word. Behind them Fred could hear shouting but it only served to urge him on faster. A second later Poppy overtook him; she'd always been quicker than him.

"Which way?!" she cried, when they broke into a small grove of trees. Dorian had told Fred about the trees. What had he said about the trees? "*Fred!*"

"Straight on!" he said, remembering. "There's an oak that almost overhangs the fence on this side. Dorian checked it out yesterday."

The two of them were running too quickly for words after that, and when they reached the tree in question they wasted no time in scrabbling up the rough bark of its branches and vaulting over the tall stone wall.

With no regard for the fall on the other side.

It was perhaps lucky that Fred fell on top of Poppy, lending credence to how he remained unhurt from a fall that otherwise should have broken his arm or his ankle at the very least. Poppy cursed, pushing him off but then taking his hand to help her hobble back onto her feet, but a second later she was sprinting faster than Fred was.

"Th-there," he panted, pointing towards a gleaming white car, its engine ready and revving. Even as he pointed two of the doors were flung open. Poppy threw herself in the back, Fred in the front; they barely had the doors closed before Casey yanked up the handbrake and hurtled them down the road. Behind them Fred vaguely heard gunshots, but he didn't care.

He'd done it. He'd actually done it.

"You scaled the cliff," Dorian said from the back, staring at Fred in blatant disbelief through the rear-view mirror as his arms crushed Poppy to his chest. Her shoulders were shaking, wracked with unspoken sobs of relief. In the driver's seat Casey was doing her level-best not to cry, glaring with determination down the road towards freedom.

Fred cracked a smile. "I scaled the damn cliff."

BREATHING SPACE

DORIAN

He couldn't believe they'd all managed it. He, Patrick, Casey and Fred – of all people – had managed to free Poppy.

He didn't remember the journey to the car park, where they swapped the getaway car for another, nor the second time they did so, nor the third. All Dorian was aware of was Poppy curled up against his cheat, her breathing slowly returning to normal with every passing minute.

Eventually they reached the hotel room Patrick had booked earlier that day, and it was time to say good-bye.

"Thanks for all your help," Dorian said, letting go of Poppy in order to crush his best friend in a hug. Patrick eagerly returned the gesture in kind.

"I'm always your guy if you need another covert, underwater rescue mission. Right, Fred?"

Fred grimaced. "Right."

Poppy blinked slowly at Patrick, then Casey, somewhat unsteady on her feet. Dorian couldn't blame her for being exhausted; both she and Fred were drenched in sweat from their breakneck escape. "You aren't...staying?" she asked Casey, confusion plain as day on her face.

Casey squeezed her hands. "We promised Dorian we'd leave the moment you were safe. We're putting ourselves in danger if we stay here, and I know...well, I know you don't want that. I know you'd hate that." When Poppy gulped down a sob Casey responded by kissing her head and rubbing their noses together. "I better see you soon, you hear me?"

Miserably Poppy nodded. "Fine. Fuck off, then. Take care of her, Patrick. And thanks again."

"Wouldn't dream of doing anything less," he said, beaming as he swung a holdall over his shoulder, took Casey's hand and exited the room together.

"Are you not going, too?" Poppy asked Fred, when he made no motion to move.

"I have business to attend to, remember," Fred told her, minutely shaking his head in a way that suggested Dorian very much wished to knows what this 'business' was. But interrogating Fred could wait; all Dorian needed right now was Poppy. When Fred caught the look on his face he rolled his eyes. "I'm gonna shower then go to bed early. I'm fucking shattered. See you in the morning, King."

She gave him the finger. "Worse words have never been spoken."

A brief silence passed between Poppy and Dorian after Fred vacated for his own room in the hotel apartment. Two. Three. Then Dorian interlaced his hand with Poppy's and led her towards the master bedroom.

He very gently undressed her. Poppy let him do so.

"Where did he..." Dorian bit out, before he could stop himself. But when Poppy flinched he immediately regretted his perverse curiosity. "Don't answer that. I'm sorry."

"It's okay. I can – I can show you." With trembling fingers

Poppy guided Dorian's hand down towards her thigh. When his fingers brushed over the now-unmarred skin he gripped into Poppy's flesh so hard she yelped.

But Dorian wasn't sorry for that. He let go of her thigh to skim both his hands over her hipbones, her waist, her breasts, her neck, then held Poppy's face tightly between them.

She wasn't the only one trembling.

"He really only took my blood," Poppy whispered, voice hoarse, giving Dorian the answer to his unspoken question. Since when had she become so good at reading him? All at once the tension Dorian had been holding left his body. "But he was..." Poppy added, "it was his real form when he – when Nick drank my blood. I've never been so scared."

"That's saying something," Dorian quipped before he could stop himself. It was a risk, going for humour considering everything that had transpired, but to his relief Poppy choked on a laugh.

"It wasn't funny, Dorian," she said, even as she continued giggling. "I was really scared."

"And so was I. If I lost you – if you were gone and it was all my fault, I–"

"It wasn't your fault."

"It was. I was gone."

"I can't expect you to be with me every second of the day, Dorian."

Dorian said nothing. What Poppy said was true but that wasn't the point. It was because of him and him alone that Poppy had been taken. Because he'd left her unguarded to do the unspeakable. Yet Dorian nonetheless took the silent – if unearned – victory of never having to explain to Poppy what he'd been doing.

He bent down to kiss her, and his phone rang. And rang. And rang. Knowing who it probably was, Dorian planned to ignore it. But still it rang.

Poppy nodded from between Dorian's hands. "I'll be in the shower. You answer that."

And so Dorian did as he was told, ensuring he was well out of earshot before accepting the call and bringing the phone to his ear.

"Good move, Kapros," Nick said before Dorian could get a word in. Doran frowned.

"What else did you expect me to do? Leave her with you?"

"Of course I expected you to try some stupid shit like this," Nick laughed. He sounded, for all the world, genuinely impressed. Like he was enjoying himself. "What, you didn't think I'd let you take her from me so easily, did you? I was testing your resolve. Good to know you have a fucking backbone."

"I–"

"See you at the auction."

Nick hung up, leaving Dorian with a dead phone line and the creeping weight of inevitability filling his stomach.

The auction. He had to go to the auction.

Dorian glanced in the direction of the bathroom. He couldn't tell Poppy; she'd want to go. But given that Fred had known about it already, and he and Poppy had discussed things as yet unexplained to Dorian, he had a sneaking suspicion Poppy already knew about it.

Even so, Dorian couldn't let her near the damn event. Not with Aisling's threat hanging over his head, and everything that could go wrong ringing in his ears. Dorian had to hide Poppy as far away from society as he possibly could. Away from harm. Away from everyone she held dear.

That was the last thing he wanted for Poppy King, but Dorian would do it.

When Poppy emerged from the shower Dorian silently took her place to wash off the guilt and shameful resolve that had seeped into his skin now he'd made his decision. It was only after he scalded himself burning red that he felt ready to face her once more.

It was Poppy who took Dorian into her arms when he joined her in bed, cradling his head against her chest as she nuzzled her face into his wet hair. "Can you..."

Dorian stilled. "No. You can't possibly want that." But Poppy tilted his chin up to meet his gaze, and he realised she did.

"I can't have him be the last one who drank from me," she whispered, wide-eyed and trembling. "So please, Dorian, please..."

And he wanted to. Even though it was shameful, and Poppy was vulnerable, and he'd betrayed her in so many terrible ways, Dorian wanted to. So he craned his neck back, shifted his hand to curl through Poppy's hair, and pulled her lips towards his. He bit them, just barely, revelling in the way Poppy's breath hitched at the sensation. He kissed along her jaw, the edge of her ear.

Then he pierced her heck, quick and clean.

Poppy sighed in relief when he did so, perhaps just as perverted as Dorian was in her need for such a release. It didn't make sense that she needed this just as much as he did, but in that moment Dorian believed it to be true. Down to his very soul – if he still possessed one – Poppy King *needed* him, *wanted* him, more than anyone else.

"Let's not talk," she murmured in the dark, when Dorian pulled away from her neck and licked her blood off his teeth. Poppy's legs wound their way around Dorian's hips, rocking against his need for her so painfully he groaned. "Just for tonight. Just for tonight, I want—"

"You," Dorian finished for her, breathless. "I want you."

And so he said nothing, and Poppy said nothing, and they

lost themselves in that nothing.

Even though it terrified Dorian how final that nothing felt.

QUINTESSENTIALLY POPPY KING

POPPY

Poppy wanted to sleep for three days but knew she couldn't. The auction Nick was holding was today. Tonight.

Poppy knew she had to be there. Even though Dorian hadn't told her about it she had a feeling he already knew *she* knew, which meant he must have realised there was no way he could stop her from going.

But when she woke up that morning – it was closer to noon – Dorian wasn't beside her. They'd fallen asleep cradling each other the night before, neither of them wishing to ruin things between the two of them by talking. Even though there was so much to be said. So much Poppy had allowed Dorian to get away with *not* saying, simply because she was sickeningly relieved to be back in his arms and safely away from Nick. Yet Poppy wasn't so dense as to believe it was only relief that had stayed her tongue.

No, Poppy didn't want to have a conversation for which she

was so afraid of its conclusion. Dorian had been hiding something from her, that much was obvious. Even Nick seemed to be in on it.

But more than that, Poppy needed to talk to Dorian about what their future together looked like when he was in love with her and she was not in love with him. She couldn't string him along the way she'd done thus far.

Again and again Poppy's thoughts circled back to what Nick had told her. She hadn't had time to figure out what exactly he'd meant about the balance between men and monsters coming to an end. Now she was done feigning disinterest; she wanted to know. Truly, badly, deep in her bones, Poppy King wanted to know what was going on – and what that meant for the rest of her long life.

She never wanted to see Nick again, but she knew he held the answers she needed. *The auction,* Poppy though grimly, staring at her pale reflection in dissatisfaction. Her hair was a tangled mess from sleeping on it wet all night; Poppy would need to wash it again to make it behave. *I'll ask him at the auction, where there are enough distractions for m to sneak away. I have to.*

And so Poppy showered, washing her hair and shaving her legs to make herself feel more like a functional, not-on-the-verge-of-a-breakdown woman. After drying her hair she found a floaty blue mini-dress in Dorian's bag that he must have packed for her to wear post-rescue, for which Poppy was supremely grateful. By the time she left the bedroom Poppy was starving, and wondered what to do about food. She froze at the sight of Fred sitting out on the balcony of the hotel room, eating a croissant whilst staring at a gun on the table in front of him.

"I thought you'd be gone by now," Poppy admitted, cautiously making her way towards him.

Fred offered her the other half of his croissant but Poppy refused; she never planned to be close enough to the man to share his food for as long as she damn well lived. "I had to reassess my plan to face Aisling in the wake of everything that's happened."

Poppy supposed that made sense. She sat down beside him. "Truthfully I thought I wouldn't see you again after...well. You made it clear you didn't want to see me again."

"I made it clear I wanted you to be as far away from trouble as possible so you wouldn't die, you mean. That's different."

Poppy sucked on her lower lip, an insult moments away from being formed. But there was a more important matter at hand, and it was gun-shaped. Poppy waved towards the offending item. "Where'd you get this?"

Fred shrugged. "Nicked it from Nick." Poppy glared at him. "I figured it would be useful."

"Useful how? I—"

With a gentle *shush* from Fred Poppy stopped talking, and he slid the gun out of sight. "That'll be Dorian with breakfast for you," he said, when the door into the hotel room clicked open. "I mean, we *did* order room service earlier but you were still out of it, so he went out to get you those custard pastries he knows you love."

Poppy quirked an eyebrow. "Seems you know I love them, too."

"I was the one who always bought them for me and Rachelle. *You* were the one who stole them."

"Touché."

A tired smile crossed Dorian's face when he joined them on the balcony, though in truth he didn't look tired at all. No, now that Poppy was looking at Dorian in broad daylight, the trauma of the previous day behind her, she saw that he looked great. Better than he'd done months.

Had saving her really changed Dorian that much?

"Breakfast," Dorian said, putting a bag down on the table for Poppy to peruse. "Custard pastries plus all your favourites from the shop. Chocolate cereal, about forty bags of paprika crisps—"

"Healthy," Fred surmised. Poppy gave him the finger.

"Thanks, Dorian," she said, before digging into a pastry with ravenous fingers. She glanced at the suit bag draped over his other arm. "Is that for the auction?"

Not even a single flash of surprise lit up Dorian's face. He sighed good-naturedly. "I suppose it was inevitable that you already knew."

"It doesn't look like you got much else whilst you were out," she said. "What am *I* supposed to wear for it?" When Dorian didn't answer Poppy understood that he never had any intention of letting her go. She rushed to her feet to stand toe-to-toe with him. "Don't you dare say I'm not going, Dorian. Don't you dare —"

"What do you expect me to do? You can't go there. Nick will—"

"If you're putting your neck out for information then you can't stop me from doing the same. You can't make these decisions for me, Dorian. You can't keep me safe forever."

"At the rate you're going it'll be impossible to save you at all!" Dorian bit out, firing a warning glare at Fred when he got up to stand by Poppy's side. In her defence. She'd never get used to it. Dorian pinched the bridge of his nose, and his shoulders sagged. "Can you listen to me, just this once? If you had only *listened* to me last summer then—"

"Oh, what was I supposed to do, then, let half my friends die? Just so you could run off with me the day before Nick showed up to *claim* me?" She shoved Dorian's chest, then again when he didn't react. "He would have still been hunting you – hunting me! We were always going to be in this situation. So why are you stopping me from going to the auction with you?"

Dorian said nothing. Even though it was clear he wanted to, he backed away towards the door, opened it, and rushed out before Poppy could say anything.

"You're a coward!" she spat after him, though she didn't follow down the hallway. She had too much pride.

"King, listen—" Fred murmured, making to touch her elbow, but she waved him off.

"Don't tell me to listen to him, Fred. I know Nick will be there. I *know* it's dangerous. But I need to be there. It might be my only opportunity to learn more about what Nick was telling me when I was captive." It was only then she realised she hadn't even told Fred anything about what Nick had told her.

But Fred didn't seem confused, only amused, as he shook his head. "All I was gonna say was that you can't go dressed like that. So how about we use this credit card of Dorian's that I stole from his wallet last night" - Fred brought said credit card out of his pocket with a flourish - "and splash the fuck out on some fancy clothes?"

"*We?*"

"Naturally. You're not going alone. And I have a harpy to intercept."

"...and if you show up with me then Aisling will think you convinced me to come along, like she wanted you to," Poppy said, understanding finally dawning on her. It was a good move.

"Exactly. Then just maybe she won't kill me. Maybe." Fred brought out the gun he'd stolen from Nick. "I have protection now, anyway."

Poppy was silent for a moment. If Fred had a gun, and she was there to help him out...

She pulled a deep breath into her lungs. "We could kill her first. We could, Fred."

"That would be incredibly difficult," he said, though a slow, manic smile was creeping up his face that implied *difficult* wasn't a bad thing. "Stupid. Reckless. A classic Poppy King move."

"Is that a no?"

"King, I've never agreed with you more."

A DIFFERENT PERSPECTIVE

DORIAN

Though the auction was being held in a massive hall Dorian felt uncomfortably claustrophobic.

In true Richardson family style, the building was as ostentatious as the mansion from which Poppy had been rescued. Tall stone columns held up the ornately painted ceiling high above their heads, which was just as well – for every two monsters choosing to retain their human guise there was a monster who dropped its second skin entirely to reveal its true self.

There were gigantic lizards and spindly, razor-legged insects. Cats the size of horses with human faces and claws that were longer than Dorian's horns. To his left was a stag with the jaws of a wolf, snapping attentively when a multicoloured harpy swanned past it.

Despite the fact most of the guests maintained their human forms it was easy to tell who the *real* humans were. Some of them were naked in cages to allow interested buyers to investigate them. Others were being made to fight each other for their freedom, surrounded by a ring of bloodthirsty onlookers.

Dorian knew fine well the victor would not escape alive, but the *promise* of freedom was what kept them fighting.

The worst fights were those held between humans and monsters. The looks on their faces when their opponent shed their human guise was something Dorian was innately familiar with, given his line of work. The pale gray skin. The unbridled terror. The tears. The hyperventilation. They couldn't hope to win against a scaled and slimy creature twice their size.

When a fight between two humans and an elephant-tusked creature almost as large as Nick ended with one of the unfortunate men being summarily torn to shreds, the other man lost complete control of his bowels. The stench filled Dorian's nose, but then this man, too, was torn apart, and the tang of blood was all that was left.

The spectators laughed. Cheered. The tusked monster carelessly tossed the entrails of its doomed opponents over the crowd for guests to catch and feast upon. Dorian was struck, then, by the reality of the event he'd walked in on. It was horrific. It was cruel. It was terrifying.

It was no different than any of the other fancy events organised by his kind for their own enjoyment. Dorian had been to them before; the difference this time was that, alongside the spectacle of the party, an actual auction for high-quality specimens was running in the back for those who could afford it.

It wasn't a style Dorian enjoyed. He had always been low-key and understated with his events. There wasn't a frivolous bone in his body, and neither had there been in his father. It was why the Kapros name was held in such high regard when it came to maintainable human trafficking. But Dorian couldn't remember *ever* feeling as disgusted as he was now when he'd attended such events in the past. Had he always been, but he'd pushed his feelings deep, deep down, or had Poppy King and her friends really changed him that much?

He wondered what Patrick would think. Patrick had come to one of these fancy events, with Dorian and his father, but had refused any and all invitations after it. Upon reflection Dorian realised his friend clearly had not enjoyed the violent party. He lived by the sea, after all; it was easy for him to live off the lost souls thrown to the waves. It was either him or the sharks.

So why did their kind feel the need to be this indulgently brutal?

Yet I stalked that jogger for weeks, Dorian thought, hating himself. Once more the desire to follow his mother's advice rang in his head. To disappear. To live away from humans and monsters alike. Dorian could live in the mountains, picking away at the doomed souls up there the way Patrick lived off the sea. He didn't need to follow poor women on the streets or break the neck of a dog to stop them from noticing he was there.

But most of his kind would always live that way. Dorian falling off the map would change nothing. They had to eat humans, and that was that.

But it might save his soul, and Poppy's, too.

As Dorian wove through the crowd he noticed some people watching him curiously. Considering he'd been a wanted man for months his face was well-known. But since he could walk around unscathed clearly Nick hadn't been lying to him when he told him he was welcome to attend. That he wanted to work with Dorian once more. Once upon a time he would have leapt at the opportunity.

But not anymore. He had to get Poppy off the grid. No more city-hopping across Europe. He'd hide them away somewhere good and obscure for the next few decades, then a few more for good measure, until surely even Nick would lose interest in Poppy.

It was then that Dorian saw her. Appearing as if to taunt him for deciding to spirit her away, Poppy appeared before Dorian's very eyes. She was a sight to behold, glamorous and made up in a way Dorian had never bore witness to before. A dark blue, thin-strapped, low-backed dress swept down to her feet, hugging

Poppy's figure like a second skin. A daring split slashed the material all the way up to her right hip. Her hair was tied up in an artfully careless bun, loose wispy fragments perfectly framing her face, whilst large hoop earrings and bold scarlet lipstick finished off the look.

She was dazzling. She was radiant. She caught the eye of more than a few guests. But Poppy was oozing confidence, and the sultry smile on her painted lips ensured not a single soul imagined she might be anything but one of their own.

So lost in staring at her was Dorian that he failed to notice Fred standing right beside Poppy until he handed her a glass of champagne. The damnable man was annoyingly handsome in a well-fitted tuxedo that Dorian knew he could have never afforded. Indeed, Poppy could certainly have never afforded her dress, either, unless...

Dorian patted down his jacket to pull out his wallet. One of his credit cards was gone.

Well played, he sighed, impressed and resigned in equal measure. He should have known the two of them would find a way to slip into the auction even if he hadn't wanted them to be here. For how else would he have expected Poppy to react to him warning her to stay away? The woman who climbed through ceilings, and set buildings on fire, and could tell Dorian she loved him without meaning a word of it, all to save herself and her friends?

Dorian knew that, whatever Poppy and Fred had planned, it was better for him to be involved than to stand on the sidelines. Forcing his irritation back down when he watched Fred slide a hand down Poppy's spine to the small of her back, Dorian made a beeline for the pair. But then another group of familiar faces in his periphery gave him pause.

Familiar. Faces.

Dorian noticed them at the same time Fred and Poppy did. Poppy's previously practised, easy smile slid from her face the moment she did so, both her and Fred frozen to the spot in abject horror.

For standing there, right in the entryway to the hall, were Andrew, Nate, and Rachelle.

Into the Lion's Den

ANDREW

Andrew didn't like crowds at the best of times. People were loud, noisy, too close, wearing overbearing perfumes and colognes or eating strong-smelling foods.

The crowd he now found himself in was so much worse.

There was blood in the air. He could smell it. See it. Almost taste it. People were literally being ripped apart before Andrew's very eyes. He couldn't look away. He thought he might be sick. Once upon a time Andrew had been frustrated that Poppy, Fred and Casey had all laid eyes on monsters in their real form. He'd been *jealous* of them. He'd felt left out.

He wished he could go back to blissful ignorance.

Why had Andrew forced himself into a stiff-collared tuxedo to walk right into a lion's den? To what end could he, Nate and Rachelle achieve anything? They couldn't stop this thing, that much was clear. They couldn't save a single soul. Seeing it now, with own two eyes, Andrew became aware of how small he was in the grand scheme of things. Glancing at Nate and Rachelle confirmed that they felt the same way.

They should never have come here.

Then Andrew locked eyes with Poppy, and he forgot about every single one of his fears. She was okay. She was alive and well and right in front of him. She was the most beautiful sight Andrew had ever seen, right in the middle of a nightmare. He took a step towards her. "Poppy, you—"

"Why are you here?" Poppy rushed out, closing the distance between them with lightning-quick strides. She stared at her three friends, aghast, as pale as if she'd been drained of all her blood. "What are you - you can't be here. Leave. This is—"

"Fred?" Rachelle said, frowning at him. "What are you doing here?"

"We have something to do," he said, indicating towards Poppy. "What are *you* doing here?"

"We had something to do, too," Nate explained, his lip curling at the sights all around him. "Though now I can see that we really didn't."

"Damn right you didn't," a familiar voice growled behind Andrew. He turned; Dorian stood there, almost unrecognisable with his hair slicked back, face shaved clean and dressed in a tuxedo that looked like it had been made for him. Andrew had never seen him in anything but casual clothes. It made Dorian look taller. More intimidating.

Andrew felt as if he faded away standing next to him, Poppy's eyes drinking in Dorian's appearance as if she simply couldn't help herself. The way Dorian fired a glare her way told Andrew all he needed to know about whether she was supposed to be here.

"Before you say anything, Dorian," Poppy said, anticipating his anger, "you know as well as I do that you were never going to keep me away from—"

"To hell with that," he bit out quietly. Instinctively the group leaned in closer to hear him over the din of the crowd. "If the lot of you don't stop acting so damn *human* then I swear to God, nothing and nobody will be able to stop you from getting ripped apart."

The group stared at each other in turn, taking note of everyone's faces before turning their attention to the monsters wearing human skins all around them. Dorian was right. Even Andrew could see it.

With some effort Rachelle shook out her shoulders and forced on a winning smile. "You're right. Thanks, Dorian. Honestly we didn't expect the auction to be so...you know. But if we want to keep our heads on our shoulders then we need to pretend like we like it."

"What you *need* to do is get out of here."

Dorian, Poppy and Fred had spoken in unison, their voices taut with the same sense of urgency. Andrew cringed at how synchronised they were.

"We can hardly leave right now, can we?" Nate muttered in a low voice. "It'll look odd."

"Why are you here in the first place?" Poppy pressed again. "How did you even know about...this?"

"Nate saw it on the Dark Web," Andrew explained. "We were tracking everything for a while. Disappearances and stuff. We wanted to be *doing* something, but we couldn't be out here helping you and then Robin suggested Nate look on the Dark Web so—"

"I get it," Poppy interrupted, looking as if she wanted to slide a hand across her face. "Thanks, Andrew. I get why you did all that. But you seriously need to get out of here as quickly as you can."

"So what about the two of you?" Andrew countered, pointing at Fred. "What are you doing here?"

"I could ask the same thing but I somehow doubt I'll get a truthful answer," Dorian muttered. When he caught Andrew's eye a flash of understanding passed between them that Andrew wished he didn't have to share with the satyr: Poppy didn't lie to anyone, but that didn't mean she didn't keep things to herself. And now she had a secret with Fred.

Andrew hated it.

"Can't we just...call the police on this?" Nate suggested, "and ge tit shut down?" Andrew knew just as well as Nate did that such a suggestion was in all likelihood redundant.

"What do you propose the police do, when faced with a room full of monsters?" Dorian countered. "Never mind the fact that Nick has some of his own men on the force. All you'd do is get yourself killed."

That shut Nate up.

"King, there's something in your hair," Fred said, distracting Andrew with the gentle way he reached forward to brush away a piece of fluff by her ear.

Poppy scowled, though she didn't flinch away from his touch. "Don't you dare be affectionate. It's disgusting."

He laughed. "I've spent years wondering how to get under your skin when, all this time, the only thing I had to do is be creepily nice to you. I'm hardly going to stop now."

"Fuck off, Sampson. I need to go to the bathroom. Why don't you fill everyone in on the plan, since it doesn't seem like they're going to leave?"

Just what was this new dynamic between Fred and Poppy Andrew was witnessing? He hated it. Dark and ugly emotions bubbled inside him, daring to be unleashed even though now wasn't the time.

"Poppy, you shouldn't go alone," Dorian said, making to go after her. But Fred held him back.

"Don't. You need to hear this."

"Like hell is she going off *on her own*—"

"You really think you'll stop her? She's already gone."

Dorian's nostrils flared, and for a moment Andrew was

certain he was going to do a whole lot worse than punch Fred in the face. But Fred stared him down unflinchingly, and eventually Dorian calmed down just a little.

"Fine. Tell us what the two of you have been concocting all on your own."

"It is, quite possible, that Poppy and I may be planning to kill a certain bird," Fred said, looking at each of them in turn. He shrugged when they returned his confession with abject looks of disbelief. "I don't know what else you expect me to say. The harpy bitch has been blackmailing me into tailing Poppy and Dorian for months now."

"You—"

"It was either that or die," Fred cut in across Nate. "Do you think it was only *my* life on the line if I said no? Fuck off. She'd come after you, Andrew, and you, Nate, and especially you, Rachelle."

Rachelle flushed a furious red. From outrage, fear or embarrassment Andrew had no idea. But that didn't stop her from saying, "You should have told us from the very start. Christmas, even. We could have worked things out together. Just like how we used to work out everything else."

"Oh come off it! No one has honest with each other about anything all year. Just look at the state we're in!"

"Well speaking of not being honest," Nate growled, rounding on Fred, "why don't you tell us what was going on with Poppy the last few days?"

"Yes," a voice that didn't belong to anyone in the group said. A sultry, low, feminine voice. A taloned hand curled over Rachelle's shoulder, pushing her to the side so that the newcomer could enter their circle.

Aisling's smile was wide and inhuman. "Just where is Poppy King?"

A DARK AND BURNING FUTURE

POPPY

POPPY HADN'T WANTED TO GO TO the toilet, not really. But she needed to escape the increasing pressure put upon her by Dorian and her closest friends.

It was too much to bear.

They'd all been keeping things from each other. Every single one of them. There were no exceptions – except Fred. How had things ended up this way, that Poppy could trust Fred to be frank and honest with her but nobody else?

They shouldn't have hidden the fact they were researching the disappearances, Poppy thought, heading up a grand flight of stairs that led to a balcony overlooking the venue proper in her quest to find a bathroom. When finally she found one she stood in front of a floor-length mirror and rubbed the pads of her index fingers beneath her eyes to wipe away a few errant tears that threatened to ruin her make-up.

"Why did they come here?" Poppy whispered at her

reflection, her breath fogging the mirror with the ghost of her guilt. Unable to stand looking at herself any longer Poppy fled the bathroom as quickly as she'd come, for she knew fine well why her friends had shown up at the auction. Whether in a misguided attempt to protect her, or lessen the burden of responsibility on her shoulders, or simply to be involved in her life, Poppy's friends had put themselves in danger for *her*.

And she had never felt so alone.

"We really must stop running into each other like this, Poppy."

Poppy froze, not having looked where she was going as she threaded her way towards the stairs. And there – directly on her left barely three feet away, leaning on the balcony to survey the horrific event he'd put on – was Nick, dressed as if he were the leading actor in a Hollywood noir film from the forties. The atmospheric lighting of the balcony played across the angles of his face, reminding Poppy of Nick's *real* face even though his human form was still and solid. The smile he gave her was genial, but all Poppy felt was fear.

She made to leave, but Nick lunged forward and grabbed her wrist before Poppy could take a single step away from him. "*Let me go*," Poppy bit out, struggling uselessly against Nick's full strength. He twirled Poppy to face him, her back against the smooth stone of the balcony's edge, one of his arms locked on either side of her. Unless Poppy wished to jump off the balcony – if there weren't monsters beneath it, she would have considered it – she was stuck.

"Clearly you and Dorian made up, then," Nick drawled, bending his head to Poppy's neck. When he breathed in deeply through his nose a shiver ran down her spine. "Pity. I don't like smelling him on you. But it won't last long."

"You keep saying that," Poppy muttered, resisting the urge to push Nick's head away simply so she didn't have to touch him. "I don't believe you."

Nick raised his head from her neck, keeping his gaze level with Poppy's as his mouth split into a feral grin. "Don't you think he seems much better than he did, say, two weeks ago? More himself. Don't you think that's *strange*?"

"He's been under a lot of stress. From you, you son of a bitch."

"Oh, Poppy, I can't wait until you finally understand that a monster is a monster."

"You say that a lot but you don't explain a damn thing."

"If I say the condition for me explaining things is for you to remain by my side, will you?" Poppy tried to kick him; it was pitifully easy for Nick to stop her with the brunt force of his leg between hers. Her breath caught in her throat, having him so dangerously close to her. Reminding Poppy that it would be the easiest thing in the world for Nick to overpower her, to have her helpless and struggling beneath him, to have her black out into oblivion.

Sensing where her mind had wandered Nick put fractionally more of his weight against Poppy, then some more, only to pull away a moment later with a low, dangerous chuckle. "Relax," he murmured, "I'm not making a move on you tonight...unless you want me to. I have enough of your blood in my system to last me years, after all. Now that I'm looking at a much longer life I could do without having any kids for another few decades. I've got lots to organise. You and I can wait until later."

Poppy was rendered speechless in the face of Nick's comment. She was...free? To walk out of the damned auction, knowing he wasn't going to keep chasing her? All she had to give up in return was her desire to know what *Nick* knew. What he planned. All she had to do was remain in the dark.

That was what she'd wanted, in the beginning. Could Poppy do it once more, for the sake of her freedom?

When Poppy remained silent Nick's gaze travelled from the top of her head and down, down, down, arousal obvious on his face. "You clean up well. Though I have to say I think I preferred you writhing beneath me, covered in—"

"Go to hell."

"I believe we established before that we're already there." He removed one of his hands from the balcony, running it down Poppy's arm until he met the top of the outrageous slit in her dress. When he slid his fingertips beneath the material to grip her thigh Poppy gave up on her resolve not to touch him and latched onto his wrist, trying in vain to wrench him away. But Nick's hand was strong as iron; Poppy had no choice but to let him touch her.

Poppy's skin was cold, but inside her body was searing hot. She could do nothing against the monster pinning her place. Nothing. If she remained unscathed it was because *he* willed it, not because *she* wanted it.

"It really is remarkable," Nick muttered, eyes roving across the exposed flesh of her thigh. "There isn't a mark on you. It's as if I never..."

"Never what, sucked half the life out of me?" Poppy spat, when Nick didn't finish his thought. But then his grip slackened on her thigh, and he spun Poppy around. He cast his curious gaze downwards, eyesight far better than Poppy could ever hope hers would be. When his ears twitched she realised his hearing was superior to hers, too.

"It seems your friends may need your help," he said, resting his chin upon Poppy's head. "I won't let you come to harm, of course, but your friends...well, I'm not so attached to them. Best see what you can do."

"The hell are you..." Poppy began, frowning as she tried to see what Nick could see through the throng of monsters and men-who-were-monsters. But then she saw what had drawn his attention.

Aisling, in her real form. Her talons resting on Rachelle's shoulder.

Poppy's eyes grew wide. She made to leave at once, but Nick kept her boxed in against the balcony. She gnashed her teeth as she forcibly turned to face him, the entire length of her body pressed up against his. Poppy's heart throbbed when she felt Nick shudder at the contact. "If you've deigned to let me help them then *let me go.*"

"I will. But listen to me first." Knowing he wouldn't let her go until she did, and she couldn't fight her way out, Poppy listened. "You'll be back," Nick said, sure of himself as always. "Whether in one year or thirty, you'll be back. You can't be alone and in the dark forever. One day you'll grow tired of knowing nothing, of *having* nothing. That's when you'll come back. All you have to do is wait and see, if you don't believe me."

Nick let Poppy go. She felt as though his touch had branded her like a hot iron; running her hands up and down her arms and hardly daring to tear her eyes from his predatory, covetous gaze, Poppy fled down the stairs.

You better be ready, Fred, she thought, as she closed the distance between herself and her friends. Around them the guests of the auction were blessedly unaware of what was currently going on. Poppy had to hope they would remain that way, until she and Fred could dispatch with Aisling and get the people they cared most about away from this hellish night.

And then?

And then Poppy knew she had to disappear.

An Inevitable Tragedy

RACHELLE

The past year of Rachelle Cole's life had been one never-ending nightmare.

Even before the summer spent at the Highlands Outdoor Sports Facility Rachelle had already been on edge. Her best friend and her ex-boyfriend were at each other's throats even more than usual, whilst that same ex-boyfriend clearly still wanted to get back together with her. Rachelle knew she didn't want to be with Fred in that capacity anymore, but she still loved him as much as she loved Poppy.

That's why it hurt so much, the way Fred had grown so obsessive and bitter. When Rachelle first met the two of them she'd thought their feud was childish. All fun and games. Until she discovered it wasn't. Perhaps because she never witnessed an actual monster until this evening, or prior to Christmas hadn't witnessed what Poppy's blood could do, but the news that Fred had tried to murder her best friend continued to hang heaviest in Rachelle's head over everything else.

Which was insane, give everything she had experienced in the last year. The memories of carrying the injured members of her club out of Dorian's facility haunted Rachelle most every night. That Poppy had remained behind instead of escaping with her friends made it even worse. Rachelle could no longer sleep longer than a few scant hours at a time without waking up in a cold sweat.

Never mind the fact that she still couldn't look Fred in the face, despite the fact Poppy insisted things were fine. Never mind that Dorian was apparently one of the *good* monsters. Never mind Rachelle was expected to get over her trauma and move on with her life. Things *weren't* fine.

Once upon a time Poppy would have confided all the things that were currently troubling her to Rachelle. But Andrew had taken even that from her. Rachelle had been upset about that for a while. Jealous, almost. But it felt unfair to be jealous of Andrew, given the circumstances under which Poppy and Andrew had grown so close.

And Andrew loved her. He loved her so much that Rachelle still didn't have it in her to tell him that Poppy not reciprocating his feelings would never happen. Screw Nate giving Andrew three options to choose from. Screw him giving Andrew even one iota of hope. But Rachelle didn't see Poppy being unable to return Andrew's love – or anyone's – as a flaw. It was just the way she was. Sometimes selfish, yes, but always genuine. Her best friend had never tried to pretend to be anything other than herself, so how could Rachelle hate her for it? Rather, Rachelle loved Poppy for her honesty. For how she barrelled headlong into any challenge that stood in her away.

Which is what made it all the more dreadful for Rachelle as she watched Poppy charge towards the group, her fear palpable as she honed in on Aisling's horrific talon piercing insistently into Rachelle's shoulder.

"Let her go," Poppy said the moment she reached them, low enough that the group didn't garner attention.

The harpy laughed heartily. "Oh, I knew it wouldn't be long before you joined us. Interesting conversation you had with Nick up there."

Rachelle watched as Poppy flinched. Clearly the harpy with the inexorable grip on her shoulder had hearing far superior to that of humans. Unbidden she glanced at Dorian, wondering if he'd heard the same conversation, but he was just as confused as she was.

"Let her go," Poppy said again, painfully, singularly focused. There was nothing else on her mind than ensuring Rachelle's safety. She loved Poppy for it, of course. Poppy would do anything for her friends.

Bleed for them.

Die for them.

But that was the problem. Now Rachelle knew how difficult it was for Poppy to die she understood the true extent of what Poppy was willing to do for her. She would put herself through death, again and again and again, beyond the pain that any normal person could endure, just for her.

"I'm okay," Rachelle said, even though she wasn't. She winced when Aisling squeezed her shoulder, and though Nate and Andrew watched her do so, they were frozen with the inability to do or say a single thing when the tip of the harpy's talon drew blood.

Fred took a step forward. "You swore—"

"I promised nothing, Frederick Sampson, other than to *consider* leaving your pitiful friends alone in exchange for Poppy. Well, at least you kept that end of the bargain. Oh, Dorian, nice to see you again," Aisling added on, almost as an aside. "Not covered in blood, that is."

A low growl rumbled in his throat. "Get away from Rachelle," he said, doubling down on Poppy's orders. But that only seemed to amuse Aisling further.

"You're so protective of your little humans, aren't you?" she teased. "Ironic, considering the way you tore that poor girl apart the other day."

The entire group flinched. Poppy's gaze slid from Rachelle's to Dorian. "What's she talking about?"

"Don't listen to her. She's trying to distract you from—"

"I don't need to distract her," Aisling cut in, smiling viciously. "It's the truth, after all. Going by her face I can tell she believes me already. Ah, Poppy, your beloved satyr couldn't deal with his hunger any longer. You should have seen him; he was truly a nightmare to behold! The girl's entrails were spread halfway across the alleyway. You would have hated it."

Poppy grew pale. Which was saying something, because Poppy was always pale. "Don't listen to her," Rachelle insisted, wishing even now to protect Poppy's feelings. "She's trying to get a rise out of you. Out of him. You must know that."

"See how they're all wrapped around your finger?" Aisling continued, gleeful. "Well, that's a satyr for you. He'll have you falling on a sword for him before you know it. It's the way of his kind. But I'm telling the truth, and I can tell that little Poppy King knows it."

Around them Rachelle noticed that people were beginning to pay attention to them. Their nostrils were flaring, monsters and men-as-monsters alike. It was then she realised how much blood Aisling was drawing from her shoulder. But it hadn't escaped *Fred's* notice.

"Let Rachelle go, Aisling," he begged, a note of desperation in his voice. "You promised—"

"Oh, Fred, darling," she crooned, stroking Rachelle's hair almost fondly. "You're so easy to manipulate, aren't you? But here's the thing." Aisling dropped her air of humour, of familiarity, of cheerfulness. Her talons caught in Rachelle's hair, forcing her head painfully back. "Because of your precious Poppy King I lost my closest friend. Dorian would know, since he was the one who did it."

"He was my friend, too," Dorian said, sad and resigned,

because he could see what was coming just as Rachelle herself could.

"And yet you killed him for your humans. And so..."

Rachelle felt nothing. She saw the reaction of her friends, but she didn't feel the pain. It was strange to know that Aisling had sliced her talons across her throat. Even stranger, then, that as she buckled to the floor, the crowd brought into a frenzy with the smell of so much fresh blood, Rachelle dazedly wondered where all of that blood had come from.

In her periphery she saw Fred pull out a gun and fire it into the harpy's face, one, two, three, four, five, six times.

Poppy collapsed by Rachelle's side in an instant, tears streaming from her face as she cradled her head. "It'll be okay," she lied. "I'll fix this. I will."

Usually when Poppy said she could fix something Rachelle believed her, because she always *did* fix it. But it was clear even from her best friend's wretched face that she knew it was no good. Rachelle could not be saved.

But Rachelle had made peace with this. What else could she do?

She didn't say anything. She didn't have the strength.

Poppy was still telling her she'd be fine when she took her final breath.

NUMB

FRED

HE DIDN'T HEAR POPPY SCREAMING, NOR Nate yelling for him to stand up and help him carry Rachelle's body out of the auction. All Fred knew was that he was running on cold, hard auto-pilot, and before he was aware of it he found himself in a dark alleyway with the rest of his friends.

Had he really killed Aisling? Had Fred really held up a gun, aimed it at her face, and fired every bullet in the chamber until her once beautiful features had been reduced to meat?

Part of the adrenaline now coursing through his system wasn't due to fear. It was because he enjoyed killing her.

Blithely Fred realised Aisling had sliced deeply into his chest when she clattered to the ground, but it was healing up before his very eyes. Despite the now gaping cut in his tuxedo nobody even noticed he'd been hurt. Why would they?

Rachelle lay on the pavement, dead and gone.

No amount of immortal blood could save her.

Dorian hung back from everyone. After what he'd done Fred wished he'd disappear entirely. He wasn't one of them; he wasn't human. Despite their time spent together at Christmas. Despite the way he cared about Poppy. Despite the fact he actively tried to keep them all safe on her behalf. No, Dorian was still a monster, and Dorian was the reason any of them had become embroiled in their current nightmare in the first place.

He had run the auction that put all their lives on the line, then had guiltlessly killed an innocent human being the moment he was free and able to do so.

Fred turned from the deplorable satyr to look at his friends. Nate was on his knees, covered in blood and shaking in disbelief. He held Rachelle's hand as if he expected her to squeeze his fingers and tell him she was fine. Andrew was standing still, looking at nothing, eyes as glassy as Rachelle's. A chill spread across Fred when he realised he'd seen that look on his face once before, when Fred had sought to end Poppy's life and Andrew had brought Dorian to save her, because he could do nothing to save her himself.

Fred turned to Poppy. He had never seen her so inconsolable. Not when he'd attacked her. Not at Christmas, when she'd broken down. Not even after they rescued her from Nick. Poppy was sobbing, screaming, bent double over Rachelle and pounding a fist against her chest as if that might make her friend's heart sputter back to life.

Fred wanted to help her. Help Nate. Help Andrew. But what could he do? The only girl he'd ever loved was lying dead between them all. The lynch-pin that had kept Fred attached to their group of friends even when he'd hated Poppy. She was gone, gone, gone, because of Poppy and because of him.

It was his fault just as much as it was hers.

Fred dropped the gun in his hands, heaved in a gulp of air, then fled the scene. He wasn't needed here. His friends were better off without him.

He would have to grieve on his own.

OLD AND NEW ALLIANCES

POPPY

"...Poppy?"

Poppy didn't respond. There was nothing left inside her. Rachelle was gone. The girl she'd gone to university with. The girl she'd travelled with. The girl she'd lived with. The girl who nursed Poppy's hangovers, who in turn was nursed by Poppy. Until last summer Rachelle had been Poppy's closest friend in the world. Her closest person.

Now she was gone. Because of her.

"Poppy," Nate's voice said, cracking on her name. "We need to get her...we need to get her out of here. We need to call...an ambulance. The police. But you can't be here. You're meant to be..."

He couldn't say dead. In the face of Rachelle, lying in front of them, she knew he couldn't. And so she nodded, for what else could she do?

"I'll text you where to meet later," Andrew said, which was the first thing he had said since Aisling appeared. Even now it looked as though the words caused him physical pain to speak. "I'll text you, so don't disappear."

The way Andrew said it broke Poppy's heart. Andrew fully expected her to do as he said. She'd spent the last few months doing exactly that, calling him and giving him updates on her life and listening to Andrew do the same in return. She'd given him a masquerade of a relationship. The ghost of one. A complete and utter sham.

So Poppy did what she had never done before: she flat-out lied to Andrew.

"Of course," she said, forcing a smile to her face as she nodded. "I'll see you later."

She hated that Andrew believed her. That relief washed over his blood-spattered face at the certainty that this would not be the end. In Poppy's heart she knew Nate didn't believe her, so she avoided his gaze, but he didn't call her out.

They both knew what she had to do.

Poppy walked away from the alleyway, from her friends, from Rachelle, but she barely made it past the front entrance of the auction before she realised Dorian was following her.

Dorian, looking like a red carpet movie star with his perfectly styled hair, clean-shaven jawline and dramatic tuxedo, save for the blood spattered across his shirt and the miserable expression on his face.

A white glimmer of rage ignited the emptiness inside Poppy. She rounded on him, surprising Dorian by crashing straight into his chest.

"*You killed someone.*"

"Poppy, I—"

"Was that what you were doing whenever you snuck off?" she demanded, stabbing a finger against his heart. "Warning me not to do anything dangerous only to go out and *murder* people?"

"Not people, plural," Dorian said, panic-stricken. His hands grasped at Poppy's arms, keeping her close when she struggled. "It was only one, and—"

"And that makes it better?!"

"I was *starving*. Poppy, you don't understand, I—"

Poppy slapped him. Dorian let her. "You didn't give me a chance to understand, did you? Instead you kept everything to yourself, letting me worry in silence instead of being honest with me. Dorian, what did you think I would have said, if you told me you were hungry?"

"I didn't want you to believe your blood wasn't enough," he said, taking hold of Poppy's wrist to bring it to his lips. He kissed the skin there, so gentle it was almost painful. All the while his eyes – wildly, inhumanly blue eyes – were trained on hers, his entire body shaking. "I thought you wouldn't stay with me if I told you."

"Well what do you think I have to do now? You lied to me. I thought – hoped – that the one thing we had going for us was that we never lied to each other. And yet here you are, standing before me, having lied to me about the worst *possible* thing."

"Poppy—"

"No," she mouthed, wrenching free of Dorian's grasp and backing away from him. When Dorian made to close the distance once more Poppy held out a hand. "Stay away from me," she warned, "and let me fucking finish." Her voice was shaking, but Poppy knew if she stopped to take a breath she'd never get the words out. "These last few months we both pretended things were fine. You knew I wasn't able to sleep. You knew what kind of nightmares were plaguing me. But you didn't do anything, because you didn't know what to do, and I didn't say anything, because nothing you could do for me would fix me. And all that time I was stopping you from being able to satisfy your true nature. So what are we doing here, Dorian? What's the point of being together when all we do is pretend?"

Dorian's heart looked like it was breaking; Poppy couldn't afford to care any more. "I love you, Poppy," he said, so softly. So sincerely. The harsh glow of the street lights exaggerated the planes of his face, hollowing out his cheeks and reminding Poppy of the way he *really* looked. The form he took, when he murdered people in the night. "You know that. If I didn't then I wouldn't have gone so long without—"

"Oh, so everything's *my* fault? It's my fault that you'll live forever but are still hungry? It's my fault that—"

"I never said that!"

"So why is everything bad happening to everybody I love *because of me*? I - I..."

Poppy couldn't take it any longer. Her head was going to explode. If she looked into Dorian's eyes one more time then she'd give in. She'd fall into his arms, cry against his chest, let him comfort her. He'd whisper blissful sweet nothings into her ear using his sinful, silky voice to assure her that everything would be okay. Poppy would fall for it, because she had nothing left, and be with him forever.

Trapping them both forever.

Dorian worked out what she intended to do a moment before she stepped away. "Don't, Poppy," he begged. "Please."

She did it anyway.

Poppy fled into the night.

DORIAN

How was it that Dorian had ended up alone? Despite the fact that Aisling was dead, and the threat of Nick was somewhat tempered by him now containing Poppy's blood, how had Dorian ended up losing that which was most important to him?

Poppy was gone. He had nobody to blame but himself.

"Well don't you look fucking miserable."

"Fuck off, Nick," Dorian said immediately from his position slouching on the kerb. He couldn't bear to look at him.

"Hardly likely," Nick drawled. "You're sitting right outside my auction, covered in blood. You're garnering attention."

Dorian ignored the comment. "I know calling me last night was all a ploy to get Poppy here," he said, finally looking up to give Nick his full attention. "What did you say to her up on the balcony?"

His former friend grinned. "That's a secret."

"You son of a—"

"And besides, it wasn't just a ploy to get her here."

"What does that mean?"

"Work with me," Nick said. His eyes shone bright, dangerous and *genuine* in the dim evening light. "I'm serious, but I won't ask again. At this point what do you have to lose? You've already lost it all."

"I told you before I've lost my taste for the business, Nick."

"So find it again. You know you want to." He held out a hand for Dorian to take. "Come on; you're better than this."

Dorian wanted to tell Nick he was wrong. Wanted to say he had no desire to be better than this if *better* meant slaughtering more humans whilst Poppy was out there, hurt and betrayed by him doing that very thing.

But he was a monster. He had to eat. And others did, too.

He took Nick's hand.

VERIFICATION

FRED

FRED SAT ON HIS BED AND CALMLY watched as he wrenched out the knife he had lodged in his thigh and threw it across the floor. He'd barely felt the pain as it bit into his flesh.

Months had passed since Aisling murdered Rachelle, and in so doing destroyed a part of Fred he would never get back.

He didn't want to think about that, so he retrieved the knife once more and slowly skewered the palm of his left hand to the bedside table. It was with grim satisfaction that Fred observed his flesh begin to heal around the blade, then seal itself entirely when he removed it from his hand. Fred now healed as quickly as Poppy had when he so viciously attacked her back in Dorian's facility. For all intents and purposes there was no discernible difference between them anymore.

They were both immortal. Fred would no longer age, and would not grow old.

To what end? he thought grimly, wiping his bloody hand on the bedspread before moving to the window of the small flat he was renting in Berlin. Peter was grateful for his quiet, unassuming company, certainly, but providing his great-great-

great-grandfather with a companion had not been why Fred accepted his immortal blood.

So why, then? What is the point of living forever if I don't have a purpose?

Fred had broken what felt like almost every bone in his body over the course of the last three months, testing the limits of his healing ability. The pain didn't even bother him now – not the way it bothered Poppy, when he'd attacked her. When Fred had murdered her over and over and over again only for her body to heal itself before any permanent, mortal damage could be done.

As with Rachelle's death, Fred pushed the thought to the side. For Poppy had run away; not even Andrew had heard from her since the auction in Barcelona. If she didn't want anything to do with her friends – or with Fred – then Fred had to find another meaning to his life besides continuing to make things right with Poppy.

But nonetheless Fred's fist shook, and anger began to cloud his mind. Aisling had murdered Rachelle in front of them all. In front of Poppy, her best friend. On top of which Dorian had also given into his true nature and devoured an innocent human being, destroying Poppy's trust in him.

Fred had expected Poppy to respond with righteous, glorious anger. To want to take revenge against the entire realm of monsters for what they'd done to her. To make them feel the pain they had thus far inflicted on their victims.

On her friends. On Fred.

Instead Rachelle's death had broken her, and Dorian's betrayal had numbed her, and now Poppy was gone.

But Fred's lust for revenge was only growing stronger with every passing day.

So far none of Fred's friends had killed anyone in the fight against the monsters who sought to consume them. It was only Fred who had been violent. Only Fred who had killed.

I'm okay with that, he thought, touching the window with the tips of his bloody fingers. The faintest trace of red was left upon the glass where he grazed it. *I'll kill so they don't have to. I'll spill blood in return for every drop the monsters have taken from us.*

And so it seemed that Fred had known his purpose all along. Nobody else was up to the task. It was only him.

He'd get revenge for all his friends. He would not fail.

Then, perhaps, if he came across Poppy King at some point in the future, Frederick Sampson could look her straight in the face and know he had finally been redeemed for what he himself had done.

EPILOGUE: ANOTHER GOODBYE

DORIAN

A YEAR PASSED SINCE THE OUTDOOR Sports Society first had the misfortune of falling into Dorian Kapros' trap, then five, then before Dorian knew it twenty-seven years had been and gone. Considering how agonisingly slow and stressful his singular year with Poppy King had been, the remaining twenty-six raced by mind-numbingly quickly.

Dorian didn't know why he was at Nate Richards' funeral, lingering well in the back where nobody would recognise him. In truth there was hardly anyone at the funeral who *could* recognise Dorian; of the Outdoor Sports Society members who escaped his facility just a small handful now remained.

Some had committed suicide. Some had eaten their trauma away and fallen to heart disease and diabetes. Others had broken down mentally and spent the rest of their lives within institutes before finally dying in their sleep. There had been panic attacks and strokes and accidental overdoses.

Everyone knew the reason for their early deaths, and that reason was currently sitting at the back of a church pretending to mourn.

For Nate it was his heart that had given up. Just one year past fifty and that was it: the life of the once vibrant, daring, loyal man was over.

Andrew was sitting in the front pew, as were Rich and Robin. Frederick Sampson was nowhere to be seen. At the back, with Dorian and with Patrick, stood Casey.

There was no sign of Poppy King.

Dorian didn't pay attention to the ceremony, instead distracting himself with how much older the remaining Outdoor Sports Society members looked. Aside from Casey, whose ageing had been slowed by virtue of birthing Patrick's five offspring. Looking at her one would believe her to be scarcely older than thirty-five rather than forty-eight.

Andrew look good, Dorian supposed, sitting in the pew stock-straight with much the same punishingly fit body he'd possessed half his life ago, but even he could not escape the trappings of time. His brown hair was greying at the temples, and there were lines on his face that betrayed the fact Andrew was almost fifty.

Unlike Dorian, who alone out of everyone in the room remained entirely unchanged.

Just where was Poppy King?

Dorian had attended in some manner or another the funeral of every deceased Outdoor Sports Society member in the hopes of catching sight of her. Poppy hadn't shown up to a single one. She never visited Andrew, nor Casey and Patrick. Nobody knew where or how she was.

Poppy had become a ghost, and Dorian was alone.

When a low murmur filled the church Dorian was finally pulled out of his own head. "What's going on?" he asked

Patrick in an undertone. His friend was frowning at his phone when it buzzed insistently in his hand.

"I think someone must have – oh. *Oh.*"

"What's wrong?" Casey murmured when Patrick did not elaborate, but before she could look at what was on his screen the doors of the church were thrown open.

"Glasgow has been overrun with m-monsters!" a white-faced man yelled at the assembly.

More and more people pulled out their phones to stare in horror at what the man was talking about. On Patrick's screen a heavily shaking video documented a gargantuan, spiderlike creature crawling out of the subway and grabbing a busker by the arm, guitar and all. The instrument exploded into shards of wood and metal strings when the creature's pointed fangs smashed straight through it.

A reptilian ox stood out in the background. Dorian recognised him as Nick's uncle: his one remaining, living relative. The monster ripped apart a couple trying to run away as if they were made of paper, not flesh and blood and bone.

Then there were too many monsters flooding the screen for Dorian to focus on a single one, then the person recording the footage – Dorian realised dully that they'd been screaming the entire time – was caught between the pincers of another creature, and the phone clattered to the pavement.

Dorian could not believe what he'd just witnessed.

Monsters, out in the open. Slaughtering people everywhere they go.

Patrick and Dorian stared at each other, mouths agape. "What do we do?" Casey whispered, taking Patrick's phone with white-knuckled hands to replay the video. "What are we supposed to do?"

"Continue living," Dorian said simply. There was no other answer he could find. "If this is the way things are going to be then this is the way things are going to be."

"But Dorian—"

"He's right, Cass," Patrick cut in, smoothing Casey's hair away from her face. He took her hand, nodded at Dorian, then the three of them used the commotion in the church to disguise their swift exit before Andrew or Rich or Robin could notice their presence. "We knew this was a long time coming. The best we can do right now is go home."

"But what about Poppy? What about—"

"If she needs our help she'll find us."

Dorian could only laugh at Patrick's suggestion. *Poppy King, admitting she needs help? From me?* It was more likely that Dorian would die of old age before such a thing happened.

The world was changing, for monsters and for humans. Nick had warned it would for decades now, and though Dorian had always believed him he nonetheless hadn't thought it would change quite this quickly.

He hoped Poppy was prepared.

Dorian certainly wasn't.

THE STORY CONCLUDES IN

THE STORY CONCLUDES IN

INVINCIBLE MONSTERS

ANDREW

IT WAS RAINING, SO ANDREW BROUGHT the goat in. Penny was delighted by this; she knew fine well she wasn't supposed to be allowed inside. But it was quite literally blowing up a storm, and Andrew didn't have the heart to leave her out on her own in her little shed. Besides, once Hazel, David and Lily arrived Penny would have so much company she would be as hyper as Andrew's grand-daughter would inevitably be. This was the last night Andrew was likely to have with his pet in relative peace and quiet.

Even though he liked that peace and quiet, Andrew was looking forward to his family coming to join him. The world had fallen into pandemonium, after all. Glasgow wasn't safe to stay in any more; most any city in the United Kingdom was dangerous. It made sense for his daughter, her husband and their little girl to come and stay with Andrew up in the hills, away from everyone who could do them harm.

If someone had told Andrew thirty years ago that he'd be living a fully self-sufficient life away from the hustle and bustle of the city he would have laughed at them. Yes, he'd never been one for large crowds, but he'd been brought up in Glasgow. He'd bought all his food and clothes and necessities from supermarkets and high street shops, just like everyone else. But as time wore on Andrew had wanted to move further out. To enjoy all that the Highlands of Scotland had to offer, despite the lingering nightmares that still occasionally haunted his sleep about the place. So when he and Nate sold their climbing company three years ago in order to enjoy early retirement Andrew was quick to move further out.

Given that Margaret had lived barely twelve months after that, Andrew wished he'd sold the company sooner.

Margaret had been delighted. Though she was a city girl through and through the idea of living in the hills excited her more than Andrew could have ever hoped for. She liked the drive into the closest village to sell goods at the farmers' market. She liked knitting and painting weird landscapes and having their grand-daughter over to play with the goat and the chickens.

And yet she'd been gone for two years now, and Nate for one.

"Come here, Penny," Andrew complained, corralling the animal into a corner of the kitchen so that he could clean off her hooves. She chirruped and bound away across the tiled floor, completely ignoring Andrew's request in favour of butting her horns against the fridge. He sighed good-naturedly; this wasn't the first time he and Penny had danced this dance, and it wouldn't be the last.

From the living room the news reported on another monster

attack in Glasgow. So many shops and public services had closed down – it was simply too dangerous to go outside – but still the news reported on what was going on, so long as there was electricity to run the TV stations and people to watch the shows. Andrew supposed, dully, that monsters themselves enjoyed these luxuries. It wouldn't do for the most basic of amenities to shut down completely.

That reminded Andrew of something Dorian had said, a lifetime ago. Who did they think was running the police force in Barcelona, thus allowing that fateful auction to go ahead? The one where Andrew first witnessed monsters in all their bloody terror. The one where Fred murdered a harpy. The one where Rachelle was murdered before Andrew's very eyes.

And Poppy King walked out of his life forever.

Andrew rubbed at his forehead. He hadn't thought about Poppy for a long, long time. That in and of itself was technically a lie – barely a day went by without Andrew's thoughts flickering to Poppy in one way or another – but this was the first time Andrew had actively, *willingly* thought about her for years. Even at Nate's funeral he hadn't allowed himself to hope that she'd be there. Even though she should have been there.

She *should* have been there, but she wasn't. Just as she hadn't been there for all the previous twenty-six years of Andrew's life, with this year making it twenty-seven.

Well, tomorrow he was fifty.

There was still the rest of his life to go, but Andrew didn't have any hopes of seeing Poppy again.

He wasn't even sure he wanted to.

Eventually Andrew got Penny cleaned up, then relented and allowed her to curl up on a blanket with him on the couch to watch TV. Reruns of game shows, to alleviate the atmosphere after the heavy news that preceded it. Andrew worked on a crossword as the presenter called out her inane questions, scratching a pen into each box in time to the ticking of the grandfather clock in the hallway. Tick, scratch, tock, scratch.

It helped settle Andrew's nerves. He felt uneasy, though he couldn't pinpoint why. He supposed everyone felt uneasy nowadays. But Andrew had a rifle in a glass cabinet by the door – locked now, with his grand-daughter imminently coming to live with him – and he knew how to fight. He hadn't known how, back when he'd most needed to, but Andrew had been quick to rectify that.

He never wanted to be in a situation where he couldn't defend someone he loved ever again.

Andrew was broken out of his reverie when he heard a knock on the door. He paused from his crossword, cocking his head to the side as he listened hard. *Did I imagine that?* he thought, frowning. His family wasn't due until tomorrow, and Andrew didn't have any post due. He wasn't expecting anyone else.

The unwanted visitor knocked upon the door again, more insistent this time.

Groaning, Andrew eased out of his armchair and walked over to the front door, eyes glancing at his rifle before unlocking the case and taking the weapon into his hands. You could never be too careful these days.

"Hold on a second," he called out, peering through the peephole to see who was so desperate to see him. But the storm had fogged up the glass; Andrew couldn't see a thing. Clinging to his rifle he eased the door open a few inches.

But Andrew could not have possibly prepared himself for who had come to call upon him. For standing there, relentlessly shivering and soaking wet from the pouring rain, was a ghost. His gun clattered to the floor, useless and unnecessary.

"Hi," Poppy King said, unchanged in every fathomable way.

ACKNOWLEDGEMENTS

Holy hell did this take me ages to write. Well, actually, it took me two months, but it took me three years of thinking about it to get the outline done. You'll be happy to know I have the outline for book three sorted and have already gotten to work on it, so it should be out in early 2023.

Middle books are always hard. With *Insatiable Monsters* I knew the tone was going to border on melancholy due to the fact everyone was processing immense amounts of trauma, but I hope there was enough excitement, drama, and bad choices sprinkled in there for everyone to enjoy! Andrew definitely got the short end of the stick with the narrative this time, because Fred had his spot in the limelight, but fear not! Andrew has much more to do in book three.

I really liked shifting Fred from secondary antagonist to anti-hero. I hope you did too. He's a complicated, horrible person, but I think he's super interesting. His arc going into book three is a fun one!

Whenever I wonder how bad I can make things for Poppy I just make things even more terrible. I should feel bad for it but it's only going to get worse. Don't hate me for it! She's such a resilient character that it was satisfying to have her actually break at the edges in *Insatiable Monsters* with no intention of fixing herself back up.

And don't get me started on Dorian.

Who ended up the winner in this book? Nick? Most likely. I like my antagonists complex, so you'll see more about what makes him do the things he does in book three.

Anyway, thanks as usual to all of my amazing fans for waiting it out for this one, and to my partner, Jake, who's had to put up with me listening to the same playlist two hundred times in a row whilst I write this.

Until the next one!

ABOUT THE AUTHOR

Hayley Louise Macfarlane hails from the very tiny hamlet of Balmaha on the shores of Loch Lomond in Scotland. After graduating with a PhD in molecular genetics she did a complete 180 and moved into writing fiction. Though she loves writing multiple genres (fantasy, romance, sci-fi, psychological fiction and horror so far!) she is most widely known for her Gothic, Scottish fairy tale, Prince of Foxes – book one of the Bright Spear trilogy.

You can follow her on TikTok or Twitter at @HLMacfarlane.

ALSO BY H. L. MACFARLANE

FAIRY TALE SHARED UNIVERSE:
BRIGHT SPEAR TRILOGY
PRINCE OF FOXES
LORD OF HORSES
KING OF FOREVER

DARK SPEAR DUOLOGY
SON OF SILVER (COMING 2023)
HEIR OF GOLD (COMING 2023)

ALL I WANT FOR CHRISTMAS IS A FAERIE ASSASSIN?!

CHRONICLES OF CURSES
BIG, BAD MISTER WOLFE
SNOWSTORM KING
THE TOWER WITHOUT A DOOR

OTHER BOOKS:
GOLD AND SILVER DUOLOGY
INTENDED
REVIVAL (RELEASE DATE TBC)

MONSTERS TRILOGY
INVISIBLE MONSTERS
INSATIABLE MONSTERS
INVINCIBLE MONSTERS (COMING 2023)

THRILLERS
THE BOY FROM THE SEA

Rom-coms
The Unbalanced Equation
Courtney Can't Decide (Coming 2024)

Short Stories
The Snowdrop (Part of Once Upon a Winter: A Folk and
Fairy Tale Anthology)
The Goat
The Boy Who Did Not Fit